Wei Hui is the daughter of an army of her childhood living in an army-o monks had been expelled during the Revolution. She studied literature at the prestigious Fudan University in Shanghai.

First championed by the state media as a rising star of her generation, Wei Hui is now dubbed 'decadent, debauched and a slave of foreign culture.' *Shanghai Baby* was banned by the authorities in April 2000 and 40,000 copies were publicly burned, serving only to fan the flames of the author's cult status. Wei Hui calls the novel a semi-autobiographical account of her spiritual and sexual awakening. 'I grew up in a very strict family. My first year of college was spent in military training. What happened after that was natural. I rebelled. I went wild. That's what I wrote about.'

Wei Hui (*pronounced Way-Way*) has written five previous books and lives in Shanghai.

'*Shanghai Baby* possesses . . . beauty and rhythm, but it's younger and more decadent . . . a new literary personality has entered the scene, and a new kind of urban novel has been born in China. *Shanghai Baby* is beautifully written, and the young author clearly combines the qualities of natural feeling for writing with intelligence.'

Jianying Zha, author of *China Pop*

'China's most popular writer . . . one of the first in China to portray Wei Hui's generation of urban women, born in the 1970s, as they search for moral grounding in a country of shifting values . . . Wei Hui sees herself a feminist helping her generation of women understand themselves.'

Craig S. Smith, *New York Times*

'Steamy, contemporary and Western in style. It tackles the battle between love and passion in a semi-autobiographical work that looks terrific.'

Sarah Broadhurst, *The Bookseller*

marrying buddha

wei hui

ROBINSON
London

Constable & Robinson Ltd
3 The Lanchesters
162 Fulham Palace Road
London W6 9ER
www.constablerobinson.com

First published in the UK by Robinson,
an imprint of Constable and Robinson Ltd 2005

A copy of the British Library Cataloguing in
Publication Data is available from the British Library

ISBN 1 84529-170-0

Printed and bound in the EU

1 3 5 7 9 10 8 6 4 2

For all those people who love me and help me,
you are all my Buddhas

1

Return to Shanghai

At fifteen, I had my mind bent on learning. At thirty, I stood firm.
At forty, I had no doubts. At fifty, I knew the decrees of heaven.
At sixty, my ear was an obedient organ for the reception of truth.
At seventy, I could follow what my heart desired, without
transgressing what was right.
Confucius, *Analects* (as translated by Arthur Waley)

Just being in a room with myself is more stimulation than I can bear.
Kate Braverman

Shanghai – Autumn

In the first few days after returning from New York to
Shanghai, my head was spinning. I was utterly exhausted, but
I couldn't get to sleep at night, and during the day I couldn't
stay awake.

I had no idea whether I could be happy again, which way to
turn, or if I could ever face the world with wise and fearless eyes.
I didn't know whether Muju still loved me, or whether I wanted
to have a child with him. I didn't know whether the dense layers
of moss that had so covered up the tracks of my memory meant
that I would never be able to turn back and run.

Shanghai hadn't changed. It was still wild with ambition,
speeding headlong down the road to capitalism. It was more
hectic than New York – the noisiest and the most bewildering
place in the world.

The city had long ago earned a name for glitter and romance.

Now its practical and crude sides had begun to show. It seemed that everyone had a get-rich-quick scheme, everyone was hurrying to catch the last train to fame and fortune. Everything was in flux, unpredictable; a crazy rush caught up in a great hallucination. It was exciting, but it left me reeling.

The second week after I got back, I started smoking again, and drinking, and swallowing sedatives one after the other in the bathroom. The toxins Muju had helped me expel when I was in New York entered my body all over again. But instead of bringing the sense of security and comfort I'd hoped for, they just offered a moment of anaesthetic blankness in which I could catch my breath.

Upon returning to my city, I'd returned to my former habits as well. It seemed I had once again become a bouquet of tranquil-lized narcissis.

I spent the entire first week holed up in my flat, an old French-style colonial. I had a local restaurant deliver meals at regular intervals and left the answering machine on to field calls from my father, who had taken a teaching position in Singapore, and my mother, who'd accompanied him; and from my friend Xi'er, my cousin Zhu Sha, my agent, and a host of other people (some of whom I knew and some whom I didn't). Everyone was trying to reach me.

Everyone except Muju, that is. I kept waiting for his call.

During occasional moments of lucidity, I had to marvel at my own incredible persistence when it came to Muju. You could call it love, perhaps, or maybe you could call it my way of making atonement.

Xi'er called again and again. 'Hi, Shanghai Princess, there's a party tonight. They're calling it 'Sex in the City', and everyone's expecting to see you there.'

'Hey, it's me. Wanna go shopping? Plaza 66 is having a sale.'

'Coco, for the last time pick up the phone! Or I swear I'm not calling you again . . .'

'God, you haven't changed a bit. No, I take that back. Your

temper is even worse than before. What's all this pretending to be a hermit? Let's have dinner together tonight. I'll drive by and pick you up in front of your building at seven o'clock. And if you're late I'm leaving without you!'

Xi'er's personality reminded me a bit of my old friend Madonna, although Xi'er was more likeable.

After I had left Shanghai, Madonna got into trouble for using her contacts with city officials and customs agents to smuggle Mercedes, BMWs and other luxury cars into China. When the police issued a warrant for her arrest, she went into hiding and seemed to disappear without a trace. Last I'd heard there was still no news of her.

From prostitute to wealthy widow, from Shanghai socialite to wanted criminal, Madonna's sombre beauty remained fixed deep in my memory like a scar.

As for Xi'er, I'd known her even longer than I had Madonna. We first met ten years ago, when she was still a pale, delicately built young boy suffering from the twin torments of adolescent acne and the male sexual organ between her legs, the periodic eruption of both of which threatened to drive her to the brink of collapse.

But three years ago when I ran into her again, she seemed reborn, like a butterfly emerging at last from its chrysalis. The adolescent acne on her face and the organ between her legs had both disappeared. She had acquired an ample chest, her two round breasts shaped perfectly to roll right into the palm of one's hand, graceful and voluptuous, sexy and alluring, like ripe fruit surrendering to the seduction of gravity.

Thankfully Xi'er had been born without a prominent Adam's apple. Whether walking down the street or hanging out at a nightclub, dressed provocatively and meticulously made-up, she managed to attract even more admiring glances from men than I did.

That night, she arrived promptly in her little green Volkswagen Beetle to pick me up.

I had finally changed out of my filthy pyjamas, taken a shower, and put on a white sleeveless dress. I wore no make-up, going downstairs with my face unadorned.

When I appeared, Xi'er shrieked and gave me a big hug. 'You awful thing . . . what would you do without me? How could you ever survive without me?'

I took a deep breath. She was right. Eccentric and fragile creature that I was, I'd never survive for long without understanding friends. 'I missed you,' I said simply.

We stood there for a while, the two of us, laughing and hugging, touching, sizing each other up and trading compliments like 'You just seem to get more and more beautiful!'

When good girlfriends get together, time seems to stand still. We start to giggle, our postures growing more relaxed and our bodies soften like warm toffee. It's a different feeling from a date with a man.

We had dinner at her restaurant.

It was called Shanghai 1933, and doubled as a tearoom. It was decorated with pale green bamboo, crinkly paper lanterns, delicately wrought birdcages, and antique furniture from all over China and Southeast Asia, arranged appropriately throughout the restaurant. Floor-length gauze curtains swayed softly in the breeze, and the low strains of popular Shanghai songs from the 1930s played on an old gramophone. The whole place was permeated with the tasteful, slightly morbid air of its owner.

Even the paper towels in the bathroom were decorated with Chinese ink-brush paintings, paintings that Xi'er had designed herself.

Before opening the restaurant, Xi'er had been a painter, and a fairly successful one at that. The *New York Times*, *Asahi Shimbun*, *Stern* and the BBC all did features on her – not because her paintings were especially extraordinary, necessarily, but because she was the first person in post-liberation China to have had a sex change. She was famous at first for speaking publicly about it, but after that she was simply famous for being famous. She could command high prices for her paintings, afford luxurious, extravagant clothes and jewellery and get into all of the trendiest clubs in Shanghai.

When she got tired of painting, Xi'er decided to open an expensive restaurant. At Shanghai 1933, a bowl of Shanghai wontons was 125 *yuan* ($15), and a cup of green tea 150 *yuan* ($20). No one else in Shanghai would have dared charge such prices. Every evening there was a queue. That's Shanghai; anything is possible. Places spring up overnight and disappear just as quickly.

Every night when Xi'er arrived at the restaurant, impeccably dressed and made-up, she would spend her time shuttling between the guests, the kitchen and the cash register, dazzling everyone with her agility and shrewd business sense. Before long, she'd earned herself a nickname: 'The Cut-throat Concubine'.

We sat down in a quiet corner, and I took out the presents I'd brought Xi'er from New York: several pornographic magazines featuring nude men. Xi'er took one look at them and laughed, thanking me with a kiss. These days, Shanghai had everything, but technically speaking this kind of magazine was still illegal.

I ordered the grilled salmon, spring rolls with duck, braised tofu and vegetable soup, and Xi'er had the waiter bring over a bottle of red wine.

'A year ago I'd never have guessed it would just be us two girls sitting here, having dinner on our own,' I said, lighting a cigarette.

'What's wrong with that? At least with no men around, we can have some peace and quiet.' Xi'er instructed the waiter to pour the wine into a glass carafe and set it aside for a while to breathe. 'There are more single girls in Shanghai than ever, and they have a lot of buying power. Most people who come to my restaurant are either groups of single girls or groups of gay men. Of course there are always the fat, balding perverts who get corner seats so they can fondle their nubile companions.'

I laughed. Xi'er and I always seemed to laugh a lot when we were together.

Of course it wasn't all laughs. Sometimes she would barge into my house in the middle of the night and sprawl on the couch in the living room, weeping bitterly – like so many spoiled peaches because she didn't have a man who truly loved her. She'd nearly died on the operating table and her parents still refused to see her, but after all her trouble becoming a woman she had suddenly lost her confidence in men. Instead she discovered their insincerity, their selfish indifference, and all kinds of other laughable and repugnant qualities. Men, she complained, were filthy animals. They thought with their dicks and not with their brains. Anyone in the world with a dick should be shot.

Presumably she was quite sincere about this. She had cut off her own dick after all.

We loved each other like sisters, a love we didn't really understand. We didn't know why we liked each other so much. Perhaps it was just that we drew comfort from each other's existence; it allowed us to forgive ourselves because there was someone else even weaker and more confused.

We would argue too, sometimes not speaking for a month at a time. We never particularly liked each other's boyfriends, often cautioning each other, 'He's just not good enough for you, you're wearing silk embroidered with pearls before swine, it's totally not worth it.' But to no avail, for sometimes when a woman makes love with a pig it's to punish herself, and later rise like a phoenix from the ashes. For women, this is a kind of self-improvement.

We laughed a lot, drank good wine, smoked cigarettes and ate delicacies: a lovely meal together. We hadn't discussed the men in our lives.

Xi'er obviously knew from my latest e-mail that Muju and I had got to a difficult place. And as for her, I knew that she'd been lonely for a while now, that she was famous for her sex change, and that men only occasinally wanted her for a one-night stand. Since breaking up with a Swedish guy six months ago, it seemed she'd never date again.

When I still didn't feel like going home after dinner, she

suggested going for a foot-massage at a parlour she frequented on Fuxing Road.

'Don't take your Beetle – let's call a taxi. You're too drunk.' I bit my lip and laughed, languid and heavy-eyed. I was drunk too.

We sat in the taxi, me clutching two wine glasses, Xi'er wielding a bottle of decent wine from the 1990s. It was her habit, she told me, to get a foot-massage while sipping red wine. She said she found it ten times more decadent than an orgasm. It was how she consoled herself when she craved sex and just met frustration.

Sunk into the plush cushions of the sofa at the massage parlour, in the dim lamplight and amidst the calming music, I could hear the faint sound of a client snoring.

Xi'er generously gave me a young male masseur that she often used, so that I could experience his outstanding technique for myself. Then she found herself a girl.

We sat down next to each other, taking turns pouring wine into each other's glasses. Instead of laughing as we did in the restaurant, we fell into a languorous reverie. After soaking in herb-infused water for ten minutes our feet were rubbed gently dry. One foot was then wrapped in a towel and rested on a small stool, while the other foot was placed on the warm knees of the masseur.

Then a pair of hands proceeded to rub the acupressure points on the sole of my foot, pinching, pushing, pressing and kneading. I love the indescribable feeling of having someone rub my feet and head so much that sometimes, when I'm down, I'll even visit beauty parlours or shoeshops just for the sublime comfort of having someone touch my head or feet. It's a kind of comfort for which men and cigarettes are no substitute.

A jet of heat throbbed lightly up my thighs as the young masseur adjusted his pressure and shifted acupressure points, and the towel that rested on my legs inched towards my waist. My womb grew warm and my vagina swelled with blood, just as it did with the rhythmic stroke of a penis when making love. Every cell of my body sighed, trembling, and I could picture the rose-petal of red between my legs as it slowly began to contract and unfold. Gorgeous and shocking.

Fine red wine was the perfect complement to such pleasure. I thought of what Xi'er had said: a foot-massage with wine was ten times more decadent than an orgasm.

We drank the wine sip by sip, relaxing our eyes, completely enslaved by the hands at our feet.

2

Sex and Escape

Free from desire, you realize the mystery. Caught in desire,
you see only the manifestations.
Lao-tzu

Perhaps man invented fire, but women invented how to play with fire.
Candace Bergen, *Sex and the City*

The next morning I awoke to the sound of birds.

The air was fragrant with osmanthus, roasted chest-nuts, petrol, and the scent of stir-fry from the street-side restaurants – all the usual smells of a morning in Shanghai. I opened my eyes slowly. Although the bedroom curtains blocked most of the light, I could already tell it was going to be a beautiful day outside.

When I turned my head, I discovered with a shock that I wasn't alone in bed. Lying next to me was a boy. He seemed to be sleeping peacefully. On that giant ice-skating rink of a bed, he looked especially delicate, youthful and fragile.

It took me a moment to recognize him as the young man who'd given me a foot-massage the night before.

I took a deep breath to clear my head. God, I had no idea how I'd got home last night. Had I raped him, or had he raped me? Or was it mutual? Try as I might, I couldn't remember a single thing about the night before.

He was waking up too. To alleviate some of the awkwardness, I went into the kitchen to make breakfast. He followed me into the kitchen, and I was relieved to note that he had at least thrown on a t-shirt and a pair of jeans.

'How's cereal and milk? Oh, looks like I've got some eggs too.' I tried to keep my voice perfectly neutral, so that I sounded neither happy nor unhappy. In fact, however, I was terribly confused. After all, how often do you wake up to find a complete stranger lying next to you, along with two used condoms and a mound of tissues scattered over the carpet? And why two condoms, I wondered, instead of just one?

We sat down together at the breakfast table. The boy helped me cut some melon into slices. Neither of us spoke.

I wasn't sure why I didn't just ask him to leave. I was even making him breakfast. Damn. Even when I was alone, I usually didn't go to the trouble of making breakfast. In fact, one of the reasons that things had cooled down between Muju and me was that I didn't enjoy cooking, while Muju was a bit of a gourmet. Whenever we discussed cooking we always wound up arguing about feminism and post-feminism, topics about which we never agreed. Once, Muju's ex-wife even came to the apartment that he and I shared and instructed me in cooking, housekeeping and finding the hidden beauty and Zen within my kitchen. Drop-dead beautiful and voluptuous, with a full head of blonde hair and two children by her wealthy current husband, she seemed happy to spend a quarter of her time in the kitchen. Any woman who wasn't good in the kitchen, she'd advised me, was a failure.

As I thought of Muju, I suddenly grew very uncomfortable. I couldn't help but wish the young man in my kitchen would just disappear. Maybe the floor would open up and swallow him.

I couldn't bring myself to think that Muju and I were really finished. I'd come back to Shanghai to work on my new book, but it was becoming apparent that he and I needed some time to let our feelings cool down before deciding whether to continue as lovers or just become friends. I hadn't been back in Shanghai two weeks and already I'd had a man spend the night in my bed. I couldn't stop feeling I'd betrayed Muju.

I was reminded of China in the old days, when a widow had to wait three years after her husband's death before she could remarry. Of course, I wasn't Muju's widow; for all I knew, I wasn't even his lover any more But that wasn't the issue. The issue was that I was still in love with him – deeply.

Without Muju by my side, I became nothing more than an exquisite corpse pining for his love, a body adrift on the sea, bobbing in the waves, numb and unfeeling, in a world that no longer existed . . .

Indulging with the strange boy last night might have been a way of punishing myself – punishing myself for loving Muju too deeply. By the time you love a certain person or thing that deeply, you've probably already lost them.

Restless and uneasy, I paced around the kitchen and smoked. I had no appetite for breakfast. I watched as the boy buried his face in the enormous bowl and shovelled cereal into his mouth. A faint milk moustache on his upper lip made him look even more childlike.

At last he seemed ready to leave. I breathed a sigh of relief. As we stood at the door, I asked him casually, 'How old are you, anyway?'

'Fifteen.' He flashed an easygoing and supremely unconcerned grin, draped his coat over his shoulders and galloped down the stairs. I heard the clatter of his footsteps on the way down, and then he was gone.

I stood there for a moment, my hair a mess, wearing only a flimsy robe I'd thrown on, the smell of sex still hanging in the air around me, smoking my cigarette and staring at the empty staircase. God, he was only fifteen. I'd taken a fifteen-year-old to bed!

Later when I talked to Xi'er on the phone, she chuckled mischievously and asked, 'So, how was it? A taste of fifteen – could be worse, no?'

I sighed and shook my head. Finally, unable to contain it any longer, I laughed. 'He looked about twenty-one, don't you think?' I said. 'Or at the very least twenty.'

After that, I somehow muddled through another week in Shanghai, a city bursting with noise and economic fever, a city that seemed to inspire in me so much lust.

The living room, bathroom and even the space beside my pillow still bore many traces of Muju. Before leaving New York, I'd stolen a few things from his apartment: an old toothbrush, several locks of hair I'd collected from his bathroom floor, a pair of unwashed Calvin Klein briefs, a fuzzy velvet peach, an old snapshot of Muju when he was in college.

And of course there was the large pile of cards that I'd saved, as well as all the little notes we'd written to each other, ticket stubs from concerts we'd seen together, plane tickets from trips we'd taken together, cards from restaurants where we'd dined together, and a small collection of little trinkets and gifts. They were like numerous tiny antennae radiating from Muju's person, ashes of my preserved memories. They were things to fill up emptiness and loneliness.

I tried to call Muju but kept getting his answering machine; I sent him e-mails but he never wrote back. His evasiveness left me feeling more helpless and distant than I'd ever felt before. We were now separated by twelve hours, by the Indian and Atlantic oceans, and by the entire continent of Eurasia.

I decided to stick with my original plan and get out of Shanghai for a while.

One fine afternoon, I loaded a few small bags into a taxi and took the overhead high-speed expressway out of Shanghai. We passed brown, golden and russet autumn canopies of broad-leaved parasol trees, forests of skyscrapers and spires, and old-fashioned baroque villas before finally arriving at Pier Sixteen on the Bund.

The little white steamer that greeted me at the pier looked even older than I was. It was covered with spots of rust, an old coat of yellowing paint, and some crudely hand-painted black characters that identified the ship as '*The Sea and Sky* – Zhejiang Province, Zhoushan Steamship Company'.

As the steamer set out slowly down the Huangpu River, I was overcome with an inexplicable feeling of excitement and happiness. Children ran about the decks, shouting, while the adults occupied themselves with card games, mah-jong, drinking, reading and chatting. On every face there was an expression of happiness, as if leaving this city of sixteen million people was a cause for celebration.

That's one of the nice things about living in Shanghai. You're always happy to get away.

As evening fell, a frosty moon appeared in the sky, the ocean winds grew chillier, and the sea air grew damp and heavy.

The steamer fell silent again, and the only sound to be heard was the putt-putt-putting of the boat's engine. We were surrounded by water on all sides, ocean as far as the eye could see. From time to time small pine-covered islands would come into view, their irregular shapes complementing the full moon that hung in the sky like a disc of jade. It was like a scene out of a Chinese ink painting.

I didn't feel like sleeping. My head was clear at last and my thoughts lucid. I felt truly happy for the first time since returning from New York. I had something to look forward to. My lungs could breathe again, my brain could think again, and though in my heart I felt real loneliness and confusion, at the same time I felt a sense of calm and courage.

I stood at the bow of the boat for a long time, gazing into the pitch-black water-world and drifting gently back to a place long since forgotten, a tiny island to which I had frequently returned in dreams while I was enmired in loneliness and uncertainty in New York. It was the little island with over fifty temples, shrines, monasteries and nunneries – that Buddhist paradise of sea and sky known as Putuo Island.

3

When She Arrived in New York

There's still plenty of sex in Manhattan but the kind of sex that results
in friendship and business deals, not romance. These days, everyone
has friends and colleagues; no one really has lovers – even if they have
slept together.
Candace Bushnell, *Sex and the City*

You smiled and talked to me of nothing and I felt that for this
I had been waiting long.
Rabindranath Tagor, *Stray Birds*

I was born twenty-nine years ago on Putuo Island in a temple known as the Temple of Righteous Rain.

My mother was a devout Buddhist. When she was pregnant with me, she and my father took a boat to the temple to pray for the future of their unborn child and for the peace and prosperity of the family. My mother had arranged for the senior abbot of the monastery to offer a half-day prayer service to secure the blessings of the Buddhist patriarchs.

That evening at dusk, as the temple lamps were being lit, my mother felt a sharp spasm of pain in her belly and realized that she had gone into labour prematurely. So it was that I entered this world earlier than expected. Needless to say, it caused something of an uproar in the temple, but luckily there were no complications and both mother and child came through the delivery safely.

The next day, my parents held a baptismal ceremony in which

they christened me with the rather weighty devout Buddhist name of Zhi Hui, or 'One Who has Embarked on the Path of Wisdom and Enlightenment'.

I had a healthy, happy childhood. My parents showered me with love and attention until I was thirteen, at which point I got my first period and became a rebellious teenager who gave my parents their fair share of grief. My mother used to say it was as if I'd turned into a monster overnight, as if I'd woken up one morning with horns sprouting from my forehead. A few years later, a fair-skinned and bright-eyed seventeen-year-old, I passed the entrance exam for the prestigious Fudan University and had my first chance to move away from home.

I had my first sexual experience at nineteen, an unfortunate encounter in which I neglected to remove the condom from my vagina afterwards. At twenty-two, a painful unrequited love affair with one of my professors became fodder for my first novel. At twenty-four, difficulties with my writing and the surprising discovery that my then-fiancé was mixed up with the Chinese mafia drove me to attempt suicide by slitting my wrists.

My novel *Shanghai Baby*, published when I was twenty-six, met with huge success at first – then it was banned on the Chinese mainland. To date it has been published in over forty countries and was recently adapted for a feature film. Few people would ever connect Zhi Hui, the little girl born at the Temple of Righteous Rain, with the writer whom the Chinese press had dubbed 'the literary beauty who shatters taboos'.

At twenty-eight, I moved to New York and witnessed the terrorist attacks on the World Trade Center. At the time, I was a not particularly diligent visiting scholar in the East Asian Studies Department at Columbia University. In the wake of 9/11, I struggled with the difficulties of trying to promote the American edition of *Shanghai Baby*.

But all of this seems insignifiant. In the words of my favourite French poet, Rimbaud: 'I have come to know the skies splitting with lightnings, and the waterspouts, and the breakers and currents; I know the evening, and Dawn rising up like a flock of doves, and sometimes I have seen what men have imagined they saw!'

For I have seen almost everything there is to see of human illusion. I have glimpsed what lies beyond the lavender haze. I have witnessed the slow dissolution of life in all its guises and illusions, and watched it fade.

When I first spied Muju at an Italian restaurant called I Coppi in the East Village, it wasn't love at first sight.

At that exact moment I had no way of knowing that following his destiny from a distant past, he would soon drift spirit-like before me and become my intimate lover, my eternally-bound family, my god and my child. I didn't know that we were fated to hold each other close and make love, to share the same dreams in the cold moonlight, to love each other, to fight, to laugh, to scream with love.

At dinner that evening, I remember that there were two others at the table with us – my British publisher and a female divorce lawyer born and raised in New York. This was the same lawyer who, ten years previously, had helped Muju's Jewish ex-wife walk off with most of his net worth. In the process she had inadvertently fallen in love with him. She'd been Muju's girlfriend for two years and they were still friends. She also just happened to be the best friend of the wife of my British publisher. It sounds complicated, I know, but such are modern relationships.

During the meal I talked mainly with the other two people and didn't pay much attention to the tall, well-built Japanese (actually a quarter Italian) man who was missing a portion of the little finger of his left hand. Historically, most Chinese aren't too fond of the Japanese, but that bothered me less than the stereotypes I'd heard about Japanese men: that they were stubbornly rigid, womanizing and chauvinistic.

Before dinner was over, however, I'd found myself forced to notice him. There seemed to be a faint current flowing between us, a sort of chemical reaction. I didn't know if it was his laugh, the way he talked, or the frank and unconcealed glances that he cast towards me. Or perhaps it was his insistence that I taste a piece of veal braised in soy that he had cut for me from his own plate. In any event, something finally compelled me to take a closer look at him.

His shirt, with a floral pattern on the collar and front, looked like something a South American man might like (it was only much later that I discovered it was a three-hundred-dollar shirt by Comme des Garçons). The giant bag at his feet looked big enough to be a small tent, I imagined it would come in handy if he ever needed to run away from a lover at short notice. His features, which betrayed not a hint of his mixed heritage, were supremely ordinary and impassive as if cloaked in an impenetrable fog. Compared to the outrageous shirt and the giant bag, his face seemed refined. Then his eyes . . . I had to admit that his eyes had an extraordinary light, as though it came from deep underground, like a lamp buried within a mine, glowing with a strange radiance.

It was the kind of light that could inspire a sudden lust in women. Particularly a woman like me, who so often found herself dazzled.

After talking on the phone three or four times and exchanging almost daily e-mails, Muju and I finally had our first date about a week before Christmas.

That evening at seven o'clock, I was still in the bathroom frantically drying my hair. The sofa and living room floor were strewn with shoes, clothes, books, newspapers, and several pairs of stockings that I hadn't had time yet to check for runs. When I heard the doorbell ring, I rushed to the intercom and begged: 'Please, just give me five minutes!'

Whenever I arrange to meet someone, I never seem to have enough time to do everything I need to do beforehand. At the moment of my birth, it seems, my fate was sealed with the words: 'Doomed to be late.'

I finally decided on a pair of brown, pointed-toe Ferragamo

heels, topped off with a coat of dark purple wool. But I could only find one of the hand-embroidered leather gloves that I'd bought in Rome. I took a deep breath, refusing to let the other glove ruin my mood.

I closed the door behind me and went downstairs to find a tall man standing outside in the freezing wind. He was stamping his feet on the ground like a grizzled brown bear, looking as if he might pass out from the cold. Muju.

He breathed a sigh of relief when he saw me and flashed a warm, sincere smile, a smile that could thaw ice. Standing there before him, I felt oddly shy.

He bent down to give me a hug, and I noticed that besides the giant bag slung over his shoulder, he was also carrying a paper shopping bag emblazoned with the words 'Sakura Nishi Department Store' and decorated with an elaborate green and red butterfly knot. It wasn't until then that I realized Christmas was right around the corner.

'This is for you,' he said, handing me the bag.

'Thanks . . . that's too kind of you. Is it a Christmas present?' I examined the huge package, but couldn't guess what was inside.

'I don't know,' he said. 'I guess so. I just felt I had to get it for you, and luckily the store was having a sale.'

His answer was so frank that I had to laugh. 'What's inside?'

'I guess you won't find out until you open it!' he answered with a mischievous smile.

Quickly I tore open the wrapping to find a box inside. When I read the words on its side I could hardly believe them . . . it was a humidifier!

As I stared in disbelief, he asked me anxiously, 'Don't you like it? I realize it's not a very romantic gift, but I remembered you telling me once on the telephone that New York was too dry, and that it was even worse with the heat on indoors. You said it gave you nosebleeds . . .'

My eyes opened even wider and I struggled not to laugh. 'Did I really say that on the phone?' I mumbled. 'But actually, I really need one of these. I'm quite a practical girl, you know. I'll take a humidifier over roses any day . . .'

With these words of thanks, I gave him a hug and a big wet kiss on the mouth. The moment our lips made contact, I felt a sudden shock of static.

We released each other immediately and started to laugh. 'You see? New York really is too dry.' His comment helped me mask at least some of the excitement and embarrassment I was feeling.

'Maybe it would be best if I, uh . . . put this in my apartment first,' I said, blushing a deep crimson.

I picked up the humidifier and darted back up the stairs, while Muju waited in the small, cosy entrance hall downstairs.

As I dashed up the stairs he called up to me, 'Coco! There's no hurry. Take your time. Oh, and you might want to change into something warmer. That's a beautiful coat you've got on, but it's really windy outside.'

'Now that's not a suggestion you usually hear on a first date . . . ' I mused in surprise, shrugging my shoulders.

When I came back downstairs, I was bundled up in an enormous down-filled black parka that looked more like a sleeping-bag than an overcoat. Muju just smiled.

Already I was deeply attracted. He had a strange sort of warmth about him; not the warmth you get from a stove or a man's naked body, but the sort of warmth that held odd associations for me: a mother's womb or the reading of sutras in a temple lit only by oil lamps. The former perhaps was a pre-natal memory, while the latter might be the baptismal ceremony performed for me by the monks of Putuo Island the day after I was born. Memories like these came from a vague intuition, as if they were stored not in my mind but in some of the cells of my skin – memories that could be released now and then by the slightest touch. Subtle intuition like this can often be far more accurate and reliable than logic.

And so, armed with a new humidifier and a big black parka as cosy as a sleeping bag, I decided I was falling in love with Muju.

We walked the seven or eight blocks to Grand Avenue and arrived at a Malaysian restaurant called Nyonya. Run by a Chinese-Malaysian, the restaurant served food very similar to Chinese cuisine. My stomach was so incorrigibly stubborn that I had eaten Chinese food almost every day since arriving in New York. The food at Nyonya wasn't as good as the food in China, but was certainly better than nothing.

Our meal wasn't bad, particularly the coconut rice, steamed fish in fermented soy sauce, and fermented tofu with stir-fried greens. Muju loved to eat, and insisted that he could eat four or even five meals a day. Eating badly put him in a bad mood and, he claimed, a bad mood affected his health.

'For me, health and happiness are the two most important things in life,' he told me.

'What about money?' I asked.

'Less important. As long as I have enough to get by, I'm happy.' With that, he immersed himself in his fish and kept eating until the bones were picked clean.

'Of course, if I had the chance to strike it rich I'd grab the opportunity,' he added. 'I've discovered that it takes a lot of courage to become a mult-millionaire. A lot of people don't have the courage to imagine that they could ever earn that kind of money.'

His judgement about being rich, I thought to myself, was certainly unique.

Besides writing travel books, Muju also volunteered at a city college medical clinic, where he taught Taoist meditation techniques and Indian yoga. His main job was producing independent documentary films (which I suppose is also a kind of volunteer work, as so few people make any money from documentaries). He had his own office on West Broadway in Soho, not more than a hundred yards away from my apartment on Watts Street.

In one of his e-mails he'd mentioned that he was working on a new project. The star of his film was an energetic Latin singer name Julio, who'd been dubbed 'The Conscience of the Dominican Republic'. The two were also good friends, as close as brothers.

'How's the documentary going?' I asked.

'Oh, there are more problems than I ever thought possible. One minute, there's a problem with the equipment; the next, someone's gotten food poisoning. And to top it all off, Julio and I have been arguing a lot.' Muju smiled. 'Latin Americans make great friends, but working with them is incredibly difficult.'

'Oh, that's right!' he said suddenly, as if he'd just remembered something interesting. 'I really liked your book.'

'So you finally got around to reading it.' I let out a long sigh of relief and allowed myself a victorious smile. He had told me once on the phone that he had gone out and bought both the English and Japanese versions of the book, but that he wasn't too sure he wanted to read them. He said he worried that if he didn't like the book it might have a negative effect on his romantic feelings for the author.

'First of all, my book and I are two entirely separate things. Second, it's not imperative that you like me.' That was my immediate retort on the phone. I regretted my words the minute they were out of my mouth, knowing that my hurt tone proved I cared about his opinion. If male-female relations were a battle of wills, then I knew my salvo had put me at a distinct disadvantage, even though I'd been the one to shoot first.

There had been a moment of silence before Muju said quietly 'I'm sorry.'

I hate that way of saying 'I'm sorry.' Of course, I hate it that Chinese men aren't in the habit of saying 'I'm sorry' to women. But the way Western culture smears 'I'm sorry' around everywhere as if it were Vaseline is sometimes even worse. It sounds perfectly polite, but it has the effect of dropping a glass partition between you and the speaker. It freezes you out.

'Not a problem. Well, thanks for calling.' I yawned deliberately and quickly ended the call.

It wasn't an amicable parting.

The next day, Muju sent me an e-mail cartoon that he had drawn himself of a little clown eating a peach. If he'd been trying to get a laugh out of me, it worked.

'Lucky you still like me after reading the book,' I said now, with mild sarcasm.

'I read both the English and the Japanese versions, but I thought the Japanese translation read better,' Muju replied, ignoring my sarcasm. 'Your descriptions are very perceptive, and poetic.'

He seemed so frank and sincere that I decided to believe him.

We smiled and looked into one another's eyes. For a split second I had the strange impression that I was gazing into a mirror.

4

As Sexy as it Gets

Love me without fear/
Trust me without questioning/
Need me without demanding!
Want me without restrictions/
Accept me without change/
Desire me without inhibitions.
Dick Sutphen

. . . he was brought low,
Burning in the bride bed of love, in the whirl-
Pool at the wanting centre, in the folds
Of paradise, in the spun bud of the world.
And she rose with flowering in her melting snow.
Dylan Thomas, 'A Winter's Tale'

New York – Autumn

The day after I arrived in New York, the September 11th terrorist attacks took place. I saw those two huge buildings come tumbling down before my eyes.

The month that passed after the attacks was miserable. There was the smell of death in the air, envelopes filled with anthrax, planes that kept dropping from the sky, the dry summer heat, bad Chinese food, rapacious lawyers and dinner dates with men who expected you to split the bill with them afterwards.

Speaking of the New York dating scene, I'd never seen such a depressing city. The men of this city were unique on the planet. Much of the time their testosterone-driven quest for supremacy was exciting, but even more often their selfishness and insecurity left one feeling hopeless. In Woody Allen films and in episodes of *Sex and the City* you could see the shadows of these people. There are physically, emotionally and financially healthy and centred men in the world, but I guess they aren't in New York.

Once, at a charity benefit thrown by a certain VIP, I met two men: forty-three-year-old John, a powerful producer at CBS, and thirty-eight-year-old Milton, a rising star on Wall Street.

As he talked, the former several times carelessly let slip his natural racism, while at the same time showing that he desperately wanted an Asian woman to rescue him. I saw why one day when he found the opportunity to take off his trousers in front of me, and I discovered he had one of the tiniest dicks I had ever seen. Alarmed, I scurried out of his luxurious flat as quick as a bunny. Thinking about it later, I felt sad for him, but also a bit flattered on behalf of all Asian women that some Western men believe certain parts of our bodies to be a bit more petite, even if that's just a cliché.

Handsome thirty-eight-year-old Milton, on the other hand, perhaps because his father had killed a young pair of twin sisters in the Vietnam War, seemed to combine guilt and infatuation in his feelings for Asian girls. For some reason he also thought I was only twenty-three. After several dates, I discovered he had a sweet and romantic side – he sent me a big bunch of roses. Milton liked to fantasize that he was either destroying the girl he was dating, or that he was rescuing her. However, at the tail-end of the third date, he suddenly started to call me 'Pussycat'. I was extremely shocked. My poor English made me extremely sensitive about some words, and, over a candlelight dinner, any word connected to 'pussy' absolutely enraged me.

After a few dates like this, you start wishing that you were a hermaphrodite so that you could just do it yourself and get it over with – and save a lot of money and hassle. It's not easy being a single woman in New York, and being a single woman from Asia is even harder.

But being a married woman isn't much of an improvement.

Before coming to the US, I had heard of an American couple who went halves on everything, including petrol and dog food. At that moment I lost faith in the women's movement. Next time around, women marching for equality should hold up signs reading: 'We want equality, but we don't want to pay for dinner, petrol or dog food.'

Anyway, that night at the Malaysian restaurant, Muju made a point of paying the bill. Perhaps we were off to a good start after all.

We met again not long after that, on the night before Muju had to fly to the Dominican Republic to continue working on his documentary; I remember that it was Christmas Eve. After sharing a nice meal at a restaurant, we went back to Muju's apartment on the Upper West Side.

His apartment wasn't especially large, but it had an atmosphere that made guests feel comfortable.

Through the large floor-to-ceiling windows adorned with simple Japanese bamboo blinds, I could just glimpse the faint dark outline of Central Park and the skyline of the buildings around it. There was a long black leather sofa and a large television set, on top of which stood a toy wooden elephant that Muju had brought back from India thirty years earlier; a specimen of coral that he had fished from the ocean floor; and a few hardy pot plants, one of which was a gift from his ex-wife on the occasion of their divorce ten years before. I doubt he watered them more than twice a year. Nearby stood a few cabinets and chests of drawers, including a lacquered antique cabinet bought in Brazil, which looked as if it might fall to pieces at any second.

What left the strongest impression, however, were the painted little knickknacks scattered around the room, a wide collection of tiny peaches and nude female figures made from all sorts of things: plastic, painted wood, porcelain, metal and velvet.

Standing there in a room so genuine, so lived in, so part of someone, made me feel like an invader, a voyeur trying to satisfy her curiosity.

I felt a wave of physical longing rise through me. It was lust, mixed with innocent memories of childhood: peaches, summer, milk, infants, conspiracies, enigmas . . .

I stood under the soft lights and stared into Muju's eyes. The light that shone from them held me. He stood so close that I could hear the sound of his breath, smell the scent of his body, see the faint flush spreading across his skin.

He raised a cup of Japanese green tea to my lips. I took a sip and – without swallowing – brought my mouth closer to his. Trembling ever so slightly, his mouth closed over mine.

Our tongues entwined. There is nothing in the world more intimate than this – this slippage, this needy searching. The clean, fresh, slightly bitter flavour of the green tea, the heady smell of sex, everything being filled at once, spinning, revolving, melting . . . We had rehearsed the scene of this intimacy many times in our heads, and now, here, it unfolded exactly as we desired.

The way his hands caressed me left me spellbound, thinking how truly fortunate I was. No man had ever caressed me like this before. Gently, with great tenderness, and yet at the same time savage, without the slightest hesitation, with the indifferent authority of a king.

And beneath his gaze my body gave up its final line of defence, was reduced to a ball of mud shredded petals, a grain of dust, the sound of a sigh. And shortly after, he made me feel like he was flying high into the sky. His fingers and lips drove my body, making me fall and rise again and again, making me climax again and again. I would never let flow another drop of water; I thought I might die of thirst, parched and dry.

And then at two or three in the morning, when at last he ceased his games with fingers and lips and prepared to give himself to me, he became impotent.

This didn't disappoint me in the least. Perched content and powerless on the soft pillows, I slipped into unconsciousness.

In the morning, the sunlight came in from the window and washed over the bed like a layer of watered honey. It was the first time I'd slept well since arriving in New York three months ago.

The pillow to my left was empty, on the sheets the faint impression of a body. To my right – on the floor by my side of the bed – a rather familiar humidifier sputtered out white steam. Looking at it, I smiled to myself.

I stretched lazily, eased out of bed, and walked barefoot towards the living room.

Muju was sitting cross-legged in his pyjamas on a round indigo cushion. His back was utterly still. Something about it aroused in me a feeling of awe.

With some men, it's only once their penis is inside you that you feel they belong to you and then as soon as they get out of bed they might as well be strangers you've never seen before in your life. But Muju wasn't like that.

What caused me to feel awe, and unfamiliarity, was his stillness. From this contemplative, meditative posture of some Indian or Taoist origin, a kind of miraculous energy emanated outward.

I curled up quietly on the sofa, observing Muju's back as he meditated. The sunlight filtered in through the venetian blinds, speckling the furniture and all those peaches and women of different shapes and sizes. Like a dreamworld.

I don't know how much time passed, but when I awoke from unexpected sleep Muju was still in the same posture. Time didn't seem to have touched him. He was here, but he was not here.

I stretched with contentment. Ever since setting foot in this apartment, something safe and warm had acted on me, body and soul. It was as if this was a home in which I'd lived for several decades and not just an evening.

Muju lifted himself up from the cushion at last and walked towards me with a smile 'Aren't you cold?'

He kissed me on the lips, rubbed my still-naked body vigorously with the palm of his hand.

The chill had left goosebumps all over my skin.

'I'll get you a bathrobe,' he said, and turned towards the bathroom.

I pulled him to a halt. 'It's all right.' I was a little flushed, but I turned his face firmly towards mine and kissed him slowly. 'What I want is . . .' I said falteringly, one hand reaching furtively below his waist. He moaned lightly, and then pushed me firmly down onto the sofa.

This time there was no lingering foreplay of fingers and lips. He sprinted to the bathroom and quickly returned, a condom in hand, and then he bored into my body with quick, powerful movements.

As I came I thought, 'He could be anyone, anything.'

He came too, but didn't ejaculate.

That afternoon, Muju left on the Dominican Air flight. We would be apart for three weeks. As far as I was concerned, that was a great deal too long.

5

Her 29th Birthday

Time flows as far as water!
Confucius

The hardest years in life are those between ten and seventy.
Helen Hayes

On January 3rd in New York, there was no song of the nightingale, no jazz music floating in the air, no Muju, no fabulous twenty-ninth birthday party. There was only the wind blowing incessantly from the East River, and the Hudson River. It puckered my skin with its sharp cold.

Twenty-nine is a truly awkward age. You don't know if you're still a girl, or if you're already a woman. The old mini-skirt in the dresser gives off a wounded air, the air of rapidly departing youth. Although you can come more easily at twenty-nine than you could at nineteen, you have no idea whether your present self is happier or unhappier.

At twenty-nine, my mother already had an eight-year-old daughter. At twenty-nine, Marilyn Monroe had the love of all the men in the world, and at twenty-nine that most beloved of Asian goddesses, Guanyin, had gone from princess to nun, perfecting her practice and becoming immortal in the 'Buddha Land of Sea and Sky' on Putuo Island.

At twenty-nine, I left my motherland behind and was adrift in a strange land. Fortunately, I rather liked New York – especially a New York with Muju in it.

When I got up that morning, Muju called me. As soon as I picked up the phone he said, 'Hi and happy birthday! Now keep quiet for a second.'

I laughed, but he quickly shushed me. I pressed the receiver against my ear, and sure enough could make out a melodious sound, like some kind of birdcall.

'What is that, a bird?' I asked.

'Do you like it?' He didn't answer me right away.

'Yes, it's like I can almost smell the rainforest. What kind of bird is it?'

'It's not a bird, it's a special kind of frog that can only be found here. Local people call it a *coqui*.' He laughed, a bit proud of himself.

'Wow, frogs that can sing like birds. Bring one back for me!' I laughed too, happy.

'I'll bring you a present, but not a *coqui*,' he answered.

It's said that Japanese like giving gifts. From my perspective that's hardly a flaw.

When I turned on my computer I found quite a few birthday greetings from friends. My girlfriend Xi'er wrote that she'd just sent me a short silk nightie, in white, and that she'd painted a big black lotus blossom on it in acrylics.

Lotuses, the colour black, a silk nightie – these are a few of your favourite things. And according to our established custom, I've naturally made two pieces, exactly the same: one for you and one for me. Long live our friendship! May you be a happy woman at twenty-nine, finish your book, and find a good man. P.S. Oh, and, I've already ironed the lotus blossom, so you don't have to worry about it fading in the wash.

I couldn't keep from smiling at the computer.

Of all the birthday presents I received each year, I always looked forward to Xi'er's the most. She liked to have a few things that were exactly the same as mine. Before long, buying two sets of presents became a kind of custom between us. Once I bought two Italian ovulation predictor kits, one for myself and one for her. When she opened hers, she nearly killed me. I'd forgotten that she had no need of such things.

My cousin Zhu Sha, who was older than me by four years, and her painter husband Ah Dick sent me an e-card together. On the card was a picture of their three-month-old son's goofy little squeezable, grinning face.

The smiling face of this little baby involuntarily generated in me a fine thread of envy. Ever since we were small, I'd been jealous of Zhu Sha's beauty and intelligence, her popularity and her sweet nature in elementary school. I'd done some horrible things, like smear blue ink on the white georgette skirt that she had to wear for a school recital.

Now she was not only a happy mother, she was also a manager in a American-owned public relations consulting firm in Shanghai. Attending simultaneously to both business and family, she was one of the rapidly developing Chinese middle class.

While the orbits of our lives never seemed to cross, nevertheless we still appreciated each other and, at times, even longed for the completely opposite life led by the other. We both knew about cherishing our opportunities, about developing ourselves, and that this generation of women had far more opportunities than the last generation.

My old friend Jimmy Wong called and we arranged to have dinner that evening.

Jimmy Wong and I had met thirteen years ago. At the time he was a famous young poet in China, proud and arrogant. He didn't like the government and the government didn't like him.

After the Tian'anmen incident in 1989, he hurriedly emigrated, bringing his wife – like him, a poet – and his newborn daughter to New York. As soon as they arrived, he and his wife both gave up the poet's life simultaneously so they could support themselves. It's an expensive city. His wife got a job in a clothing factory and in a restaurant in Chinatown, and he went to law school, waiting in agony for the day when he would earn his licence to practice. He became an immigration attorney and soon opened offices in both Flushing and Lower Manhattan so he could provide services to the more than one million Chinese seeking green cards. But later he got divorced. His ex-wife started a company that specialized in importing imitation antique furniture from China. Now it made profits of more than a million dollars a year.

I'd heard that ninety per cent of poets were naturals at earning money; they just weren't willing to go out and try.

After I arrived in New York, Jimmy Wong would call pretty much every week or two to ask me to a meal. He was plumper than before and had a bit less hair, and his face wore the anxious, alert expression of a lawyer. Since his divorce he'd remained single, and still liked his beer cold and his women hot. But the more women he slept with, the lonelier he got.

He once said that I made the best dinner companion. Sometimes he'd be disappointed when I couldn't attend meals with him regularly every two weeks, but that would only last a few seconds.

Come to think of it, our friendship was nearly flawless. We appreciated each other, cared for each other, and strangely enough never argued; but neither did we love each other too much. Even now we had never been plagued by lust or desire, and could discuss our sex lives freely.

This time, we chose a Shanghai-style restaurant on Mott Street in Chinatown called Old Zheng Xing. They had authentic Shanghai cuisine.

As soon as we saw each other, Jimmy's always-impatient face lit up. He spread his arms wide and gave me a huge hug. 'I really can't believe we've been friends this long!' he said, looking me up and down.

I wore a rice-coloured angora turtle-neck sweater and a black leather jacket. 'Time hasn't touched you,' he said. 'Look at you, you're still exactly the same as the first time I met you in Beijing, still with such an innocent face!'

I laughed when I heard this. Flattery always has its place. But I'm not very tall and with my long straight hair and round face I can sometimes pass for innocent.

From his pocket he took out a red satin box tied with silk ribbon and passed it to me. 'What's this?' I took it curiously, and rattled the box next to my ear, trying to see if I could tell what it was. Ever since I was small I've been used to getting all sorts of presents, and more than one person has felt that I took them for granted. Even Muju would one day accuse me of being 'needlessly arrogant'.

Jimmy seemed to really enjoy my childish conduct. 'Can you tell what it is?' He smiled. 'It's a jade bracelet. Very sophisticated. Ten years ago, I'd definitely have given you a poem.'

'Lucky it's ten years later,' I giggled. Perhaps he thought I was just kidding, but the truth was that even at my most frenzied, most manic periods of writing, I never neglected material beauty. Silk was beautiful, jade was beautiful, Prada was beautiful, Ferrari sport cars were beautiful, and American money, especially imprinted with the likeness of Franklin, was also beautiful.

Old Zheng Xing's waiters all spoke the Shanghai dialect, and their clothes and hair were tidier by far than those of the immigrants smuggled over by the Chinese mafia to work in Fujianese restaurants.

A male waiter with long narrow eyes brought over menus, and we ordered Shanghai crab-marrow steamed buns, 'One Hundred Leaves' braised pork, salted greens with bamboo shoots, and 'tasty' marinated pork soup. The latter was pure old-school Shanghai cuisine. There was no trace of it in present-day Shanghai. Who'd have guessed it would survive intact in New York?

Every Chinatown overseas was like an old-style freight train, chugging slowly along with its cargo of traditional Chinese memories. In contrast, China was a super-high-speed bullet-train, rocketing ahead.

The food was good, the wine was good, and the conversation flowed.

Jimmy's poetic sensibilities seemed to have returned. We had a rare discussion of the religious views of Dostoevsky and Hermann Hesse. The conversation then turned to homes, cars, gardens, and then inevitably, quite naturally, to our favourite subject: sex.

'New York isn't as sexy as Shanghai,' I said.

'I think so too.' He swallowed a big mouthful of beer. 'And what's worse, New York can turn a guy into a sex maniac one minute – over-confident about sex – and then make you impotent the next, so you don't feel like having sex for a year.'

'When I'd only been here for a month, I intentionally dressed down in order to reduce the likelihood of getting mugged or raped,' I said. At this, Jimmy and I laughed.

A few days ago my mother, far away in China, had telephoned anxiously to tell me that she'd just seen a news report that said that some pervert had recently pushed a foreign girl off the platform in a New York subway station. She demanded repeatedly that I be careful when I go out, that I should take care not to dress too ostentatiously and that I should try to stay towards the back of the station in the subway.

Who told me to live in this infamously disreputable city anyway?

Sex here was like a small hard coin one could pick up from where it had been thrown carelessly on the ground. People here had lost sight of the most classic sexual pleasures, had forgotten what it was like to sit in a café casting glance after glance full of innuendo and charm, to flirt at one's leisure, refusing, fawning a bit, stopping for a moment, then teasing again, refusing again, stopping again for a moment . . .

This type of tango is something that takes time. And in New York, time was precious.

Shanghai was becoming increasingly like New York, but it would never *be* New York. In Shanghai, at least, the air was always moist and humid; it was air that reminded you of a garden after a rainfall or a woman after her bath.

'In *The Brothers Karamazov*, Dostoevsky said through the mouth of the Grand Inquisitor that man desires not only to live, but to have something to live for.' Jimmy raised his glass high. 'A toast,' he said, 'To Something to Live For!'

6

Snow

Elegant Things: A white coat worn over a violet waistcoat. Duck eggs.
Shared ice mixed with liana syrup and put in a new silver bowl.
Plum blossoms covered with snow.
Sei Shōnagon, *The Pillow Book*, Ivan Morris' translation, 1967

The weather turned cold and windy.

One morning I got up, pulled open the heavy black velour curtains, and discovered with surprise a coat of plain silver wrapping outside the window. It was snowing! A real snow-storm.

Snowflakes as big as my palm danced in the air, filling the sky. So pretty it didn't seem real. Buildings, streets, cars, trees – all disappeared into a world so transformed that only poetry remained.

When I was little snow for me meant the New Year, firecrackers, tangerines peeled and eaten while sitting around the kitchen stove. But no real snow had fallen in Shanghai since my adolescence.

New York's first snowfall awakened all my memories of snow. Mind wandering, I sat on the toilet, brushed my teeth, combed my hair, did some simple yoga, and ate last night's leftover dumplings, all while gazing out the window at the white snow outside. In a daze I imagined that I had been transformed into one of those flying snowflakes, that I was dancing lightly, just so, in the air, pure white, unique, no control over my body, and then falling to the muddy earth below, melting or being crushed by the heel of a boot . . .

The process of life could be as simple as a snowflake fluttering down from the sky or the extinguishing of a lamp; or two of the most magisterial buildings in the world being reduced to ash in the space of an hour.

But snowflakes on the ground melt into water, and then evaporate into the sky; a day comes when they once again become snowflakes flying in the air. Maybe death is similar, a kind of interlude, so that when you open your eyes again you find that you've already begun a whole new life in a totally different part of the world.

Everything is ephemeral, changing, a void. Yet this kind of transformation and emptiness is eternal. There is a road that seems to wind slowly towards perfect knowledge, and every step down this road is eternity, is rebirth.

I put out my cigarette, surprised by the thoughts that had lapped like waves into my brain.

The snow was still falling, but it had slackened a bit. A few snowflakes fell on the glass of the windowpane and melted straight away.

I sat down next to the window, opened my laptop and went through my e-mails. Apart from the junk mail you constantly see such as 'How to Make Money Without Working' and 'How to Be Multi-Orgasmic', there were messages from publishers, from the media, and from East Asian Studies students and scholars, and naturally there were quite a few personal ones. Among the many messages, I always picked out Muju's first. We wrote to each other every day, sharing what had happened to us both, sharing our yearning.

In today's letter, he told me that he was about to leave for Havana. Julio was giving a free concert for the workers of Cuba. Twenty thousand people would watch as he sang out in support of a small nation's brave resistance to American imperialism. Castro would attend. Two months ago concert playbills had been posted throughout the streets, and the two local television stations had been constantly broadcasting announcements about the show.

At the end of his e-mail, Muju told me he had just had breakfast with Julio's first and third wives, both Latina, one a blonde and one a brunette.

As soon as we sat down to eat they started talking dirty about Julio, in the sweetest voices, like milk and honey. At first you want them, but at the same time both ladies are highly destructive, like two engines turning over relentlessly.

That was how he described them, anyway.

Muju's observations and descriptions of all sorts of things sometimes surprised me. Through his eyes, I could see colours, shapes, characters and stories that I'd never noticed before, or taken an interest in. I have to confess that before meeting Muju I wasn't even sure what corner of the world the Dominican Republic was in.

So he'd be off to Cuba with a band to a concert for the proletariat, a concert that Castro would also attend. That sounded pretty cool to me.

I pressed 'reply' and wrote that it had snowed heavily in New York that day.

'A very beautiful snow scene, and I really wish you were by my side . . . I've been sitting by the window watching the snow for hours, and I don't know why, but some odd thoughts kept popping into my head. I was thinking about things like death, eternity, rebirth . . .

I took a drag from my cigarette, hesitated a moment, and then continued tapping out the line:

I'm thinking about having a child. I used to detest the whole idea of pregnancy. Just imagining it, something stuck in your stomach, squeezing away your youth, growing bigger and bigger . . . but now I've started to consider it. Perhaps with you. Love –

I paced back and forth, excited, happy, and alone, but not feeling especially lonely.

It was peaceful. The heating pipes occasionally made a soft hissing sound, and now and again from the left came the sound of my neighbour's dog barking. To the right another neighbour's doorbell rang when the delivery boy from the Chinese restaurant arrived. Downstairs a male and female college student couple made love loudly. Such frequently heard sounds were part of everyday life in my Soho apartment building. When sometimes I didn't hear one of these sounds, it was like a tiny black gap where one tooth was missing from an otherwise orderly row.

I lay on the sofa and read the biography of Eileen Zhang's later years in America that I'd borrowed from the Columbia University East Asian Studies Library. Before long I fell asleep.

When I awoke, the sky was black, the neighbour's television was blaring and the scent of fried beef had wafted in, hanging smoky in the air and floating warmly into my nose.

The snow had stopped falling and outside the window a thick layer had accumulated on the nearby rooftops off-setting the dusky blackness of the sky. Its soft glow on the rooftops reflected the light like a ribbon inlaid with blue and silver, deep and still.

The light illuminated the night, and through the tiny window, it also illuminated my eyes. There was a kind of cold and beautiful air about it that went beyond colour.

I put on a thick down coat, wrapped an angora scarf inlaid with fine golden threads around my neck, pulled on a pair of embroidered lambskin gloves, and spent some time searching among the crevices of the sofa for my keys. I opened the door and went into the street.

The snow plough just passed. There wasn't much snow on the ground, and the wind wasn't blowing hard. Alone, I walked slowly towards the Old Zheng Xin restaurant in Chinatown where I often went. The waiters there all knew me, and knew the dishes I liked.

Lying in bed later that night, I discovered it was just as many other days had been: an entire day had passed in which I hadn't said a word.

In a city as restless and rash as New York, there was nothing like doing nothing and saying nothing, sensing the time trickling slowly from the creases in your fingers. It could make you happier. Or even more lonely.

7

Sex and Zen in the Kitchen

Eat drink, man, woman: Herein are man's great desires.
Confucius

Every day, eat the food that grows in season.
In Japan, in the spring we eat cucumber.
Japanese proverb

At last Muju came back. He was due to arrive in New York that evening.

As it happened, it was the same evening I went to a birthday party at the home of a famous Columbia University professor.

The professor was ninety-two years old, but he had such vigour and spark that he could eat a whole steak in a minute. Furthermore, he always carried an instant camera with him, so that when he encountered, as he invariably did, one of the pretty young girls who worshipped him he could suggest taking a picture together. A few shutter-clicks later, you could see his smiling face floating slowly to the surface of the film, followed by the smiling or unsmiling faces of the girls, his arms resting on their shoulders or round their waists.

I figured to myself that I'd make my getaway around the time that Muju's flight reached JFK. When the time came a book critic of some authority was standing next to me discussing, with great animation, whether there was room for women authors to expand beyond topics like menstruation, sex, changing diapers and so on, as well as whether cultural differences between the

East and West were decreasing, or not, or whether, like men and women, there existed a fundamental difference between the two.

I hemmed and hawed but my heart wasn't in it. Then someone bumped into me and the glass of red wine in my hand splattered all over the book critic's expensive woollen shirt, while his vodka drenched my equally expensive slant-sleeved Chinese silk shirt.

Amidst the chaos of the huge number of apologies that ensued, I took the opportunity to find the professor, give him his birthday present (a Japanese-made disposable camera) and say a hasty goodbye.

The apartment building where Muju lived had a luxurious and roomy entry hall decorated with massive planters, and five or six doormen with haughty expressions, dressed in black.

This was my second visit. Like the last time, the doormen had to call upstairs before letting me in. When the lift reached the forty-fifth floor, I flew through the open door and turned left towards Muju's apartment, not glancing to my side. Then behind me came the sound of footsteps and laughter. I turned to look and saw that it was Muju.

When the doormen called him, he'd lain in wait by the lift door, hoping to give me a romantic surprise. Unfortunately I'd walked out too fast.

We laughed together. Ever since he'd given me the practical gift of a humidifier on our first date, our romance had seemed very different from any other. I remembered chatting with him on the telephone once and suddenly looking up at the sky outside my window, where I saw the impressively white, round moon daubed like a droplet of white paint onto the pitch-black sky. 'Hey, right now I'm looking up at the sky, looking at the moonlight. Ah . . . so romantic . . .' The phone fell silent for a few seconds, and then we both laughed out loud.

The word 'romantic' is something one must experience for oneself, with one's own heart. It's a word that must absolutely never be used lightly, for once its spoken, 'romance' becomes something of a farce.

His luggage lay on the floor of the living room; he hadn't had time to put everything away. In the bright light of the kitchen he looked for a knife and two cups, and then placed two lustrous lemons on the countertop.

'Do you want some lemon tea?'

'Why don't I make it?' As soon as I said that, he immediately stopped what he was doing.

'Great – you make it.'

He held the electric tea-kettle out to me, wiped his hands dry, gave me a kiss, and hurried out of the kitchen.

It wasn't that I was better in the kitchen than he was, but it seemed to me that to make a cup of tea for my boyfriend who'd just returned from afar would be a loving gesture. I got started.

Honestly, it was the most kitchen-like kitchen that I'd ever seen. Roomy, warm, bright, with a white foundation, and modern almost to the point of absurdity.

The massive refrigerator was eye-catching, like a small truck that had been stood on its end. The door to the fridge had a drinking-water machine and an ice-maker, and inside the fridge there was a shelf for drinks that could fit a gallon; a sturdy separate cabinet; an airtight snack tray; and a full-size sliding storage shelf.

Looking around me, I saw a woven basket filled with coloured Japanese *furoshiki* cloths, and a white porcelain vase for which flowers hadn't yet been bought. Above me was a set of white cupboards loaded with more than two hundred pots, pans, bowls and cups; and below, a floor-level cabinet with twenty kinds of multi-purpose woks and basins and a dozen different types of knife. There were thirty bottles of spices in different colours and flavours as well, all arranged on two wooden racks in neat alphabetical order. In the corner were several books. I picked up a few and glanced at their titles: *Cooking From the Right Side of Your Brain* and *Zen and the Art of the Kitchen*.

Located as I was in such a magnificent, ambitious and intelligent kitchen, a hunger both biological and psychological – along with a certain pressure – surged up in my stomach.

I busily poured the boiling water into two clean mugs decorated with pictures of peaches, and threw in slices of lemon.

'Where's the honey?' I shouted.

Muju walked in, and found within the great refrigerator a big amber-coloured jar of honey mixed with ground flower-petals.

'Look, I brought this honey back from the Dominican Republic. It's very fresh. I brought you a jar too.'

Then he found another jar in the fridge and handed it to me. 'A present for you.'

'Thanks! Oh, it's heavy.' The jar felt like a little weight from an old-fashioned set of scales.

If I were Muju, perhaps I'd have brought back a fresh-picked, pollution-free cotton-flower, a lighter gift. But I'm just being clever. It was a lovable quality of Muju's.

Just as I was about to take the mugs into the living room, he grabbed hold of me. Gently removing the mugs from my hands and placing them to one side, he leaned down and began to kiss me.

I closed my eyes as the current of sweet electricity struck home, flowing like honey until it was everywhere, flowing onto his clothes, flowing onto his hair, onto his face, into his every pore. I had waited for this moment for three weeks.

It has to be said that of all the men I've ever met, Muju could transport me the highest, to a state where I desired both immortality and death. No skill could compare with his, and most astonishing, this special ability lay beneath a calm and warm exterior. In the deepest recesses of his body there was a bottomless and irresistible ocean of mystery and passion.

As the days went by and my understanding of him deepened, I saw his uniqueness even more clearly.

Sex for him was a kind of spiritual experience, but with a faith peculiar to an Eastern religion. It had a mystical aesthetic, pure and dazzling.

As for me, writing and social contact made me aware of my existence as a person, but it was sex – especially sex combined with love – that made me aware of my existence as a woman. I thought of this every time I heard Portishead's lead singer croon mournfully: 'Give me a reason to be a woman.'

With Muju, I couldn't contain my thirst for his skin. It was a sexual thirst so deep that my body ceased to exist. I *became* this thirst, a walking, talking, screaming thirst.

That's the truth of it. I wanted to make love with this man night after night. I had to.

Wordlessly, with a smile both enchanting and inscrutable, he undressed me quickly.

I sat on the white countertop. To my left was the great, gleaming basin; to my right were chopsticks, a whisk, a juicer. There were also a great many things for which I could not find names.

In this super-kitchen, I was like a super-fruit. Trembling with anticipation, anticipating and trembling.

'You're really shivering. Are you cold?' he asked me in a low voice, smoothly picking up a *furoshiki* cloth and draping it over my shoulders.

It only took him a second to pull open the zipper to his jeans and another to pull on a condom quick as a magician. It was a little obvious and a bit shameless but very tantalizing.

I stared wide-eyed at the ceiling and tried not to scream. The fire of the flesh had been lit, the electricity of Yin and Yang flowed. I was Yin and he was Yang; I was the moon and he was the sun; I was water and he was the mountain, breathing his breath, being in his existence. Such ecstasy left me senseless. My orgasm exploded in the warm embrace of the kitchen. 'I'm coming,' I murmured, looking into his eyes.

At that moment, I was suddenly overcome with a feeling of both emptiness and love combined. A kind of blankness, a floating sensation that went deep into my bones, deep in that way that makes people knit their brows when they climax, groaning as if they might die at any minute.

'I'm coming – ' I closed my eyes, holding him close. It was as if I had already held him for a thousand years, as if we'd never been apart.

He came then too. With a great cry, like a wounded general flung suddenly from his horse.

And this time, as before, he didn't ejaculate.

Drinking reheated lemon tea, we chatted off and on, nestled against the tall pile of pillows.

'You seem to really like it in the kitchen,' I ventured.

'My kitchen is even more lavishly decorated than my bedroom.' He laughed a bit awkwardly. 'But don't you think a woman is especially feminine when she's in the kitchen?'

'Oh?' I commented noncommittally, picturing myself desperate and fumbling in the kitchen: dirty and dishevelled, body covered in smoke and grease. 'Am I to gather from this that you'd love me even more if I cooked you a meal?'

'Correct,' be said, only half joking, his arm resting on my shoulder.

'There's something else I'm really curious about.' I leaned down closer to his ear, hesitated briefly. But seeing his look of encouragement I continued, 'You . . . do you never ejaculate?'

He looked at me. 'How could you tell?'

'Ah, I have a sixth sense or third eye, that kind of thing,' I said jokingly. In fact I had been able to feel the subtle difference. Plus I'd stolen a peek at the discarded condom the first time.

'Is that so?' He rubbed the tip of his nose against mine. 'Sometimes I ejaculate. But not often.'

'But why? Doesn't that affect the sensation when you come?'

I honestly didn't understand. Chinese Taoist manuals spoke of how 'refraining from ejaculation will conserve the essence and nourish the brain', thus prolonging life and preserving youth.

And according to the ancient classics, the Jade Emperor's manual of bedchamber arts from two thousand years ago claimed that if you can master three thousand women you will become immortal.' But I had never encountered a man who could successfully practice the Taoist arts of the bedchamber.

'No, it doesn't.' He shook his head.

I looked at Muju's face, a face that didn't reveal his age, a face that lit up with warmth when he smiled, and said nothing.

'You don't like it?' he asked, hesitantly. 'Does it affect how your body feels?'

I shook my head.

'Sex with you is an addiction that I could never kick. I crave it day and night. I'm like a spectator on New Year's Eve who's waited all year for the fireworks, her head up, her mouth hanging open, waiting for them to go bang,' I said.

He laughed, touching my forehead with his finger. 'You!'

We lay there with our eyes closed, didn't speak.

It wasn't exactly late, but after having come such a long way Muju seemed exhausted. He fell asleep quickly and began to snore softly.

Without a curtain to cover it, the window let in the light of the city at night. The sky was neither black nor deep blue, but rather a leaden grey mixed with deep red, like the background in a vampire movie. On the street forty-five floors below, cars flew past one after another, and the whooshing sound they made mingled with the hum of the humidifier by the bed, sounding like rainfall.

Or such were the impressions of a chronic insomniac.

I don't know how much time had passed when I suddenly felt hungry. I got quietly out of bed, pulled on some clothes, and stole into the kitchen. When I turned on the light, an imaginary kingdom materialized before me. Grand, warm, safe.

I opened the refrigerator and ate three slices of whole-wheat bread, two tubs of yoghurt, four small pickled cucumbers and a bar of chocolate.

As I sat at the small kitchen table, the urge to sleep gradually overcame me, spreading from my stomach to my head to my limbs, until I must've drifted off.

. . . softly, as if lifted up, my body drifted like a cloud to the bed, falling from the sky to the soft sheets below. At which point I woke up again.

Muju had carried me back to the bed. Gently he patted my back. 'Sleep well. You can sleep now.'

8

Making Dinner for Muju

There is no spectacle on earth more appealing than that of a beautiful
woman in the act of cooking dinner for someone she loves.
Alice Adams

You must do the thing you think you can not do.
Eleanor Roosevelt

It was very cold out, but it hadn't snowed again. New
Yorkers said it was the least snow there had been in twenty
years.

The restaurants no longer offered a glass of cold water before
meals except when customers specifically asked for it. Car-
washing and watering the garden were also regulated by new
water conservation rules established by the city. I went from
bathing once a day to bathing once every other day.

The weather was cold as well as dry, and after each shower I
had to spend ten shivering minutes squirting on a layer of
moisturizer, and then rubbing in a layer of skin lotion. Bathing
once every two days used less water but also was less hassle.

On a day when even a cockroach would freeze to death, a
blessing fell from the sky. My agent called me, his voice
quavering. I'd never heard him this excited, even last year when
the CBS programme *60 Minutes* wanted to give me a five-minute
interview.

'Your publisher, S & S, is very happy,' he reported to me
solemnly. 'Your book has made the *San Francisco Chronicle*'s top-

ten best-seller list, and it's number one on quite a few online best-seller lists as well!'

'Oh . . .' I felt I ought to shout, since he seemed to be waiting for a shout on the other end of the line, but the book that was being greedily gobbled up like fried chicken all over the world – with its close-up of my face on the cover – had already consumed all my enthusiasm itself. Consequently I was struck dumb for a few seconds, cleared my throat, and then said hoarsely: 'Oh? That seems about right. Isn't it on the best-seller lists in a lot of countries?'

A picture drifted into my mind of me dragging along a huge box with a dozen *qipao* dresses and all different kinds of medicine inside, masking the big black circles under my eyes with sunglasses as I appeared in different international airports, one after another.

Or the year before in London, after finishing up the last interview on the BBC, when I cried from insomnia, loneliness and my hopelessly broken English, until the publisher paid for me to get a massage and a facial at a classy beauty salon that was said to have catered to the former Spice Girls.

And there was the fourth day after 9/11, when to keep to the publicity schedule I had no choice but to fly alone to San Francisco. Including me, there were only seven passengers on the plane.

No, I had no desire to shout over this book. No matter how truly great it all was.

'The publisher wants you to pick a day. They want to find a place in the Village and have a celebration, but not the kind where a hundred people show up. Maybe just forty or so people would come.'

I called Muju and arranged a time to see him that evening, telling him my news in the process. Only when I heard his enthusiastic reaction on the other end of the line did I start to feel excited.

'I'm so proud of you,' he said earnestly.

'You are? Thanks!' A sweet taste flowed to the tip of my tongue.

To make him even prouder of me, and to my own great surprise, the words just slipped out of my mouth, before I had time to think: 'Then tonight, I'll come over and make dinner. In your kitchen. That way maybe we can have a little more time at home and we can watch a video or do something else.'

You can imagine how delighted he was. He agreed instantly. We arranged for him to come over from his office and pick me up at my place at six-thirty, and then go to his apartment together.

I put down the phone, perplexed. I couldn't believe it. I'd actually volunteered to cook a meal! I must've lost my mind. It was one of the biggest challenges I'd ever set for myself.

The only person who could save me now was my mother. And she was on the other side of the world. But when I'd had a chance to cool down and think for a minute, I recalled the dishes that I'd eaten with Muju at restaurants, as well as several of the favourite family dishes that my mother used to make. And I recalled several dishes that I'd liked ever since I was a child. And then finally I wrote down the names of a few, as well as a list of ingredients I'd have to buy in Chinatown. After that, it was like the Nike ad says: 'Just do it!'

Chinatown was crowded, cramped, dirty and chaotic. A dizzying number of restaurants and signs with words like 'Dragon', 'Phoenix', 'Joy', and 'Prosperity', as well as all kinds of medicine shops, acupuncture studios and massage parlours.

A group of tourists had gathered around a small open-air stand selling fake Gucci and Fendi bags, picking and choosing among them, when a cop suddenly appeared and started to confiscate the fake merchandise. The proprietor of the stand answered the policeman's questions expressionlessly.

Off to one side there were peddlers selling freshly-made steamed tofu custard, cheap toys and fruit like the foul-smelling but delicious durian imported from Southeast Asia.

Shopping list in hand, I went to a number of grocery shops and produce stands, and ended up buying a carton of fresh tofu and some relatively fresh greens, as well as mushrooms, carrots, frozen shrimp, black rice, dates and Chinese wolfberries.

When I passed a small news-stand, I also bought a pornographic magazine chock full of pictures of hunky men. It was the kind of magazine that Xi'er would covet the most as a gift, and which you couldn't buy in China. When I received the gift that she sent me – the nightie with the black lotus painted on – I felt I ought to send her a racy magazine. But I could never be sure it would actually reach her hands if I sent it by post. Chinese Customs have a strict system of inspection.

As I waited at the light to cross the street, a cold wind began to blow, so hard that I couldn't even open my eyes. It was a typical Chinatown winter scene. Hauling a great many bags full of tasty Chinese edibles, you suddenly felt very sentimental.

At six-thirty sharp, Muju rang the doorbell. Toting several overflowing bags of stuff I got in a taxi with him, heading north towards the Upper West Side.

On the way there, a smile on his face, he glanced periodically at the bags of food beside my legs. I had to laugh. God, finally I knew the meaning of 'a man who was passionate. about food'. His expression, when he gazed at the food, was even more tender, more possessive and loving than it was even when he gazed at his own girlfriend.

When I told him what I'd noticed, he burst out laughing. I must have been the first girlfriend he'd ever dated who was jealous of food. When he laughed out loud it was stunning, as if a powerful light had suddenly illuminated his face. In a split second, every part of it came alive, especially his eyes, which glittered so bright and clear. They could pierce through any obstacle and go directly to the heart.

I found myself standing in Muju's white, perfect, frightening kitchen. In front of me there was a multicoloured heap of green, red, purple and yellow purchases brought back from Chinatown.

Muju showed me how to light the stove, turn on the exhaust fan and use the automatic timer on the wall, and gave me basic information about the spices, the wok, the dishes, the ladles and the pots. He also helped me put on a small apron embroidered with flowers and helped me tie my hair back neatly to keep it from getting into the food. Everything was ready.

At this point my enthusiasm was nearly exhausted. I hated the mere sight of the thawed shrimp that was lying there soft and sticky.

Muju sat on the living room sofa drinking Smart Water, a kind of drink supplemented with lots of nutrients that was popular in Manhattan, and watched television contentedly. A New Jersey Nets game – a team Muju really liked – was on. I wandered around the kitchen, completely at sea. There was no way out.

I began by washing the vegetables, mushrooms and shrimp, and boiling the black rice. First I placed the rice in a purple porcelain bowl, then put a lot of water on to boil, and then rinsed the dates and the wolfberries. When the water for the rice boiled I would add it to the bowl.

So far so good. I drank a cup of yoghurt, turned towards the living room, and sat myself down on Muju's lap, snuggling up against him. 'You look really sexy in that apron,' he said, nibbling my ear.

I looked down and sized myself up. I couldn't see what was sexy. Must be some sort of fantasy about women who fitted a male fantasy of feminine gentleness and virtue. Men could have foot fetishes, and hair fetishes, so perhaps Muju had a kitchen fetish, perhaps a sexy kitchen-maid frying up steaks and wearing an apron in his incomparable kitchen was his wildest fantasy.

I went back to the kitchen, and everything was going as it should. The water for the rice had started to boil. I threw in the dates and wolfberries. Now it was time to stir-fry the greens. I put a teaspoonful of oil in the wok, waited until it was hot and then emptied in all the vegetables. The water on the vegetables hit the hot oil in the wok with a great sizzling sound, and the oil splattered onto my face and neck. It stung.

Muju rushed in. 'Is everything okay?'

I bore the pain with a smile and said, 'Everything's fine. I'm still alive.'

He hugged me. 'Oh – you forgot to turn on the exhaust fan.' He quickly flipped the switch.

I covered the wok with a pan to keep the hot oil from splattering all over the place, and sighed. Chinese cooking wasn't very easy, like making pasta and salad. It called for the use of lots of different oils and sauces. Big trouble.

The greens and mushrooms were finally done, and I breathed a sigh of relief. When I called my mother I would mention to her that this was the first time in my life I'd ever made food for a boyfriend. Of course I wouldn't mention that it was my *Japanese* boyfriend. The older generation of Chinese weren't too fond of the Japanese.

Next, I would fry the shrimp, then cook the fried shrimp together with the tofu. The fresh tofu would be delicious when it had soaked up the flavour of the shrimp. Typically, you first add the oil to the wok. But this time I'd learned my lesson. Before emptying the shrimp into the wok, I held the lid of the wok in front of my face to protect it from the spatter of hot oil. It worked. Once again there was the loud sizzling sound, and once again Muju came rushing in. I shrugged and he left, relaxed.

Then I added in the soy sauce, the cooking wine, the onions and the ginger, and covered it all with the lid.

Once again I slipped out of the kitchen and nonchalantly walked in front of Muju to the bathroom. I quickly closed the door, moved up close to the mirror and inspected the places where the oil had scalded my neck and cheeks.

Approximately five or six spots were slightly red and inflamed. I felt crestfallen. Three visits to the beauty salon wasted. The scent of grease hung heavily in my hair and clothes.

I hurriedly rinsed the inflamed red spots on my face with cold water. But just when I was about to open the medicine cabinet to look for some moisturizing lotion, I heard the loud blare of the alarm, and simultaneously smelled the strong odour of something burning. Something told me this was not good. I rushed into the kitchen.

It looked as though there had been an air raid: nose-stabbing smoke and a scorched wok filled with the blackened corpses of several small organisms that had been burned to a crisp.

Muju had run into the kitchen one step ahead of me and turned off the burner. But there wasn't anything he could do about the incessant blare of the fire alarm. At this point the doorbell rang loudly and I ran to open the door. It was two of the doormen. So they were useful after all.

The two of them went into the kitchen and looked around, shrugging. 'Chinese food!' one of them whispered.

I gathered my courage and watched as the men tried to drive out the burning smell and the thick smoke from the kitchen. I didn't care what they said, as long as the goddamned fire alarm would just stop blaring.

The disaster finally stumbled to an end. The doormen went away with a bad impression of Chinese food. Muju and were alone in the room. Neither of us was smiling.

He washed his hands in the kitchen, and I washed my face in the bathroom. The sound of the alarm still rang in my ears and the stench of burning still filled my nostrils. A total catastrophe.

Muju walked into the living room and looked at his watch, saying, 'Perhaps we should go out and eat at a restaurant.'

I didn't reply, but continued dabbing carefully at my face.

'I'm tired and hungry. We should go now.' This time there was an obvious and impatient edge to his voice.

'So, you're tired and hungry?' I said coldly. 'What about me?'

Muju got up from the sofa, walked over to me, and looked at me in the mirror. My complexion was damaged and I kept nervously massaging the spots that had been scalded. Muju took a breath. 'I commend your spirit of adventure.'

I didn't make a sound, unable to stop the movement of my fingers on my face. I was overcome with despair and irritation.

'But I can't eat this. We'd better go to a restaurant,' he insisted.

I stopped what I was doing and turned to face him. I was on the verge of tears. Instead of crying, however, with one movement I threw the lotion I was holding into the toilet bowl. A powerful ego is my fatal flaw and when I lose my temper I explode more violently than a man. More like a lioness.

'Enough!' I shouted the word. 'I spent two hours in Chinatown buying these things, and spent another hour in the kitchen. Now my whole body smells like a dishrag and there are five or six places on my face that hurt from being scalded with hot oil. Then the smoke-alarm went off, and then those bigoted doormen showed up . . . and now here you are, telling me "I'm hungry and I'm tired"!'

'Why are you getting so worked up?' Muju's voice sounded angry too. But he also sounded confused.

'Why not?' I'd already lost all reason. 'You *make* me worked up!' I was like a ship that had already sunk beneath the waves.

'You don't like to cook, you throw things rashly, you shout . . .' Muju's voice rose. 'Who was it who just told me in a recent e-mail that she was thinking of becoming a mother, thinking of having a child!'

'That's right, I throw things, I shout, I can't cook, and I want children! But what business is it of yours? An old patriarch who expects women to wait on him his whole life? You not only want a woman to cook for you, you want her to chew it up and then put it in your mouth! You are the strangest man I have ever seen! You're picky about what you eat, you don't ejaculate when you come, you . . . you . . .' I hesitated about whether or not to add 'You even have a missing fingertip,' but in the end I changed it to 'You can be very wise, but sometimes you are a complete idiot!'

Actually, only the first half of this comment was true. While Muju wasn't particularly brilliant, he possessed a kind of deep wisdom. But the latter half . . . I'd never actually witnessed a single incident when he'd been any sort of idiot. The gift of a humidifier on our first date and the many big bottles of honey he'd brought back from the Dominican Republic – well, these were lovable traits. As he told me himself, sometimes he would pay for something and forget to take it with him. Sometimes the unusual expression in his eyes would make women he'd just met think he'd fallen in love with them at first sight. Some of them would invite him to dinner again and again, while the rest never wanted to see him again to stop him getting desperate.

I don't know why, but when I'd delivered this impassioned, tearful lecture I realized suddenly that the fire of anger in my heart had pretty much gone out. I even felt a bit like laughing. These flaws which had inspired my accusation weren't unlovable – they actually made him different.

From the look of things Muju didn't feel quite so much like laughing. His face had gone a bit pale. He didn't say a word, listening silently as I listed his crimes. I began to worry. After all, I'd burned one of his woks, messed up his kitchen, and conjured up a roomful of smoke and two doormen.

Had I gone too far? Would he want to break up?

This thought rolled around in my brain making me suddenly miserable and my eyes clouded with tears.

Suddenly Muju reached out and held me.

I could smell the heat of his body, lithe and huge, mingled with testosterone. It was out of my control; I could never escape his aura. My body, rigid, relaxed all at once, the fire of anger long since vanished. All that remained were tears – tears of release.

'I'm sorry,' he said, low and clear.

'It's okay. I'm just a spoiled girl, without any feminine qualities,' I said, admitting to myself only the 'spoiled' part. The 'without any feminine qualities' part was a joke, since Muju had declared that women were more alluringly feminine when they were in the kitchen.

'You!' He shook his head, tapping my forehead with his finger.

We looked at each other in silence, as if seeing ourselves in the mirror once again but this time it was as if the mirror had been scrubbed clean. We had a kind of resolve. If we were unhappy, then we could quickly make the unhappiness disappear. Because we were together, because we wanted to be together.

Soon our eyes shifted to the bottle of lotion I'd thrown into the toilet bowl. I groaned, bent down, and frowned. With two fingers, I fished out the bottle, threw it into the sink, and turned on the tap.

'What are you doing?' Muju looked shocked.

'You know what? This stuff cost a hundred and fifty bucks.' I frowned again. 'Wouldn't it be a pity to throw it out?'

'Wow!' said Muju. 'I really admire you.'

I pretended not to hear the teasing in his voice.

As he walked away he said: 'Perhaps we should stay home and order a take-out from China Fun. Didn't you already make some greens and rice?'

A strategy that served a dual purpose: saving face for me, while filling our bellies.

After dinner, I was happy to spend forty minutes in the kitchen cleaning everything up. While I was at it, I put water on to boil and made two cups of tea. Since women naturally want to please men, the truth is they can be trained quite easily – if they love the man enough, that is.

9

The Missing Fingertip

You are mine, mine, woman of steel lips, you belong to me.
Pablo Neruda

Teaching without words, performing without actions,
that is the Master's way.
Lao-tzu

As we lay together in the spa tub, our bodies submerged in the bubbling water, Muju scrubbed my back with a sponge, slowly and strongly.

Some time later, he opened his mouth. 'Do you really want a child?'

I nodded.

He confessed he'd almost had a baby with an ex-girlfriend of his, but in the end decided she wouldn't be the mother of his child. I fell silent for a while, and then told him I felt confused by the urgency of my own sudden desire to have a child.

'It's not so unusual,' he said, handing me the sponge. He turned around and I began to rub his back. 'You've reached that age when the secretion of oestrogen naturally stimulates the maternal instinct.'

We didn't talk further. We soaked for a long time at either end of the tub, letting the water flow over our bodies.

My hair drifted in the water like black seaweed, and in the lamplight lustrous rainbows of soft, captivating colours emerged.

The whirlpool bath filled with the scent of our bodies. Lust didn't take long to follow.

Tentatively at first, and then with abandon, he used his big toe to touch between my legs. It was slippery there, soft, like a fish.

I gazed at him intently, quietly letting him toy with my body. In that moment, my entire body – every single hair, each toe – belonged to him.

He moved his body closer to mine, and beneath his gaze, part beast and part saint, I was overwhelmed with desire and began to moan.

He placed a finger inside me, and when I felt that it was the little finger of his left hand – the one with the missing fingertip – the blood rushed through my whole body like lava erupting from a volcano. My face must have been intensely red, as if I had a fever, as if I'd come down with some kind of illness. The germs that caused it were called desire, a desire that was mysteriously destined to blossom and spread.

But he didn't give himself to me. He only used that finger to make me writhe and twist like a snake. The finger with the missing fingertip wasn't inside my vagina; it was inside my head. He controlled my body by seducing my mind.

'Come on,' he said softly, his voice like music floating up from the bottom of the sea, 'Give it to me . . . Give it to me.'

The pleasure accumulated in my vagina and my head like layers of powder, more and more, until finally the orgasm that exploded in my head could have turned the Pacific ocean inside out.

'I'll hate you if you leave me,' I gasped, mumbling as if in my sleep, 'Because now I can't leave you.'

That night, I lay in the moonlight, half awake and half in a dream.

He finally told me the story of his missing fingertip. It hadn't been bitten off by a love-crazed woman. It hadn't been severed by the jealous husband of a lover. It wasn't a car accident, and it wasn't some dangerous sport. It wasn't a wolf in the forest. All my previous hypotheses, numerous and all over the place, disappeared in a puff of smoke as soon I heard his story.

He had cut it off himself.

'It was more than twenty years ago,' he said.

'I was still very young and impulsive, a bit like you are now.' He gathered me in his arms, kissed my hair. 'I was student body president at one of the best private colleges in Japan, but got suspended because I liked to drink and fight. Later I became a complete punk . . . It's a long story. One day I met the old man who would change my life. Moved by his philosophy of life, I was determined to take him as my master and follow him to the most beautiful mountains and rivers in the world.' He paused a moment. 'The old man was dead set against it, so I cut off my finger to show him how serious I was. I'll never in my life forget the look in the old man's eyes when I did that. In his eyes there was a profound compassion, but also pity and regret. He said that what I'd done came from a powerful ego and sheer pig-headedness, and that it was the exact opposite of what he believed in, and that I should only go looking for him when I had grasped this. Then he just turned and left.'

I was deeply drawn in by his story. No wonder Muju had such a unique and indescribable disposition. It was because of how he'd grown up, and the choices he'd made. He was a riddle. On the one hand he made you feel warmth and trust, but on the other you were aware of a kind of distance that you could never bridge. When he was lying next to you, so close you could reach out and touch him with your hand, sometimes he just wasn't there. He was far away on a distant horizon.

'And then?' I asked.

'A year later I felt I'd grasped what the old man had said, and went looking for him. When he saw me he just nodded his head and said the words: 'You've come.' And then I travelled with him – as my master – all through the most beautiful mountains and rivers of Japan, until one day he decided he wanted to meditate on his own in the Zen style of "sitting facing the wall".'

He paused a moment. 'And then later I had an American girlfriend and came with her to New York.'

'What exactly did you learn with that old man?'

'In the simplest terms it had to do with knowledge about life and love . . . In fact, you might think it strange, but all I did that year was follow him around and sit quietly under a tree or by a river. He didn't speak, I didn't speak; he didn't move, I didn't move . . . I grew very accustomed to – even came to enjoy – that state of motionlessness. It was so immeasurably profound. It couldn't be put into words, since it was beyond my grasp then, though perhaps I understand it now.'

'What is it?'

'Between motionlessness and emptiness you can actually feel a hard and perpetual kernel of existence, like the core of an apple – the real truth. The real truth of the world and of mankind.'

'What is the real truth?'

'Being is nothingness, nothingness is being; in serenely observing all things in the world, you automatically achieve all things.'

'Lao-tzu said that two thousand years ago.'

'Words can't do it justice.' He fell silent. I could see the rough contour of his eyes, nose and mouth in profile, smooth and soft, like a child in his early teens. The corner of his mouth was slightly pursed, looked childish.

'Are you still in touch with your master?'

'He passed away.'

'I'm so sorry.' I took a breath, watching him.

'It's okay . . . life is like a dream; life and death are linked, so death isn't really so terrifying. The truly terrifying thing is that so many people are alive but do not live well.'

'In Chinese we call that a Zombie.'

He chuckled and kissed me lightly on the lips. 'Go to sleep.'

In the air, tiny bursts of blue fire seemed to glimmer and then disappeared until all that remained was the silver moonlight and myself, half awake and half in a dream.

10

So this is Love

Love is old, love is new, love is all, love is you.
The Beatles, 'Because'

There is time for work. And time for love.
That leaves no other time.
Coco Chanel.

Cars shuttled past on the street and the tops of the buildings gleamed in the thin air. I walked Manhattan's streets and alleys aimlessly, filled head to toe with things I'd never noticed before, courtesy of Muju.

Free of anxiety and loneliness, life buoyed me up like water. Sometimes you have to swim for your life, other times you have to go with the flow, fumbling and floating towards things unknown.

Having survived the kitchen incident, Muju and I grew even closer.

He took me to see a New York Yankees game at Yankee Stadium. We ate hot dogs and drank Coke even though neither of us particularly liked either. Apparently that's the thing to do at a ballgame in New York

Muju explained the rules of the game to me while we watched. It was the first baseball game I had ever seen in my life – that's how little into sports I am. In China, I'd mainly watched ping-pong and diving competitions since they were on television the most. Chinese people seem to be able to win championships in these two sports with their eyes closed.

For Chinese people, baseball was like the cloth that was once used to bind girls' feet: it dragged on too long, and it didn't smell so good either.

Nonetheless, watching those athletic men with their white trousers pulled tight over their round behinds, all concentrating intently on a tiny white ball, I couldn't help but feel amazing.

In China I'd heard a joke. At twenty, women are like soccer balls: everyone scrambles to get them. At thirty, women are like ping-pong balls: they are bounced back and forth from one person to another. At fifty, however, women are like golf balls: the further you drive them the better. When I told Muju this, he tapped my forehead with his finger, as had become his habit. 'What about when women are forty?' he asked.

'I forget,' I confessed. I've always been the kind of person who absolutely loves to tell jokes but can never tell them well. I'm always the only one giggling at the end.

'But if you were to switch it to men,' I continued, 'wouldn't you have to say that a man who is both wealthy and loving is like a soccer-ball that everyone is scrambling for, while a poor and loving man is like a ping-pong ball getting bounced back and forth, and a man who is both poor and loveless is therefore the golf ball?'

I gazed at him. This time he finally laughed. 'You're hopeless,' he said, shaking his head.

Not long after that, he consoled me when I lost my wallet and even helped me contact the bank, cancel all of my credit cards and bank cards, and apply for new ones. But I was horrified when the monthly bank statement arrived. Since I'd been a day late declaring the loss, the credit card had already been used in my name to the tune of several thousand dollars.

I took a look at how the person had spent my money: five hundred dollars in DKNY; a hundred and fifty dollars in Furla; and in Emporio Armani fifteen hundred bucks. I nearly fainted with anger. West Broadway was only fifty yards from my place.

Muju's office was there, and so were all three of these stores, all in a row. The thief had the audacity to be quite mercenary with her purchases – whereas I had agonized for more than a week over whether to buy a two-thousand-dollar wool-trimmed black leather coat at DKNY. The person who stole my credit card was far more ruthless than I was.

Muju told me that once we'd explained the situation to the bank, the money would be refunded. He then phoned the bank and ordered some incident report forms. Standardized forms like that always give me a headache, and here again he helped. But out of absent-mindedness, he forgot to send the forms out on time, and before long the bank had to post me another set of forms.

That wasn't all. When piercing menstrual cramps made me want to drown myself in the toilet-bowl, Muju gave me a back rub and made me a cup of hot ginger tea.

When I drank too much at the bar of the Hudson Hotel and picked a fight with a coquettish gay boy leaning seductively on the shoulder of a shy elderly man and it escalated to the point where we were throwing wine glasses at each other, again it was Muju who extracted me from the heap of shit I'd got myself into. And he didn't criticize me. He just corrected my pronunciation on several of the words I'd been shouting.

I resolved to stop drinking, stop smoking and to stop taking sedatives.

I gained courage and confidence from Muju. Although from another point of view perhaps he'd become an addiction in his own right – a grand, new, magnificent addiction that I might have to spend the rest of this life and future lives trying to kick.

Muju began to teach me Taoist reflective meditation and tai chi.

It's strange that an impetuous Chinese girl, who has been called 'a slave of Western culture' in China for knowing about the Beatles, the Sex Pistols, Marilyn Monroe, Allen Ginsberg, Charles Bukowski and Existentialism, should find herself in New

York – that cruel bastion of capitalism – and having found love, hope and light there, should also learn about the arts of Chinese wisdom from a Japanese man. I had to learn to let those ancient wandering spirits, exiled from their native country, return to me, let them seep into my bloodstream and into my soul, like night birds looking for their roosting place.

I had a copy of Lao-tzu's *Tao Te Ching* that I'd brought with me from China, and I'd bought an English edition at Barnes & Noble. According to Muju, the translation was graceful and easy to follow, maybe even more so than the original Chinese. I also found a Zen tale that had been passed down for several hundred years called *Zen Flesh, Zen Bone*. At university I'd heard my professor lecture about a thousand years of Chinese cultural traditions, Confucianism, Taoism and Buddhism. At the time I was hanging out with several rock bands from near the university and it seemed like the only real way to express the anger of youth and the flame of desire was through Western rock 'n' roll, through the delinquent poetry of the Beat generation, and through hot, sweaty, screaming sex. These were weapons that could kill, that could make you leap out of the rotten, suffocating grave in which you were entombed.

And now I lived in New York.

I thought about explosions, bloodshed and death in the Middle East. I saw the names of several thousand souls dead on 9/11 drifting in the air over New York. In China my book was still banned; Japan's economy was still in a slump . . . at that moment, all I wanted was to take a breather, rest for a while, and give myself over, as Dylan Thomas wrote, to the 'force that through the green fuse drives the flower'. I wanted to give myself to the moonlight, to the tides, to the secret incantations, to a thousand years of wisdom – and to the man who tasted me all over, held me, and loved me.

That day Muju took me to the Riverside Church in Harlem.

Recently, he started going every Sunday to this great church in North Manhattan where he'd volunteered to teach a healing meditation to about a dozen black girls who'd been sexually abused as children by their fathers or brothers.

I sat quietly in the back row, watching Muju as he smiled that familiar warm smile, spoke in that soft voice, and every so often cracked jokes to get the plainly-dressed girls – behind whose eyes lay deep sad shadows – to relax and open their faces.

After having explained the main points of 'smile meditation', he got everybody to stand up. 'First let your body relax,' he said, 'just like this. Watch me . . .' He relaxed his limbs, shook them out, up and down, moving his shoulders back and forth, flexing his heels repeatedly, then relaxed his chin and stuck out his tongue.

I wanted to laugh. Muju, with his big, tall body, looked like a teddy-bear with its tongue sticking out.

'Like this,' he said,' thoroughly relax, let go of the burdens and restraints on your body and mind. It doesn't matter if it looks a bit silly . . .'

A few girls blinked their eyes and beamed. 'It's just when people ought to be silly that they try to be smart, and it's just when they ought to be smart that they get silly.' Muju was smiling. 'Come on everybody, do it with me.'

Over the next two hours, the little group sat on the floor. Everything was quiet and from time to time the high-ceilinged vault with its beautifully carved sculptures, resonated with the clear and gentle sound of Muju's voice. 'Now, everybody find your own heart, and smile at it . . . take it home with you, put it down, and just relax . . .'

Time passed and before we knew it, what I and the girls had learned together was to smile. And not just the kind of smile you have on your face, but even more importantly the kind of smile that comes from the bottom of your heart, from your lungs, from your liver, and from your stomach, kidneys and uterus – from every cell in your whole body. A compassionate, forgiving, confident, serene smile.

When the mediation was complete, we slowly opened our

eyes. Everywhere I looked the colours and shapes seemed brighter and more vivid.

I stretched and checked out the oil paintings decorating every corner and the stained-glass windows. It was a beautiful church. I imagined the sound of the organ and the gospel choir ringing out in the carved vaults of the ceiling and then dropping down onto the human bodies below, falling to the ground, the dust vibrating and flitting upwards in the sunlight . . .

I clasped Muju's hand as we walked slowly out of the church.

'Now where?' I asked.

'Where do you want to go?' he asked in reply.

'I don't know. I've been in New York less than half a year, but you've been here twenty years already – where do you suggest?'

He thought for a moment. 'Let's go to Barney's. It's on the way home, so we can stop in and take a look. You can get some idea of the latest fashions.'

'All right!' I grinned. From the spiritual church to the worldly, trendy Barney's – quite the eclectic Sunday. Of all the men I'd ever met, he was the least resistant to going shopping. And what was more, I even liked the style of the clothes he wore: expensive, crazy designs that still had a cute side, the kind of thing that the majority of American men would never buy. Where ninety per cent of American men might choose Gucci or Armani over Yohji Yamamoto for the same money, Muju would always choose the latter.

From the outside you couldn't see a thing, but if you pulled open the lapel to his expensive black suit jacket, on the inside you'd find a stunningly embroidered colourful picture of a naked woman. The outsides of his trainers were plain, but when he raised his feet, you could see a large picture of a sunflower inlaid in each sole. Muju's principle was: buy expensive, high-quality clothes, but only those that seem modest from the outside, and that don't show how much they cost.

Perhaps this was a deeply ingrained, traditional Japanese aesthetic, something in the blood. Their most beloved temples have roofs thatched with straw and fences of woven bamboo. Perhaps the fact that they look as if they might be toppled by the next strong wind or by rain or by snow only makes them seem more precious. Their most admired teahouses, too, are tiny and sparsely decorated, with a straw mat for a rug, a single piece of calligraphy hung on the wall, and at each place-setting a rough-quality, coarsely enamelled tea-set.

My own clothing principle was: black; red; silk; fairly tight; even tighter; and tighter still.

I'd never worn denim or jeans. They were too healthy for me, too laid-back, too lazy. Even during my angry rock 'n' roll, youth phase, I always wore skin-tight black silk dresses. I enjoyed watching my rock 'n' roll lovers shift their gazes to my black dress. In the glimmering light, chilly to the touch like the skin of a snake, the silk clung to my body so intimately that it seemed almost ethereal, like it might disappear at any time, drifting along in time with my steps. It rippled delicately from my tightly-buttoned collar to my lap, constantly shifting in subtle ways. Although it had existed for more than a thousand years, the beauty of silk was timeless and everlasting.

Even more than the sight of beautiful silk, it was the beautiful sound of silk that I enjoyed the most. When silk is torn by a pair of strong, hot hands, veins throbbing with passion, you hear an indescribably vulnerable, elegant, thrilling 'shhaa' sound . . . the sound of torn silk could bring you tender bliss as well as explosive desire, and there was nothing like it in the world, nothing that could compare.

In my wardrobe there were always exactly thirty silk *qipao* dresses, skirts and tops, all skin-tight, delicate and beautiful. Every time I tore one, I had a new one made. So there were always thirty pieces.

After wandering around Barney's for a while, I did something I thought I'd never do. I bought a denim top. A sky-blue Marc Jacobs denim top set off by bright yellow buttons, with still more buttons on the shoulders and epaulettes, and a narrow, fitted waist. It was very retro, something a hip London girl in the seventies would've worn. Muju spotted it right away and got it down from the display rack for me.

I tried it on – yeah, right – and thought at first that it made me look like a Girl Guide. But then I felt attracted by something refreshing and something stubborn about it. It made my face look sophisticated and innocent all at the same time, quite different from my usual black-scorpion-that-always-eats-its-mate image. So I bought it.

Muju bought a new pair of Pumas, on the soles of which were a lot of tiny round air cushions, so that when he walked down the street he floated along lightly, like walking on the moon.

11

Her Melancholy

I got nineteen men and won't want more;
I got nineteen men and won't want more
If I had one more I'd let that nineteen go.
Bessie Smith

My whole face was lathered in a moist and slippery collagen mask. I lay half-asleep on a soft bed in the Eli Day Spa. Low soothing music was playing, and Natasha had switched the light off on her way out. In that moment I lay peacefully side by side with the outside world.

Natasha was from the former Soviet Union. She'd had a daughter when she was seventeen, and now that daughter was twenty-four. Natasha was still quite attractive, and when she went out dancing with her daughter she was mistaken for her daughter's elder sister and hit on by her friends. She liked to chat while giving me a facial, and this story was something she'd told me herself. Once she'd found out that I was from China, and also that – like her – my vice was smoking, she warmed to me.

'Sweetheart,' she announced to me proudly, 'you sure have come to the right place. In three months you're going to witness a miracle on your face.'

Before this I'd always been dubious about beauty salons run by Westerners. I'd always believed that Western aestheticians were too rough, and that Asian skin was so very sensitive and smooth. It was only after I'd had some bad experiences at a beauty salon in Chinatown run by someone from Hong Kong that I found this mid-Manhattan spa through an introduction by a female client of Jimmy Wong's.

The first thing I asked Natasha when I saw her was: 'Do you think you can do Asian skin?'

Natasha laughed, or perhaps it would be better to say she laughed maniacally. 'Sweetheart, don't you worry. As long as it's human skin, I can handle it.'

The impression I gave Natasha was that I was 'sweet' or 'cute'. The impression she gave me, through her speech and behaviour (besides that she was an accomplished aesthetician), was at times that of a seasoned madam, with her rattling laugh and her raspy voice and the cigarette smell on her fingers. She reminded me of my old friend Madonna.

I hadn't been in touch with Madonna since I'd left Shanghai, but a steady stream of gossip told me that she was dealing in imported cars – at this point she hadn't yet got into trouble with the police – and there was even a rumour that she was engaged to a Frenchman ten years her junior. Xi'er had seen Madonna and the Frenchman come into her restaurant holding hands, and observed the impressive, nearly three-carat diamond ring on her finger. Xi'er told me that the Frenchman seemed really shy, a bit like Ah Dick, who Madonna had once fallen so madly in love with, and who was now married to my cousin Zhu Sha. The young Frenchman was often seen picking up Madonna's Valentinos or Christian Dior evening gown from the dry cleaners.

I may have lost touch with Madonna, but I couldn't help being interested in any titbit of news about her: a good friend who'd been the inspiration for a lot of *Shanghai Baby*, a woman who'd gone from prostitute to madam to wealthy widow; a famous Shanghai beauty who'd occupied a good deal of space in my memory, scorpion-like.

Half an hour later, the mild smell of cigarettes drifted into my nostrils. Natasha had slipped back in, silently as a cat. She lit a lamp directly over my face, and I could feel her gentle fingers checking to see how much of the collagen mask had been absorbed.

'How do you feel?' she asked as she used her fingers gently to work the thin membrane off.

'I feel very positive,' I said in a low voice. My aesthetician had recommended that whenever I was lying down having a facial I should cultivate 'positive emotions', in order to maximize the skin's ability to absorb nutrients. Actually a new pimple had erupted at the corner of my mouth, and it bothered me. It was a premenstrual thing, and Natasha recommended that I didn't mess with it. 'You'd be better off coming here in between periods, when you're ovulating,' she said. 'That way all the toxins in your body can be flushed out with your next period.'

I liked that idea. I liked any idea that would help me expel toxins, even though quite a few such ideas wound up being new age garbage. One advantage of getting rid of toxins was that then you had room to put them in again next time.

Just before I left, I confirmed my appointment with Natasha for a waxing next week.

I – and of course Xi'er as well – was a great fan of waxing. We were practically obsessed with concern for that triangular patch of hair, we couldn't help ourselves. I had a tune-up at the spa probably every ten days, come hell or high water, and Xi'er had one even more often, maybe once every five days. But she didn't go to a spa to do it, she did it herself. She would never reveal her naked body to anyone. Even when she made love to a man, it always had to be in the dark: no lights and no sunlight.

Xi'er was both infatuated with and terrified of her own body and the two extremes created a stubborn kind of love. She had to take great care of her body and had to put in much greater effort that most other people. This was the source of her fragile sense of security and her primal feelings of guilt.

Her body was a mirror that reflected back not only her feelings about the world, but her feelings about herself. It was her innocence, her desires, her fears and her struggles, combined with her uncertainty about herself and the world around her, that made Xi'er even more woman than most women. I loved her deeply for it.

If she suffered, I suffered too. If her eyes glittered with lust for a man or for some material thing, my eyes glittered too.

Yes, feelings like this were beyond our grasp. It hadn't always been that way, but after she'd had the sex-change operation and became all at once the subject of argument, abuse and worship in China, I discovered how I felt about her.

Thinking first of Madonna and then of Xi'er, I suddenly missed Shanghai far away on the other side of the world. It would have been the black of night right then, everyone asleep. The lamplight on the Bund would be burning like an eternal flame, and those little winding alleys that criss-cross Shanghai would be enshrouded in layer upon layer of shadow under the moonlight.

When I passed a Barnes & Noble on the street, I went in. After using the bathroom on the ground floor, I picked out a few fashion magazines from the magazine racks, then went upstairs to the second floor with its pervasive smell of coffee in the air and ordered some camomile tea with honey. I sat down and flipped casually through the magazines. The great thing about Barnes & Noble is that you can use the toilets and sit for as long as you like in the café. I'd heard that it was an established pick-up spot for some New Yorkers.

These magazines always recommend movies and CDs and the like, and I always pause over the sections about books. Once when my father, a history professor, asked me on the phone what kinds of books were popular in America right now, I just so happened to have tucked under my arm a copy of a popular fashion magazine. I flipped through it and read out the titles of a few books from their reading list: *How to Make a Man Fall in Love with You: The Fail-Proof Fool-Proof Method*; *Why Men Don't Listen and Women Can't Read Maps: How We're Different and What to Do About It*; and *How to Hunt Ghosts*.

Upon hearing this, there was a pause on the other end of the line. Then after careful and deep thought my father said, 'Then from this it would seem that your book has a chance at making a splash in America.'

Sometimes my dad could be so sweet.

When I left the bookstore, the sky had grown dark. I looked at my cellphone as I walked and discovered a message from Muju: 'I have to work late tonight. Do you want to come over to my place tomorrow? Don't forget to bring your moisturisers, eye-cream, and saline solution for your contact lenses. Miss you.'

Tomorrow night? I had to attend a lecture on Beijing opera at the East Asian Studies department. A singer from Beijing would be giving a lecture and then performing a few arias as a demonstration. He was going to perform at the Lincoln Center a few days later.

I called Muju's cell, but nobody answered and I was cut to voicemail. I left a message telling him that tomorrow night was fine, but it would have to be a little late.

When my cellphone rang, I thought it was Muju. As soon as I answered I knew instantly that it was actually Xi'er.

'Hey darling.' I looked at my watch. It was six in the morning in Shanghai, a rather odd time for a phone call. 'How are you?' It was a bit confused.

Judging by the background noise, Xi'er was in a club.

'What are you doing? Is it a good time to talk?' she asked, giggling. She sounded as though she'd had quite a bit to drink.

'Of course. Where are you?'

'I'm at Mandy's,' she said. Mandy's was an underground club, which had the coolest music, the cheapest alcohol, and the most cynical crowd in Shanghai. People always started to arrive after three in the morning, and by five or six the place would be packed. But by ten even the people who'd managed to stretch the night out till then were forced, reluctantly, to climb out into the vile daylight, walking slowly into the distance and evaporating like bubbles into the air.

'You were up all night?' I asked her in surprise. She always needed to sleep ten hours a night. She believed that the more you slept the prettier you got. Sleep was her religion.

'I don't feel like sleeping.' Her voice was suddenly gloomy, and a moment later I heard her sob.

'Hey, what is it?' I was taken aback. I used my left hand to shield my ear from the shrill sound of a siren as a police car drove past.

'Nobody loves me.' She sniffled and heaved a great sigh.

'I love you,' I said quickly as though if I didn't say these three words fast enough she might jump off a ledge. At the same time I wondered to myself what kind of trouble she'd got into.

'Fred doesn't love me!' She began to cry again. 'He said he was sick of keeping the light off when we make love, sick of the forced femininity of my body, sick of . . .' I couldn't hear what she said next.

'He's an asshole,' I muttered, my friend still crying on the other end of the line.

It seemed as if her alcoholic tears would never end. Something acidic was on the tip of my tongue. It filled my stomach, and I was suddenly cold. Women who cry over men are like a sad strip of magnesium burning blue on their own. Women like Xi'er who cry over men . . . a little pile of ashes.

I did everything I could to block the feelings in my own heart and instead tried to send a ray of light to my despairing friend on the other end of the line. 'Darling,' I said, 'Fred is just one of thirty billion men in the world. If he doesn't love you, that doesn't mean that other men won't.' There was silence on the other end of the line.

'Frankly, if one hangs around then there's no room for a new one. I found Muju, and he's almost perfect.' She said nothing. I realized that bringing up my own boyfriend at this particular time probably wouldn't inspire her.

'Do you remember what the best fortune-teller in Shanghai said a year ago?' I grasped at a passing straw. 'He said the two of us would both find the right one for us in the end, but that we'd have some hardships along the way.'

This seemed to work. She sighed and said mournfully, 'How much more hardship will I have to take?'

'Don't worry, you've already accumulated enough good karma,' I said in a cheerful voice. But inside I was asking myself, 'Lord, what *are* you talking about?'

But what I'd said turned out to be useful. When you're feeling weak, fortune-tellers and karma can seem very attractive. Destiny becomes something not to control but to explain.

Xi'er seemed ashamed of herself. 'I'm drunk,' she said looking for an excuse. 'The truth is I knew Fred wasn't right for me from the start.' She coughed a few times. 'You're right: out with the old and in with the new. Aren't there lots of men in Shanghai?' she added, with an air both worldly and naïve. 'It's just like the fortune-teller said. It's my destiny to be filthy rich and have men who love me!'

A cold wind blew. Air from the laundromat across the pavement wafted out, warming me, and steam rose from the manhole covers in the street. Things like these often made me feel I was in a movie. They might be the most common of everyday New York scenes, but there was still something unreal and poetic about them.

An airplane skimmed through the air overhead heading in directions unknown.

I discovered I'd been walking towards The Bowery in Chinatown. The Xilingmen restaurants there were famous for their congee and noodles. I'd heard Yoko Ono sometimes went there. I decided that I'd only have a plain bowl of congee and a small dish of preserved egg for dinner tonight.

All day thoughts of Shanghai and my Shanghai friends had flooded through my head in great waves. I felt overwhelmed. Right now I only wanted the simplest and most classic of Chinese meals.

12

He Loves Gourmet Food and He Also Loves Women

. . . what is commonly called love, namely the desire of satisfying a voracious appetite with a certain quantity of delicate white human flesh.
Henry Fielding, *Tom Jones*

uju and I took a cab to a small film festival at Columbia featuring the works of the Hong Kong martial arts film master Hong Jinchuan. As we hurried towards the campus, we could see Jimmy Wong in the distance, standing in front of the East Asian Studies library. He was frowning and making a call on his cellphone. Beside him stood a stylish-looking girl in high-heeled boots, a woollen shawl wrapped around her head.

He saw us too and promptly finished his phone call. He leaned down and planted a kiss on both of my cheeks, then clapped Muju on the shoulders, shaking his hand. The three of us had already eaten a meal together two weeks ago; this was their second meeting. It looked as though they quite liked each other.

He introduced the girl next to him. She was a pretty Korean girl who'd only been in New York a short time. Jimmy had met her at a KTV in Flushing and promised to help her get a green card – a chat-up line he often used to snare girls. Her name was something hard to remember, but luckily I'd no intention of doing so: Jimmy went through girls like he went through ties.

The girl's eyes really stood out. She seemed to have had plastic surgery, and was sporting blue contact lenses and super-long silver eyelashes. And of course she had thick eye-shadow, blue mixed with white. Well-applied eye-shadow is like a good oil painting, while applied badly . . . well, it's like a bad oil painting. She had the sex appeal of a girl freshly arrived in New York, a sex appeal that girls who've lived in New York for a while lack. Then they've had to make compromises and develop a bit of cynicism. She'd become sharp-edged and calculating after a bit. She'd have to.

I noticed that the girl had caught Muju's eye. He stole glances at her while pretending to talk to Jimmy.

Of course I wasn't thrilled about it, but I didn't let it show. When I'm in public with a boyfriend I can be quite self-conscious about my manners.

I saw several familiar faces in the screening-room and acknowledged them one by one. We'd arrived a little late and the only seats we could find were towards the back. The theatre was nearly full. Jimmy and the Korean girl sat in the row in front of us, so that while we were watching the movie we could, conveniently, make out Jimmy's budding bald spot, the girl's hat, and a small patch of exposed skin on her neck. Besides this irritation, I enjoyed the movie. Chinese Kung Fu movies seem more interesting when viewed from abroad. It was the same with *Crouching Tiger, Hidden Dragon*, which was so well received in the States but had been a flop at the box-office in China.

After the movie, Jimmy and the girl bade us a quick goodbye. But before he left Jimmy took a teenage edition of *Cosmopolitan* from his bag, placed it solemnly in my hand, and announced in the voice of a proud father: 'My daughter is in this magazine!'

The odd thing was, though we frequently spoke on the phone and had meals together, I had nearly forgotten that he had a daughter who lived with his ex-wife. He rarely brought her up.

Flipping open the magazine to a full-page Calvin Klein ad, I found Jimmy's pretty fourteen-year-old daughter and four other young models of different racial backgrounds. They stood together smiling, their teeth all very white (Americans are hopelessly infatuated with white teeth), their hair fanning out perfectly behind them as if to suggest the free-flying and aggressive energy of youth.

'Wow!' I said, shocked, adding fawningly. 'She looks a lot like you!'

'Nancy has turned into a swan overnight!' said the proud father with a somewhat complicated expression. Ah, so Nancy was Jimmy's daughter's name. I examined the picture carefully. Nancy's carefree smile and healthy complexion betrayed her posh upbringing. I remembered Jimmy's brief description of his ex-wife's grand house on Long Island and her yacht worth more than half a million dollars.

'Just don't throw it out!' Jimmy urged me earnestly, glancing at the substantial magazine in my hands. Then he hurried off. He had two appointments to look at condos.

Carrying the magazine with Jimmy's daughter in it, I took a cab with Muju to a Japanese restaurant called Nippon on 52nd Street for dinner.

Muju knew the owner very well. In fact, the owner had once been an apprentice to Muju's father, who was a famous and well-respected noodle chef in Japan. He supervised a number of students and had opened several dozen flourishing noodle restaurants.

Muju's mother was Eurasian, unique for her generation. Her father was Italian, and she had inherited his mysterious big blue eyes, while from her Japanese mother she'd inherited her exquisite skin and luminous black hair. In one of Muju's photos of her, she wore a black embroidered kimono, and her blue eyes glittered. Apparently she played a key role in the family business and compared with the rest of that generation of docile Japanese women she was both individual and opinionated.

By comparison my mother seemed gentle and virtuous, making the care of her husband and child her life's work.

The day that 9/11 happened the phone-lines to New York

were so busy it seemed they'd burst, and when my mother couldn't reach me by phone she nearly lost her mind with worry. Now she calls me once a week, and the first thing she always says is: 'Are you well? Have you been eating properly?'

Confucius said: 'Eat, drink, man, woman: Herein are man's great desires.' In this placing of food and drink above desire, one can see that eating is clearly the first tier of great things under heaven. Ever since I can remember, my parents never hugged me let alone kissed me. But while they had a taboo against making physical contact with the body of the grown-up child, they would serve up table after table of fine and delicious food, every dish declaring: 'I love you, my child.'

So my father had something in common with Muju's father: a passionate appreciation of good food. Besides being a professor of history, my father was also a famous Shanghai food critic. He was often a commentator on a celebrity chefs' contest that went out in a progamme called *The Great Chinese Gourmet Gathering* on Shanghai television.

We sat down next to a picture of a green wheatfield that took up the entire wall. The owner came over to greet us and Muju exchanged greetings with him for a moment in Japanese. The owner nodded at me, smiling, and said a few words of Japanese. I looked at Muju for help, and he quickly introduced us in English.

'People always mistake me for Japanese,' I said, 'as if Asian people who dress fashionably must come from Japan and not China.'

Muju lowered his head and flipped through the menu quickly, then asked: 'Want me to suggest a few dishes? Their noodles are pretty good.'

'Okay.' Eating with him I was happy to be lazy. He almost always ordered the food.

The soba at this restaurant was made of twenty per cent wheat and eighty per cent buckwheat. The latter was produced specially for the restaurant at a farm in Canada. The big picture of the lush green wheatfields next to us was the farm.

'Tell me about your father. I'm guessing he was a great influence on you,' I said, eating cold tofu. Muju ate his noodles noisily. I've heard that when Japanese people eat noodles, the louder the slurping, the more they're expressing how tasty the noodles are.

'Perhaps. I remember when I was four or five years old, he taught me how to eat noodles.'

'Then how *do* you eat noodles?' I asked.

'Oh, you wouldn't want to learn that.' Muju turned back to his noodles.

'But I'm very curious,' I insisted.

'All right then. First, you appreciate the exterior of the whole bowl of noodles, looking at the scallions floating partly submerged in the broth. Then you take a mouthful of broth and put the bowl down. Savouring the taste of the broth thoughtfully, you roll it back and forth in your mouth; then you swallow, and then you eat the noodles. You can't eat the roast meat on the noodles first. First you have to just look at it. While consuming the other ingredients you have to look at those slices of meat, look at them with true affection . . .'

Muju finished speaking and examined my expression.

My mouth was hanging open as if I'd just heard the most bizarre story. Then we both burst out laughing.

'Very interesting,' I said.

'I never intended to let myself get too picky; as long as it's food – even a MacDonald's burger – I'd still eat it. But the truth is I don't really like that kind of food.'

'Doesn't matter That's hardly a fault.' As I spoke, I wondered secretly whether, however long I lived with Muju, I'd ever be able to please his gourmet palate. I doubted it.

'It's not a fault,' Muju said, 'it's a hobby. Gourmet food and nice clothes are both hobbies of mine.'

'Right,' I said, then, thinking ahead, 'What about pretty girls?' I thought of the way he looked at Jimmy's Korean female companion when we were at Columbia, and also of the naked-women trinkets placed around his apartment, distributed like potatoes all over the room, on the fridge, by the bathroom mirror, on the sofa, and by the head of the bed. I'd always found it very endearing, interior decoration with comic flair.

'Of course I like women,' Muju said casually.

'What do you mean?' My heart sank.

'Hey, what sort of man doesn't like women?' Muju gestured, trying to make me laugh.

I said nothing. The image of him in bed with all sorts of women floated into my mind: lying next to him, fondling him.

It wasn't a happy thought. The truth was, I was even jealous of his previous girlfriends. I remember once he was eating a meal and mentioned how he always ate a lot but that he didn't put on weight easily, while the people who ate with him did. His former girlfriends, for example, all seemed to have grown fatter after they met him. At the time I just made light of the situation by saying: 'Oh? They must have been able to eat a lot.'

'Well, have you ever cheated on a girlfriend, or your ex-wife?' My voice had an edge to it, too much of an edge. The truth was I really didn't want to know if he'd ever been unfaithful. People who ask over-specific questions of those they love often end up getting hurt.

Muju fell silent. He just looked down and ate the noodles, put down his chopsticks, lifted up the bowl, and drank a mouthful of broth. I watched his every move. His hands as he lifted the bowl seemed exceptionally large, and the scar on his little finger seemed especially obvious.

'Yes, I have.' He opened his mouth suddenly, gazing straight at me.

My heart was in turmoil. I looked down, said nothing.

'Coco, please look at me.' He clasped my hand. 'Things from before are all in the past. I only care about the present . . . The reality is I'm with you, not with someone else. It's you I'm attracted to, and I have no intention of starting up anything with another woman.'

I looked at him. He seemed a bit anxious. I shook my head to clear it of those negative thoughts. Liking women was not a drawback in a man. If a man didn't like women, I figured, women wouldn't like him either.

But to be unfaithful . . . I myself had been unfaithful to a boyfriend. This was the dark side of human nature. When you think about it, even the moon waxes and wanes, and even the great outdoors has its dangerous and terrifying qualities. Humans are complex, and flawed.

Nonetheless Muju was too honest. He didn't want to lie, even to avoid an over-complicated life. Sometimes I just couldn't stand his forthright honesty.

Sometimes people become used to hearing lies.

A few hours later, we were sitting on the leather sofa in the living room in front of the huge television.

A segment of Muju's documentary about Julio was on the TV. Muju had brought it back from the Dominican Republic and had just finished the final editing.

Sometimes Julio's eyes opened wide and round, his lips pursed, intense and passionate like a jungle prince; sometimes he crooned and swayed, deep emotional sincerity and excitement on his face.

His two former wives were just as Muju had described them in his is earlier e-mails: like milk and honey, but highly destructive.

Julio's father's ninety-eighth birthday party was attended by roughly forty-three great-grandchildren, thirty-six grand-children, and eleven children, as well as more than two hundred friends and neighbours. It was an ocean of people singing and dancing.

On the small plane to Cuba, there were three cages with roosters, several of which crowed loudly at different intervals. Next came a close-up of the chickens' wings in motion.

At the massive concert in Cuba, twenty thousand comrades of

the Cuban proletariat danced and waved their hands as Julio sang his heart out.

Big-bearded Castro embraced Julio in greeting. I noted that Castro was wearing a pair of Nikes.

13

Male Authors and Critics

I wonder why men get serious at all. They have this delicate
long thing hanging outside their bodies, which goes up and
down by its own will . . . If I were a man I would
always be laughing at myself.
Yoko Ono

I supposed I could have stayed home and baked cookies and had teas.
Hillary Clinton

Sometimes I think I'm like Linus from the Snoopy
cartoons, only it isn't the little blanket I can't do without.
It's love.

I always need love, I seem to need it even more than other
women. Without it I can't breathe, can't live. I hold love in my
mouth, hide it under my pillow, put it in my vagina, write it
down on paper.

For me, before Muji, the essence of most of my love was being
in love with love. Those men were, one after the other, merely
envelopes that could walk and that had penises. I took my love
and placed it in these envelopes for a while, pretending that
someone somewhere in the world had sent me a romantic letter
asking for my love. I pretended that I'd received these letters with
a great deal of pleasant surprise, when in truth the content of
these letters – love – was from the start my own creation. It was
love that I had to store temporarily in a man's body.

But Muju seemed quite different from these earlier envelope-men. For the first time he made me experience a kind of spiritual warmth and loving sincerity. For the first time he made me see the magic of sex and the space for limitless imagination. For the first time he made me grasp that love and sex could be perfectly combined.

He had given me a lot of things besides love. He opened some windows for me, pointing out a world I'd never seen before, or never really stopped to notice.

When we were together, we spent a lot of time reading, chatting, meditating, making love, eating, walking, laughing, and of course we had our small arguments. I didn't smoke now, drink, or take sedatives. My dreams were more peaceful than before, and Putuo Island had appeared with its beaches, mountains and temples.

By that time it was already March, and our love had reached its third month.

Hints of green began to appear on the sidewalks of New York. You could see the first stirrings of the cherry blossom. The wind was still as strong as before, but not quite so harsh. Because, as everybody knew, spring was just ahead.

That week, I was busy.

On Monday I had to give a lecture for graduate and doctoral students in the East Asia Studies Department at Columbia. I, and a group of visiting writers from China, were to be the main lecturers.

The lecture hall was more crowded than expected. I looked past the sea of black and blonde heads to see people standing in the hallway. I asked one of the organizers, and discovered that the biggest Chinese newspaper in America had made a full-page announcement about the lecture with a sensationalist headline: 'Decisive battle of the alternative vs. the mainstream. A lecture hosted by banned and official authors convened at Columbia University.' Many people had seen the ad and rushed over.

This kind of hype fed on chaos. I'd already experienced too much of it myself.

Actually, to have your book banned in China isn't something to be proud of. It carries a heavy and practical punishment that forces the author to lie low and make no public appearances for six or seven years. In contrast, the officially approved authors can sit back and relax with a government-guaranteed monthly salary for the rest of their lives.

Seven middle-aged men in ties and suits with the labels still on the sleeves and one young woman with long fingernails, long hair, and a self-protective smile stuck on her face. Eight people seated in a row, facing the audience.

After each person made a simple statement laying out his or her views about literature, it moved to the part where audience members asked questions.

Many of the audience's questions were directed at me, so I became the star of the show. But I proceeded cautiously, trying as hard as I could to direct attention towards those seven male authors who were so much older and who'd come from so far away. It got to the point that even when I was answering questions I still addressed them deferentially as 'teacher' in a complimentary tone of voice.

The questions were far from new. All had been asked of me by reporters hundreds of times before.

'Why do you write?'

'What is the ratio of truth to fiction in your work?'

'If your book had been written by a male author, would it still have been attacked by public opinion and finally banned?'

'How are you different from the last generation of writers?'

'Do you prefer Western men or Chinese men?'

I gave practiced answers. At times the audience guffawed, applauded. But from start to finish I felt that, compared to those male authors with their cheap suits and stiff manner, I was trendy but powerless. Seated before so many pairs of curious, critical eyes I was like a startled bird.

When confronted with a mainly male audience, I dug my heels stubbornly into the ground, but at the same time I couldn't help but feel deeply intimidated. Although society has progressed, prejudice and misunderstandings towards women persist. Especially when people associate you with sex and politics.

After the presentation was over, the whole group went to the Mountain King restaurant. Thirteen people sat around a big round table, seemingly equal and friendly. After the gunsmoke has dispersed you should use food to fill the troubling cracks of life that have appeared.

The Professor from the East Asian Studies Department ordered the food. Shrimp with black ginseng, grilled lobster with scallion and ginger, Peking duck, green vegetables and meatballs, claypot clams with tofu and other dishes were placed in the middle of the round table. There were different colours and smells to tantalize the nostrils – an impressive display. Eating a lot of complex Chinese food often leaves one exquisitely happy. For the majority of Chinese people, Chinese food is one of the reasons for living.

None of the thirteen diners mentioned anything about literature. The male authors spoke loudly in Chinese, laughing now and then as if they were members of some great alliance. They patiently discussed with the Professor the schedule for sightseeing in New York over the next few days, such as when to go to the Metropolitan Museum, Broadway, and of course the very popular remains of 9/11.

Afterwards, several of the men, determined to do some on-site research into the culture of capitalism, asked haltingly whether they could be taken to a sex club.

Not one among them had any intention of speaking to me in a friendly way. My English, the several hundred dollars' worth of clothes on my body, and even the pimples on my face were all things they couldn't forgive, in spite of the fact that in their minds they'd probably already torn off my clothes.

I concentrated on eating, feeling slightly stronger with each mouthful. Misunderstandings, estrangement, jealousy, hostility – all these things are unhealthy, but they can only improve your immunity and broaden your mind. When a woman drinks dirty water, it gets squeezed out as mother's milk.

Then, on Thursday evening there was that little party of forty or so guests thrown for me by the publisher. It took place at a small café in the Village.

The café was truly very small, but its size didn't show. With the bobbing heads and lively atmosphere the place seemed much bigger than it actually was.

Among the people there were the publishing company's editor, the PR person, people from the marketing and distribution departments, and some authors and critics. Among them was a local man who'd just won a literary award. He looked a bit like the character of the best-selling author Melvin played by Jack Nicholson in *As Good As It Gets*, who took pleasure in humiliating animals, women, homosexuals and people of colour, until love transformed him into a good person. I chatted with him and he was endearing, but a bit crazy. He brought a purebred German Shepherd with him to the party, making the tiny café even more crowded.

'What a lovely dog!' I flattered him.

'Ah,' he laughed, 'So that's how it is, when a charming girl compliments my dog, I suddenly have hope.' He winked at me and then swiftly reached out his hand and took a firm pinch of my bottom.

Suddenly he looked not in the least bit wise, just an old billy goat wearing a flannel shirt, with a herding dog by his side.

I walked away from him. I took a few turns around the room, greeting people with a smile, and then approached a young man.

He was a redhead, very young, with a bookish look about his handsome face. To me he looked no different from the acne-ridden students I often saw on Columbia's campus with twelve leaky pens stuck in their shirt pockets and wearing jeans that they washed once a year.

But after chatting I discovered that he wasn't a student after all. He'd recently become a critic for the *New York Times*. His name was Eric.

So I told him that I and my book had appeared in the *New York Times* three times. Sadly, once was a year ago, though it got nearly half a page; once was the week right after 9/11; and once was in a special travel section on Shanghai.

He laughed, and said that he'd just read my book and really liked it.

We got to talking about Asian culture. He told me his father was a professor working on Tibet at Columbia, and had converted to Buddhism a long time ago. He himself planned to make a trip to Tibet before long.

'Tibet is one of the places where human consciousness is preserved in its most primitive form,' he said. I agreed.

We chatted a lot. I discovered something pleasant in him, something intelligent, friendly and sensitive.

While we talked, my red silk top kept catching his eye. It had three black velvet coiled buttons in the shape of butterflies slanting from the collar to the armpit.

He couldn't stop praising the skill of Chinese tailors' button work. The liberal flattery left me floating on air. I couldn't help but tell him that this kind of coiled silk, velvet or cotton button comes in more than a hundred different shapes. There were cloud shapes, chrysanthemum shapes, lotus shapes, buttons in the shape of an old form of Chinese currency known as 'Yuan Bao', as well as goldfish and many more.

Eric's eyes widened with astonishment, and he expressed unreserved admiration. 'Can men wear this kind of button as a decoration too?' he suddenly asked.

'Why not?' Saying this, I couldn't suppress a smile. He was very cute; he wasn't pretentious or affected like critics usually are. Perhaps he hadn't yet had the chance to develop.

Before the party ended, Eric and I swapped phone numbers and agreed to get a coffee together or something sometime. I liked him. Perhaps he was gay. He reminded me of Xi'er ten years ago, before she became a girl.

14

A Secret About the Concert

. . . and first I put my arms around him yes and drew him
down to me so he could feel my breasts all perfume yes and
his heart was going like mad yes I said yes I will yes.
James Joyce, *Ulysses*

It only took Muju five minutes to walk from his office to my apartment on Watts Street. We were going to go to Carnegie Hall to hear a concert by Yo-Yo Ma.

As usual I was scurrying around, blow-drying my hair, putting on make-up, and trying on outfits; gleaming silk was scattered all over the bed.

And it was Muju who helped me make a speedy decision. He chose a skin-tight black *qipao* dress with pictures of phoenixes embroidered on the lower panel. I always joke that after putting on that kind of *qipao*, even if you've only eaten a peanut you can immediately detect its presence. Because this *qipao* was quite tight, it seemed to melt into my own skin. This kind of traditional Chinese silk garment is a bit like bound feet: both are the intensely beautiful product of a process that is violent to the point of maltreatment.

Naturally, there was no way I could complete my preparations before departure on time. As I said earlier: inscribed on the tablet of my destiny was the word 'Late'. Certainly, I'd never been on time at least to eat, watch movies, or go to parties with a boyfriend.

When we stood on the corner of Watts and Sixth Avenue

trying to hail a cab, we only had forty minutes. A gale was blowing and we started to worry. If we were late we'd miss the first half.

We waited impatiently for an empty cab. Just as one stopped, a man and a woman dashed out from the shadows, charged ahead of us and opened the taxi door.

'Hey, we were waiting here first,' I called out, rushing towards them. But they were already inside the car. I shouted to the driver: 'You saw what happened. Please ask them to get out of the car.'

'Sorry, we have urgent business,' the American woman said as she closed the car door. She had coarse skin like tree-bark and a high, arrogant nose.

Then Muju silently stepped up to the taxi and opened the door. 'Fine, in that case we'll share. Coco, would you mind sitting next to the driver?' As he spoke he got into the back seat and sat down next to the couple.

'Wait a second, sorry, you can't get in,' said the man, who was wearing a long black leather jacket. He clearly wasn't prepared for this. There was an edge of panic in his voice.

'Why can't I?' There was no smile on Muju's face. His eyes were gleaming, and the pulse on his temples was pounding. In a clear and calm voice he said: 'My friend and I have been standing here about ten minutes, and you were after us, but since you absolutely must take this cab, then fine, we'll share it. But I'm afraid it will have to drop us off first at Carnegie Hall. We're about to miss the concert.'

A few seconds of silence, then the man and the woman decided to give up. 'Okay, you can have this cab.' They got out.

The driver pretended not to have noticed anything, but after that he drove fast, rushing down one street after another.

My spirits were high, and I kissed Muju several times. At that moment, in his formal attire, he was stunning. He was my hero. In cold and crass New York, having to fight for a taxi on a street-corner was an everyday event. Compared to the foul wind and rain of blood on Wall Street, this was quite trivial and ordinary. But it was a new lesson for me. Muju showed me how to stand up for myself calmly.

The driver got us to the concert hall with only five minutes to spare before the concert began. We trotted all the way to our seats in the balcony.

It was a completely different world from a few moments ago. Our seats were side by side in the second-floor balcony, directly opposite the stage. We were gasping slightly for breath as the houselights dimmed, accentuating the light on the stage. In the air there was a kind of golden silence, a nearly intangible aroma, and a kind of clarity of memory. Classical music in a splendid, majestic concert hall can bring all these pleasures back to you, even though the things that you experienced – Bach, the anxious spring of your seventeeth year, your lover's pure smile – may have long since become history in the blink of an eye when you weren't looking.

Yo-Yo Ma, a Chinese Westerner, is a master in the world of classical music who's risen to great heights. He appeared on the stage wearing a bright smile. Thunderous applause, then after a brief silence, the music drifted upwardss. People held their breath in silence, as if they had been hypnotized.

I liked his performances of Bach's suites for cello. One morning, I opened my eyes at Muju's and heard the first movement from this same suite for cello, and could feel in the music a cool and fresh turquoise, behind which was a river, clean and deep, carrying unthawed ice along in its gurgling flow. There was the occasional sound of angels' wings beating softly. You were left too moved to speak.

I turned my head slightly and glanced at Muju by my side just as he was lifting a pair of binoculars to his eyes, completely engrossed in watching the stage. At his wrists, the flat, even white cuffs of his shirt extended beyond the sleeves of his black suit. His straight, taut back; his long hair like flames of solid black; and on his face a nobility that left one speechless.

This was one of my ideal sexual fantasies: a magnificent concert hall, a crowd of people dressed in splendid and formal clothes, the air deceptively sweet, a man wearing a black suit smooth as marble with a white shirt showing at his sleeves, sitting enigmatic and silent by your side. You have no sense of his inner spirit, nor even of his body or his flesh, which you see but do not comprehend. You know nothing of his station in life, nor anything about him, yet he sits within arm's reach, and with your hand outstretched you can reach the zip of his trousers.

Imagine that the zip can be opened wide like a door to endless possibility and that your fingers fly softly like rose-petals, until you receive the dewdrops of nectar gushing forth.

You and he both are about to faint in this absurd passion bordering on the edge of nightmare. Yet both of you remain expressionless, sitting there outside time and reality like a pair of cold and exquisite statues.

I caught my breath. The tip of my nose was damp with sweat. I had to admit, having sexual dreams like this was one of the pleasures of classical music in a concert hall.

After the performance was over, we went backstage. There was a great crowd of people there. We saw Muju's friend, the New York real estate baron Richard and his Japanese wife 'W'. From his childhood Richard had resolved to be a famous piano player, but in the end he became a famous and rich businessman. After he'd learned the unpredictability of fate, he started to subsidize all kinds of classical music concerts.

Muju's relationship to Richard's wife W. was actually even closer. W. was once Japan's most famous geisha, and was in Muju's mind's eye perhaps the near-perfect woman. She was nearing sixty, but in her elegant, stately kimono she was ravishing. A three-hundred-dollar facial twice a week and endless pampering made her look like she was thirty-seven or thirty-eight years old.

It was truly unbelievable.

She called Muju 'little brother'. She rarely made dinner for her husband, but when Muju fell ill she made sushi and hot porridge herself and brought it over to his apartment. Her skills in the kitchen, to use Muju's words, were 'Impeccable! First rate!'

Then we saw Yo-Yo Ma, still smiling. Muju had once helped organize a performance by Yo-Yo Ma in Japan that was attended by the Imperial family.

After the concert we went to a cocktail party at the Plaza Hotel.

Neither Muju nor I drank. Muju had helped me to give up alcohol, smoking and sedatives. It all turned out not to be as difficult as I'd imagined. But even though I hadn't had any wine, as the evening wore on and the night grew darker and darker I still had the feeling I was drunk. Like I was spinning slowly in the thin air. The moon rotated around the earth, the earth rotated around the sun, the sun was at the centre of the body of the one I loved, so I rotated around him.

The cello master Yo-Yo Ma could really drink, and in the end it seemed he was gulping wine like a whale. Equally able to drink, my father once said to me: 'Men who can drink but need not fear getting drunk are worth depending upon.'

I was a bit doubtful about this. But the unchanging smile on Yo-Yo Ma's face, warm and refined, seemed likeable and endearing.

Richard and W. were an odd but very interesting couple. Richard had a belly that quivered like jelly whenever he laughed. He was a big man with a prickly beard, sometimes roaring like a bear and sometimes mewing like a little kitten searching for mother's love. He was passionate about all fine art and active in philanthropic organizations and movements to protect the Brazilian rainforests.

Richard loved W. completely and he was jealous of all the men she knew including her twenty-five-year-old son from a previous marriage.

But some of his childlike actions in his daily life were astonishing. For example, he always ate in one breath any ice cream that he saw before him, and then was sick immediately. He'd get up at half past five in the morning, to get his driver to take him to the Hamptons. The parking lots there were free before 10 a.m., so you could save thirty dollars. But he'd be so happy he'd saved thirty bucks that he'd spend three hundred to treat everyone at work to lunch.

The first gift he ever gave W. was a stone he picked up in the middle of a sidewalk on his way to an appointment. He saw something precious in this rough and ugly piece of stone, and still congratulated himself that other people hadn't noticed it when they passed.

By comparison, the humidifier that Muju gave me on our first date seemed a far greater token of love than that piece of stone.

Richard was energetic, gesturing constantly, expounding to me and Muju various brilliant remarks about aesthetics.

'What is spiritual truth, and what is visual truth? Why can these things be so different at times? With your eyes wide open you see a beautiful woman standing enticingly in front of you, yet you feel nothing. But close your eyes and suddenly, when you can't see anything – Aha! You can see everything.'

'How is it possible to feel nothing with a beautiful woman standing enticingly in front of you?' joked Muju.

The exquisite and ageless W. seemed to have no expression. Beneath the flower-embroidered folds of her kimono, under the cover of her perfect make-up, W. moved with languid grace. Even her eyes blinked in slow motion like in an old movie.

But even when she didn't make a sound, W. still impinged upon your awareness. She was a swan that had drifted in from the Middle Ages, regal and poised with a nostalgic beauty.

'Even if an author were to spend his entire life using words in an attempt to communicate his emotions and beliefs, still there are some things an author would be unwilling to share with a reader. Of course, I'm not talking about private matters, but rather more metaphysical things. You know what I mean.' Richard said, gazing directly at me.

'Um . . . well . . .' I nearly capitulated. God, he didn't seem anything like a real-estate salesman. At that moment I wasn't in the mood to discuss writing with anyone, dizzy in my high heels, the skin-tight *qipao* dress constricting me so I could hardly breathe. It was time to leave the cocktail party, time to break the spell.

I don't remember what I said to Richard, but after a series of hugs and kisses, Muju and I rushed away. Returning to Muju's apartment, I couldn't take my high heels off fast enough, and I swiftly removed all the hairpins from my head. Just as I began to undo a row of buttons on the *qipao*, Muju suddenly intervened: 'Wait a second, you can't do that yourself. Let me take it off for you.' I stopped, and an ambiguous smile floated up to my face.

'Sorry, let me wash my hands first,' he said, hurrying into the bathroom. There was the swish-swish sound of the tap, and then he came out from the bathroom and walked quickly towards me.

As soon as he'd run his eyes hungrily over my *qipao*, he wrapped me in his arms. At the same time he kissed my neck below my ears and gently stroked my arms, my shoulders, my chest. This layer of skin-tight silk was my skin. Through the silk I could feel everything, even more intensely than when I was naked.

'You like it?' I murmured.

He said nothing.

'Feel like hearing the sound of silk when it tears?' My voice was muffled as if I was talking in my sleep. A kind of carbolic fizzle of excitement tickled at my heart.

This was me. I know the kind of woman I am. There's no helping it, some things are just predestined and can't be set aside. It just goes round in your bloodstream. That's the kind of woman I am.

I guided Muju in tearing it. Start with the slit at the leg, pulling upwards, forcefully at first and then progressing evenly. You must hold your breath and keep your voice down, otherwise you'll miss the beauty of that split second of sound.

His eyes again emitted a glow that dazzled and excited me. The light in his eyes made my vagina clench so tightly that it was almost painful.

Once again Muju became my god, throwing me suddenly onto the soft bed, then beginning to tear the silk in earnest.

I moaned, writhing like a snake shedding its skin. He laughed, stopped what he was doing, bent down, and blocked my mouth with a kiss. 'Shh . . .' he said, and then he delicately straightened his body and with regret for the destruction, resolutely proceeded to rip the silk *qipao* to pieces.

The sound of tearing silk, clear and crisp, is sublime, terrifying yet enchanting. The sound lingers in the ears for a long time. When you close your eyes you can still hear it, and then you get hot and wet all over again.

In Shanghai, whenever my tailor brought a delicate and glamorous *qipao* over to my house, I would always say to myself: 'There are all kinds of beauty. Most beauty should be preserved; that's eternal beauty. But a tiny part is for merciless destruction. That's temporary beauty.'

15

At the Temple of Righteous Rain

What you are you do not see, what you see is your shadow.
Rabindranath Tagore

On the empty mountain I can see no-one/
But I can hear the sound of voices
Tang Poet Wang Wei, *Deer Park Cottage*

Putuo Island – Autumn

After sailing on the ocean for the whole night, the S.S. *Sea and Sky* ferry drew slowly up to the wharf at 8 a.m. After a series of jolts, the motor died, the gangplank was dropped, and passengers began to file off the boat with their luggage.

It had just rained and the tarmac pavement was wet. But the sky lightened and sunlight spilled down through the layer of clouds. I took a breath of fresh air, and found that I was in a small valley encircled by cheery green hills. Here and there the crimson and gold eaves of temples hidden among the green folds sparkled like cherry tomatoes in a fresh salad

After asking directions, I got on a small crowded bus. My destination was the Temple of Righteous Rain.

On the way, the scenery entranced me. In the nearly thirty years since I'd been born, I had returned here with my parents on several visits. But then I wasn't so willing. I felt like I'd been forced to come. At that age, once I'd burned incense to Buddha, I was only interested in sunbathing and playing in the water on the clean white sand beaches.

The turquoise ocean rolling smooth and flat, the white sand beach, the chain of mountains showing different shades of green and chestnut brown, the dense forests, and every blade of grass, every tree, every stone by the side of the road, all seemed to offer me a smiling welcome.

How familiar it all was!

The salty ocean breeze cooled my face. It teased long hair into chaos. Every pore of my body opened. I was enveloped by an anxious, joyful mood that brought tears to my eyes.

The bus came to a stop not far from the Temple of Righteous Rain. I was the last to get off.

I could see the high memorial archway of grey-green stone on which in ruby-red characters the words Temple of Righteous Rain were carved. Behind it there was only a small bridge decorated with a row of miniature carved lions. The entire temple was concealed behind a dense stand of trees.

Only after passing over the small bridge and venturing along a shadowy path of mossy cobblestones could you find the temple and experience its solemn, remote stillness.

I decided to find a hotel to stay in first. From my last visit I recalled a small inn run by local fishermen situated on the gentle slope next to the temple. When I headed towards the slope to look I discovered that the inn was still there. The Happy Arrival Inn. It appeared to have been through a lot, just like an old friend you haven't seen for many years.

The paperwork for registering was very simple, and the room was amazingly cheap. When I thought back to life in Manhattan, it seemed like everyone there burned money all day.

A young girl with cheeks reddened by the sea breeze and carrying a thermos of hot water led me to my room. The thudding sound of her feet was loud as she walked in front of me. My room faced south with a view of the ocean.

The girl put the thermos on the table, told me the times of the three meals and the hot water for bathing, then left with a bashful smile.

I plopped myself onto the bed, lulled by the rushing sound of the billowing ocean waves and the wind blowing through the trees in the hills, and drifted off. I think I had a dream, but when I opened my eyes I forgot it immediately.

I brushed my teeth, bathed, did a half-hour's worth of Taoist meditation and it was time for lunch. I dressed in white loose-fitting clothes and a pair of comfortable shoes and went to eat a bowl of seafood noodles in the little restaurant on the ground floor of the hotel.

I was all by myself; nobody knew me, nobody spoke to me. But I didn't feel lonely.

This place seemed to have no links to any other part of the globe. It hung, otherworldly, on the horizon, floating on the great rolling surface of the ocean. It seemed not to care about the past and not to worry about the future. It existed eternally by itself in this moment in time. It was a pure white void. Dark memories would disappear into it without trace.

By now the sun had emerged and it beat on me. The autumn air smelled faintly of something burnt, but was clear and mild. It took me only ten minutes to reach the slab of green stone at the archway of Temple of Righteous Rain. I then crossed through the high, curved gate, passed a small bridge, and then on down a quiet footpath. After about five minutes, a narrow white wall and a wooden door, well corroded by the wind and rain, appeared before me. The door was partly open, and I moved to step over the bluestone threshold.

Just as I stepped across the threshold of the temple, I was seized by a feeling of *déja-vu*.

It was as if I'd crossed the threshold many times before, long ago, but with great effort. In the landscape of *déja-vu* I was still a two- or three-year-old child and the bluestone threshold of only twenty centimetres was too high for me. There wasn't a soul in sight in this vivid dreamscape. There was only a small child struggling with all her might to lift her little leg up over the stone. It all resembled a riddle-like

107

painting by De Chirico, suffused with a tranquil and transparent light that made it seem not the least bit frightening.

Hands in pockets, I slowly entered the courtyard. In the front chamber was an arrangement of Guan-yin and other Buddhas welcoming offerings in solemn splendour and on either side of this great room were lower and slightly plainer chambers with long corridors for Arhats and lower-ranked Buddhas. There was a guestroom for visitors, a meditation hall where monks recited the sutras and a small dining room for them.

After paying my respects to the Buddhas, I strolled casually over to a shady courtyard at the rear corner of the temple gardens. My eye fell on several ancient Bodhi trees, five or six centuries old.

Although I had been almost constantly immersed in the concrete walls of the urban jungle, with few opportunities for contact with nature, on those few occasions when I encountered a great tree I was always involuntarily moved by the sight of such enduring and miraculous beauty. To think that the beauty of this tree in its entirety had taken several hundreds or even thousands of years to cultivate.

The gnarled and criss-crossed roots of the Bodhi tree before me were planted silently and powerfully in the earth, while its massive canopy reached vigorously towards the sky. Looking up at it, I couldn't help but think of the brevity of human life. This was not the 'world of empty illusion' variety of melancholy. Hundred-year-old and thousand-year-old trees alike possess special healing powers, powers that flow through the trickling sap of the trees directly into your heart.

I breathed in the fragrance of the ancient trees, and walked towards a circle of people who had gathered beneath one of the trees to watch an old and a young monk play Go.

I don't know how to play Go, but these two monks, wearing their gray cassocks and belts like grandfather and grandson, caught my interest. The older one had a goatee beard; his thin cheeks made his nose seem pronounced and its tip was a bit red. I couldn't tell his age. His face had an expression of laughing without laughing, of sleeping without sleeping, and his body gave off a strange magnetic force. A close look revealed that the young monk had fine, delicate features and glittering black eyes. He seemed very intelligent. He looked to be about fourteen or fifteen years old.

I decided to stand and watch from one side.

The pair stared intently at their game, one young and one old. Little pearls of rainwater gathered in the dense leaves of the great tree and dropped down onto the wooden Go board, making a crisp 'da' sound.

The circle of onlookers came and went, but I stood there and continued to watch. Since coming to this island I'd had nothing but time, and when I got tired of standing I just sat down on a nearby bench.

The sky gradually grew dark. On the small island, it seemed one could only feel time passing by observing the colours of the sky. But the sky here grew light earlier than it did in the city, and it got dark earlier too.

Sighing, the old monk discarded a black gamepiece at last. 'You win,' he said to the young monk.

The young one smiled, his clean face glowing childishly. This was the only match he'd won out of ten.

I quietly clapped my hands, smiling.

The old monk glanced up at me and nodded briefly. I quickly put my hands together, palms facing, in a gesture of respect, and bowed gently.

'I see that the young lady is not very old. If you'll pardon my asking, is this your first visit here?' he asked me good-naturedly.

I hurriedly shook my head 'No, I've been here several times before – in fact, I was born here.'

The old monk listened and squinted his eyes, stroking his beard. He kept quiet for a moment as if he recalled something.

At this point the young monk had already tidied up the

gameboard and gamepieces. He stared at me curiously for a moment with those black eyes of his, and then transferred his attention back to his master. His master nodded his head slightly.

'Yes, I do seem to remember such an incident. A girl was once born at the Temple of Righteous Rain, prematurely to a woman who seemed to have come from a great distance and in great haste.'

A tremour ran through my body and my heart began to pound hard. What the old monk said was exactly what I'd often heard from my father and mother about my birth. 'Master remembers this?' I asked.

He sat in front of me, stroking his beard, measuring me kindly with his eyes as if in the space of only a few seconds he could see all the things that had happened to me in twenty years. All the good, bad, happy, sad, dull, violent things.

His gaze was like the fire from a stove in winter or like the sun at dusk, so warm and benevolent that I nearly burst into tears.

'Are you that little girl whose Buddhist name was "Wisdom"?' he asked me at last.

Suddenly I found myself sobbing.

16

Muju's Dripping-wet Birthday

During lovemaking, we enter the deepest part of our being.
My body's very existence melts into his body, and in the midst
of the sensation of our two bodies becoming one,
we feel the greatest pleasure.
Hindu Love Classics

When man and woman have sex and do not ejaculate after ten times,
the eyes and ears grow sharper (i.e. faculties of seeing and hearing);
twenty times without ejaculating will make your voice clear and strong;
thirty times without ejaculating will make your skin
bright and lustrous; forty times will strengthen your back and waist; fifty
times without ejaculating will make your buttocks and thighs firm and
strong; sixty times without ejaculating will drain the urethra; and a
hundred times will bring you good health and longevity' . . .
Chinese Daoist Classic
Sex, Health, and Long Life, or
The Taoist Classics: Collected Translations of Thomas Cleary

New York – Spring

April. Spring in New York. Finally a thread of happiness.
The spring thunder that occasionally rang out seemed to
awake the green shoots. The weather wouldn't be so cold
again.

My dreams came true. I gave up my apartment on Watts Street
and moved into Muju's on the Upper West Side.

The doormen there already recognized me – the girl always
dressed in silk. They gradually became more relaxed. One,

named Sieg, even became a friend. He was actually also a poet, on the nightshift guarding the door, engrossed in his writing. He gave me a thick photocopied volume of his poems. In exchange, I gave him an autographed copy of my book. When he was young, he'd been on Broadway as an extra. He was still handsome, almost suave and when he opened the door and greeted you he always gave you the feeling you were on stage.

The doormen were living guidebooks. If you were puzzled about where to copy a key or where to get something notarized, you could always get the answer from one of them.

When I moved in with Muju it felt like we were man and wife. I saw my clothes hanging beside his, my underwear in the drawer where he kept his underwear, my laptop on the desk, my maxipads stuffed into the cabinet in the bathroom, the Chinese preserved fruits I loved to eat in the refrigerator. It seemed as though my antennae were creeping into the three-dimensional space of Muju's life.

Muju would say 'This isn't bad! At least I don't have to miss you so much now.' As I expected, he stopped calling me three times a day as he'd done before.

In the evening after he got home from work, we ordered take-aways from China Fun and watched NBA games featuring the New Jersey Nets, and then sat in the tub giving each other back-rubs and using nail-clippers to clip each other's toenails. Sometimes when we remembered, we would walk into the big kitchen, open a bottle of vitamins, each place one in our mouths, share the same glass of water, and gulp down the pills. Of course there were also loud kisses when we opened our eyes every morning, like a pair of pigeons in the morning sunlight.

It was the life for two that I'd yearned for in my dreams.

And then it was his birthday.

Unlike me, Muju thoroughly enjoyed any and all festivities in life, including birthdays. He said half-jokingly that he'd begun preparing for his hundredth birthday bash when he was only twenty. It would of course be attended by all his ex-girlfriends (assuming they lived that long). When he shot the enormous scene of Julio's father's bustling ninety-eighth birthday party, it only encouraged him, as if it was a dress-rehearsal for his own hundredth birthday.

But this wasn't turning out to be a lucky year for Muju. Several of his friends were in trouble. Richard was suddenly always ill – probably too much ice-cream. Julio had planned to attend Muju's birthday dinner when he flew to New York for a Dominican Society fund raiser, but he was suddenly blacklisted by the Immigration Department and decided it was a bad time to enter the US. Meanwhile Muju's workmate of many years, the editor Carrie, had to hurry back to Sydney to look after her sick mother.

So we decided to have an intimate party for just the two of us.

After dining on oysters and lamb at an expensive French restaurant, we returned to the apartment. We put Indian music on the stereo, lit red candles all around the apartment, took a fragrant-scented bath, and both dressed in nightwear: Muju in pyjamas, me in the short silk nightie Xi'er gave me.

Gently Muju helped me comb my hair which just moments before had been soaking in the bubbling water. Both it and my skin were permeated by the strange fragrance from a perfume Muju had brought back from Bali, which smelled exactly like ambergris. Legend said that when a dragon flew over the sea, at the exact moment its spit dripped down into the ocean, it formed the famous ambergris. Indeed, as soon as this type of perfume touched your body, it was as though your heart rippled with its incomparable scent.

Then Muju led me to the bedroom, and from a small locked drawer took out several objects, which he placed on his palm and held in front of my eyes. First, a pale green jade egg trailing a long red silk thread from one end. Next, a silver ball as big as a pearl, within which were several smaller pearls, which trembled slightly since they were on his palm. He said they were called mianzi bells. There was also on a red silk ribbon, a frighteningly

113

ugly penis-shaped thing made from some kind of tuber (which, he later explained, swelled up when it absorbed water), as well as several small pieces of incense.

The calm smile on his face was effective. I wasn't afraid, just curious.

He put most of these objects back in the drawer, leaving only the jade egg and the red silk ribbon. He told me that the jade egg was used by women to exercise the muscles of the vagina, and upon reaching orgasm women could suddenly shoot out the egg from inside. I couldn't help but laugh. Muju seemed a bit embarrassed, 'It can also give you an exceptional orgasm . . . but if you feel uncomfortable, we don't have to try it,' he said.

But I couldn't resist trying it. Since the first time we'd made love, he had cast a spell over my body, and more to the point, I trusted him as I'd never trusted a man before.

We sat facing each other on the bed, already both in a trance-like state from the fragrance emanating from our bodies. First he put the jade egg in his mouth, holding it there for a second, and then he passed it to me. The pale green jade, soaked wet with his saliva, had already been warmed to the body temperature of the inside of his mouth and had a light musky odour.

'Put it in, give it a try.' He watched me.

Without taking off the white silk nightie with the black lotus painted on, two fingers gripping the slippery jade egg, I carefully inserted it between my legs.

The moment the jade egg slid into my body, I opened my mouth soundlessly, gazing at Muju in wonder. He came closer to me, holding my lips in his mouth, kissing me softly, speaking off and on in a low voice: 'Let it slide around, use your muscles to control its direction . . . slide backward and forward, left and right.' He held the long red silk cord that was left outside my body tightly between two fingers so that he could feel the movements of the jade inside my body.

I gradually fell in love with that feeling, the slippery, heavy and light friction, different from the friction of a penis, an extra kind of playfulness, even more distinct as it touched the softness and the warmth of the muscles in the human body.

I couldn't stop this strange and sexy game. The jade egg was like a little psychic being that changed and changed again along with the temperature of my vagina and womb, warmer and warmer, more and more slippery.

Muju leaned over me like an eagle, sucking on my highly protruding nipples and at the same time using one hand to pinch the red silk cord that trailed out of my body, pulling and tugging, creating minute shifts in angle and pressure. I already sensed the tide-like approach of an extraordinary orgasm. My muscles stiffened and tensed, the force first expanding then contracting, growing stronger. Then with a resounding crash the tempestuous waters burst forth from the dam.

Muju's smile looked warm and lustful. Closing my eyes, I could feel his hands slowly tugging the cord attached to the jade egg and pulling it from inside my body. I could feel him placing the slippery wet and warm jade next to my lips, could taste an air of ocean mixed with musk.

I opened my eyes. I saw him put the egg into his mouth, licking, holding it there, swallowing the mixture of saliva and my bodily fluids. He looked calm and satisfied, and in that instant I had a fantasy: this egg was like one produced by a mother hen; it came from the crystallization of the feminine power within my body.

'Want more?' he asked. I saw that his bathrobe was open. Lately he'd been more and more turned on by my orgasm; it was his finest aphrodisiac. He'd told me he felt lucky to have found such a partner. Ancient masters believed the fluid secreted by the vagina wasn't just any water, but was Yin Essence, which meant the liquid female essence. Lots of fluid indicated Yin Essence of great purity and thus a woman with copious fluid embodied both Yin and Yang.

It's up to you whether you believe it or not.

I sat up and pushed him down underneath my body, removing his pyjama bottoms and smoothly tying the red silk cord around the base of his penis. All of a sudden it was tied a bit too tightly. He let out a groan, and his rigid cock sprang up like a dragon in a violent rage. Carefully I loosened the string, and using no condom, spread my legs and sat on top of him. I'd memorized this position in college from looking at a famous pornographic book from five centuries ago called *Jin Ping Mei*, or *The Golden Lotus*. It was the first time I'd tried it. Given that the birthday this evening had become an evening of sexual education, let us educate each other I thought.

In the midst of orgasms that exploded like firecrackers I went a little crazy with passion. The sheets were soaked. The room smelled better and better. It was as though we were on a great ocean of precious ambergris. Little green flames seemed to flicker in the air like delicate flowers, silent like the night

Coming everywhere, flying everywhere. I am but your lone rose, magnificent throughout the whole night.

When I had nearly fainted, he pulled himself out of my body. His cock was rock hard like a living fossil, with the silk cord still tied there. It seemed it would never soften, as if it could carry on for several more days and nights. This was what the ancient books call the secret of the cord.

After a brief but profound and trance-like sleep, we seemed to wake at the same time as the moonlight came through the window and shone on our pillows.

Since there was still moonlight, the night would last some hours longer. We remained as before, deep within the centre of a great plain of darkness feeling each other's breaths.

After a series of tentative kisses, we discovered that our desire wasn't spent. It remained in our bodies like molten lava that had only been slightly cooled. What we'd just done seemed only a long prelude, an *hors d'oeuvre*.

'I want more,' I murmured to myself like a woman whose soul has been set adrift, 'Again, again . . .'

He asked what I would like this time, and I said, to find another woman.

He couldn't believe what I'd said. To be with two women was nearly every man's fantasy, but he hesitated remembering that I'm a woman who could even be jealous of his flabby ex-girlfriends. 'Go on, make a phonecall, find a Japanese girl,' I said in a daze. I felt sudden hunger pangs and went to the kitchen to find something to eat. He followed me in.

We sat in the bright light of the kitchen sharing a container of yoghurt and a cucumber sandwich, quietly discussing what kind of girl would be suitable.

Then I flipped through the sex ads in a magazine, and he picked up the receiver and dialled a mumber. We compromised on an American girl, mixed black and white, extremely politically correct.

The price she wanted seemed a bit high, but when she appeared before our eyes forty minutes later, we were totally convinced the real thing was worth the price. She had a beautifully proportioned toned body: long, long legs, skin that gleamed as if a layer of glaze had been applied, thick curly hair, and nipples that thrust through the wrapping of her tight-fitting red dress.

She was like a leopard, walking towards us guarded yet composed, and at that moment I felt a bit overwhelmed. Muju certainly had nearly the same feeling. I noticed that he involuntarily moved his tall body back a step. Dressed in white silk we looked like a pair of startled rabbits.

After we politely shook hands with this girl, called Mimi, we went into the bathroom and closed the door. 'Do you really want to do this?' Muju watched me suspiciously, keeping his voice low.

'Why not? Given that she's already here.' I turned on the tap and rinsed my face. 'But,' I said, 'you can't touch her.'

Muju watched me, confused. 'What do you mean?'

'You can only watch her,' I said. I'd suddenly had an idea. The apprehension vanished and I grinned brightly

Then I opened the bathroom door and went into the living room. I discovered Mimi had already taken off all of her clothes except of a pair of panties. She lay on the sofa smiling slightly at us, like a queen from the jungle. 'Okay?' She had a thick Brooklyn accent.

On our messy white bed, Muju lay quietly in his pyjamas, watching me in my nightgown as I massaged the nude Mimi.

It felt really wonderful to touch her. Especially her breasts and her buttocks, so downright elastic, so like rubber. Asian women's bodies are more like the flesh of a peach in compairson, not so plastic and with a more vulnerable kind of beauty.

She moaned softly, very professional and very alluring. You could see that she was very good at what she did. She moaned, she writhed, and then she got paid, no matter what she was asked to do.

When her legs were spread apart to what seemed like 180 degrees, I took off Muju's pyjamas. He was extremely hard, the tip of his penis moist and glistening. I made Mimi turn over, face down, lying across the middle of the bed, and lay down on top of her with my bottom just at the curve of her hips.

She was our pillow, a sexual pillow made of flesh and blood.

Muju bent over me and held my breasts with both hands, stretching his body and entering me.

With his every thrust the bed shook and the springs creaked. The feeling of three awkward, heavy bodies moving together was like a great mass being kneaded again and again.

I was told threesomes were popular in Manhattan, and apparently the majority of them were 'sex without love' games, but that even without love when the game was over someone often wound up being hurt.

But Muju and I seemed to survive the conclusion of the game and strangely we developed an extra layer of trust and ease with each other. In fact, having been through this sexual test, I started to see a wedding ring glittering not far away, for when his two previous girlfriends brought up the question of marriage, Muju had used a three-way as a kind of experiment or as a means of scaring them off. Though perhaps it was just that back then he had not been divorced for long and wasn't ready to get married.

The feeling of that night stayed with us for a number of days afterwards. We didn't make love again. It was as if we'd had our quota of sex for the next decade, though that ecstatic feeling didn't disappear and didn't stop tempting us.

Perfect sex makes women pretty; walking down the street men would compliment me on my good looks. But a bit of danger seemed to have slipped in somewhere, for Muju had become the embodiment of love and sex and was in the process of becoming my addiction, my god. I thought about him for every second of every minute. I couldn't bear to imagine the day he might leave me.

But nothing in the world is ever totally perfect. The trick is to be happy with your lot and approach life with a spirit of understanding and tolerance, especially relationships between men and women.

17

Nick the Assassin

I am a free lover!
George Sand

When Muju flew off to the Dominican Republic to finish shooting the final section of the documentary, it happened that my whirlwind-riding business woman of a cousin, Zhu Sha, was flying to New York for a meeting. Because of her outstanding achievements in the Chinese market the year before, she was the company pet, and they booked her a big suite, decked out with fresh flowers, in trendy West Union Square.

We arranged to meet at her hotel.

As soon as she opened the door to the room, we screamed and hugged each other, giggling. When you meet family in New York when they've come from far away, the feeling is a bit strange, but warm. Especially as Zhu Sha had brought my favourite red-bean cakes and dried pickled bamboo shoots, prepared for me by my mother. At first they'd worried that the treats would be confiscated by customs.

I tore open one layer after another of the carefully wrapped packages, put a piece of red-bean cake in my mouth, and after swallowing a mouthful involuntarily narrowed my eyes. Only my mother could make something so delicious. Faced with the warm but unwieldy weight of maternal love you're always happy, but also unsure how to return that love in a suitable way.

We talked non-stop – especially me. I didn't get much chance to speak Chinese here. As she listened, I poured out everything about my life in New York – including Muju.

Zhu Sha had become more mature and dignified, but the patient smile on her face hadn't changed. Originally her husband Ah Dick, who was her junior by eight years, had wanted to come too, but he couldn't get a visa. I'd experienced the same problem myself, and Xi'er, who'd always wanted to take a holiday in New York, had tried three times but couldn't get a visa. In one sense the lifestyle of young Chinese weren't all that different from young people in America or Japan, but in another their dreams clashed with reality. They couldn't fly to Paris or Tokyo or New York on a whim without worrying about a visa. It didn't matter how many holes a kid pierced through his body, he still wasn't cool.

When speaking of Ah Dick, Zhu Sha's tone of voice was casually indifferent, as if she were talking about the air. It was nothing like her irrepressible excitement and love when she talked about her son Little Worm.

Of course I'd recently heard all the gossip through e-mails and and phone calls from Shanghai: the artist Ah Dick, under the oppression of mundane married life, had entered a period of creative stagnation; the Casanova Ah Dick had started making frequent dates with women eight years his junior; the little husband Ah Dick's credit card, which had suspicious expenses on it, had been repossessed angrily by his wife, although not long after his separation from it he'd somehow got hold of another card; the father Ah Dick really seemed to love his son, but perhaps it wasn't real love so much as a form of need.

When Zhu Sha heard that I was expecting the relationship with Muju to enter a completely new phase, and furthermore that I was considering marrying him, she gazed at me in shock for a bit and then, covering her mouth with her hand, burst out laughing. When she laughed heartily she would always cover her mouth; to be shy but refined was one of her most charming qualities.

'You're crazy,' she sighed. 'It's really baffling. We seem to have switched roles. I was always seen as the type suited to marriage and having children, while people expected you to travel the world in your silk *qipao* dresses, writing and dating along the way with countless men everywhere lining up to wait for you. And now? Now you've run to the cosmopolitan world of New York and are actually thinking of getting married, and what's more it's to a Japanese man! God! As for me? This is my second marriage, and it looks like it won't last long either . . . Every time I think about marriage and holding onto someone, it's like the old saying: "First make a family and then establish a career." But it doesn't work.'

Tenderly, she took my hand. 'Coco, think carefully. Falling in love is easy, but staying together is hard.' She sighed again. 'People in a castle always want to escape it, while people outside the castle always want to get in. Life always seems to be like that.'

I shook my head. 'You can't think too much. When you think a lot, your courage just disappears and you can't accomplish anything.'

We gradually fell silent, munching the chocolate on the coffee table, looking at the stack of photos she'd brought along.

The baby boy looked strong and good-natured. The pictures alternately focused on his toothless gums and pink, dog-like tongue, or on him quietly paying with his own toes.

At the figure of the adorable child tears welled up in my eyes with soft tenderness. I couldn't help but say: 'Perhaps women are meant to have children.'

'Yes.' Zhu Sha gazed steadily at her son's smiling face, 'Many women regret finding a certain man, but no woman regrets giving birth to a man.'

In other words, men aren't very responsible, and when you stop counting on them, a son becomes the substitute for a man.

'It's natural,' Zhu Sha said, 'After all, your son comes from your own belly.'

We burst out laughing. Zhu Sha had changed. Two unhappy

marriages had left her a bit cynical about men but motherhood had given her an air of maturity and she didn't seem so fragile anymore.

We decided to have a sumptuous dinner first and then to hang out at a club.

Because of Zhu Sha's theories that there was no good Chinese food in New York, and that good Western food beats bad Chinese food by far, I'd no choice but to go with her to an expensive Italian restaurant called Babbo in the Village, although I was the kind of person who'd rather eat bad Chinese food than good Western food. She was a guest who'd come a long way, and besides she was treating me to dinner, or at least her company was treating us.

The Italian food tasted very genuine, so perhaps that was why it was so expensive. But when we tried to share our food with each other, a thin old waiter wearing spectacles walked over and in long-suffering tones reminded us that we'd best not do that, because to sample several different types of food at the same time could affect the purity of your sense of taste.

'Perhaps one day they'll ban talking while eating. That's also very distracting isn't it?' I said.

'Nowadays the world's in such a muddle. Too much freedom has led to restlessness and hassle; perhaps it wouldn't be such a bad idea to have some restrictions. If people ran up against a few rules of "can't do this" and "can't do that," maybe they'd learn to cherish what they already have,' said Zhu Sha.

After eating dessert, we discussed which bar we should go to. Like two million other Shanghainese Yuppies and proto-yuppies, Zhu Sha was fascinated by *Sex and the City*, and wanted to get a glimpse of the Bowery Bar (now called the B Bar) that was often patronized by the show's characters. At the same time she also wanted to go to Cafe Carlyle on the Upper East Side to see Woody Allen play the clarinet. But Woody Allen wasn't on the programme that evening so we went to the Bowery Bar.

The Bowery Bar was a rippling sea of heads, though at first

glance it didn't have that sense of glamour it was expected to – that feeling an adventure or a love affair could start at any time. However, about three seconds after we'd got there, something magic happened – I ran headlong into someone I knew.

To say it was someone I knew isn't quite right; we'd met once at a cocktail party put on by my publisher and had a pleasant conversation. It was Eric, the newly-promoted book critic at the *New York Times*. Beneath his mop of red hair, he had a handsome face and a bashful smile. After bumping into each other, we simultaneously gasped, 'Oh!' and then gave each other a brisk hug. When we separated we introduced our respective companions.

When I first looked at the man beside him, I gave an involuntary shiver. He looked very like George Clooney, but even more handsome, slim and stylish, dressed entirely in black Armani. His name was Nick. He seemed about forty-five years old. He was Eric's uncle.

When he spoke I was startled by his magnetic voice. Hearing him talk was like ice-cream to the ears, simply too perfect.

Over the next couple of hours, Zhu Sha and I talked and laughed constantly with Eric and Nick, who sat beside us. I didn't drink any alcohol, nor did I smoke. But Nick lit up a joint in the corner by the bathroom and for some reason I shared it with him.

As we stood in the dim corner under cover of a cloud of smoke we felt a kind of covert happiness. From time to time he ran his fingers through his thick chestnut-coloured hair, gazing at the people who came and went in front of us. Men, women – he watched all of them steadily with that curious expression unique to womanisers.

We saw Ethan Hawke, but not his wife Uma Thurman. Near him stood a short, voluptuous American girl wearing a tight-fitting red Chinese *qipao*, like a little sausage that hadn't been stuffed right. I laughed involuntarily. Nick grinned too, even though he wasn't sure why I was amused.

I moved close to his ear and giggled, 'I'll bet what that girl is wearing isn't real silk.' He took a look at the girl, then took a look at me, and said: 'Want me to go over there and ask her?' This was why he was attractive – he could make even trivia become interesting and there seemed to be nothing he wouldn't do.

After going back to our seats when we'd finished smoking, I really felt I was in the glamorous Bowery Bar with my adorable cousin Zhu Sha and two charming guys, having good time. My English suddenly improved so much that I remembered difficult words like 'aphrodisiac' and 'menopause' which even Americans didn't use very often. I told lots of stories, including the one about being so jealous of Zhu Sha in primary school that I shamed her in public by spilling blue ink all over her white skirt just before she went on stage.

Nick laughed as he watched me, but Eric was gazing at Zhu Sha.

Next Nick told a story in which he passed out from alcohol and drugs at a party and woke up with a naked girl sitting on his face. When he reached the end, our jaws dropped.

Happily, but also a bit guiltily, I watched Nick's movie-star face with the sexy playboy smile and shook my head. This was impossible. Right now I didn't need a one-night stand and I didn't need any hassle. Nick would be an absolutely huge hassle. His charm was poisonous. Before meeting Muju, I'd been helplessly fascinated by this sort of man.

As soon as they began their siren songs I'd sink my own ship and swim towards them without looking back – a leaf boat in a gale, swirling towards their laps. And then when it was finished everything would magically disappear, and I'd still be on my own, alone on the road, writing more novels about the wounded in the battle of the sexes, and living a stormy life.

When I discovered that it was already three in the morning, I realized I'd missed Muju's daily bedtime call from the Dominican Republic. Suddenly I was overcome with tiredness and the 'party' button in my brain switched off.

'Oh, it's so late.' I started to look for my handbag and coat, but with my brain spinning this way and that, for a moment I couldn't find them.

'Don't worry, kid.' Nick reached out to me. He had my handbag in one hand, and my coat in the other.

Nick had a black Mercedes-Benz and a driver waiting outside the bar. The four of us got in together. Eric sat beside the driver, and I sat between Nick and Zhu Sha. Ah, that long-lost Shanghai Princess feeling. The car glided like a boat along the weary but glittering streets of night-time Manhattan. The whole city seemed to hang between heaven and hell, between civilization and animal passion.

I felt slightly carsick. Generally speaking, if I was sitting beside a strange man in a car and felt carsick there were two possibilities: 1. I really liked him or 2. I really disliked him.

The car brought me first to Muju's apartment in the Upper West Side, where I hugged and kissed everyone in the car goodbye. When I kissed Nick's cheek a dark blue spark flashed between us, zapping our skin when we touched. It was just like the static electricity when Muju and I first kissed. I was pretty certain that the second possibility didn't really describe my feelings for Nick.

'Ow, New York is too dry!' Nick said to ease the awkwardness of the situation. We laughed loudly, both of us feeling the residual sting and stimulation of the static electricity. 'I hope I can see you again very soon.' As he spoke he closed the car door and the car drove off in a puff of smoke.

Zhu Sha stayed in New York for five days. When she wasn't in meetings with her boss, we strolled and shopped together, sat in open-air cafés watching people and being watched, looked at galleries in Chelsea and watched a show on Broadway.

On the recommendation of a New York friend of Zhu Sha's in Shanghai, we also made a special trip to the Eiji beauty salon at Madison and 65th. Zhu Sha insisted on taking the New York subway, so we took the R north from Union Square and got off at 59th. We couldn't tell which way to go and were walking confusedly towards the exit to the Oak Bar, when I realized that it was quiet all around and we were completely alone. Suddenly, as if in a play, three figures leapt out of the shadows to one side. Looking more closely, I saw they were three black kids. They looked to be about twelve or thirteen, wearing white head-wraps and baseball caps and low-slung trousers whose legs were so wide you practically couldn't tell where their real limbs were.

Zhu Sha and I were both wearing high-heels and skirts and stood out clear and bright as easy meat from a foreign country. In that nanosecond, my instinctive reaction was to take off my heels and hold them in my hand.

But after a face-off in silence for about half a minute, we heard the sound of lots of footsteps on the stairs to the platform and several overweight American tourists from the South appeared carrying cameras and maps. Zhu Sha and I quickly stepped around the three boys and bolted up the stairs into the stream of traffic on the sunlit street.

We looked at each other and laughed nervously, still not too sure what had just happened. 'Anyway it's something to brag about back in Shanghai,' I joked. After discussing it for a moment, we decided to find a café and get something to drink, and then go to Eiji's place.

Eiji had an impressive head of wild, curly hair which hung casually over his loose white linen shirt. When he was cutting hair he didn't say a word, though his eyes filled with light and enthusiasm. Apparently he'd patiently tend to every single hair on your head, no exaggeration. It was this Zen focus that was at the heart of his reputation in Manhattan, and even Shanghai.

He spent a full two hours on Zhu Sha's hair! I had mine done by another Japanese man whose long hair fell below his shoulders. It felt really good to have someone touch my head patiently and carefully, and it felt really good to be pampered. A man who can gently and patiently tend to a woman is the best. No wonder that whenever I get my hair styled or my feet massaged, I fall in love with my stylist or masseur, even if it's only for a few hours.

For a split second I wished my boyfriend Muju could have Eiji's patience and his desire to serve women.

I watched Eiji all the time, but he didn't take his eyes off my cousin's hair. I closed my eyes, calmly enjoying the gentle and busy pair of hands on my head.

As Zhu Sha and I walked towards the reception area on the way out, we passed the countertop on which a stack of beautifully folded envelopes stood for leaving tips. Americans leave tips ostentatiously, the Japanese put them in envelopes, but the Chinese – Chinese people never want to leave a tip. In their five thousand years of civilization there had never been such a custom.

Leaving Eiji's salon, I said to Zhu Sha with a smile: 'Did you notice how great Eiji smells?'

Zhu Sha was just at that moment looking into a small mirror, happily sizing up her hair. On hearing my comment she looked at me. 'Oh?' she said, raising an eyebrow.

Zhu Sha and I both love shoes (there isn't a woman anywhere who doesn't love shoes). Her legs were long, slender and enchanting, and she looked great in her high-heeled strappy sandals. At my urging, she bought two pairs of Manolo Blahnik shoes at Barney's, both with very fine straps.

Contrary to my expectations, Eric turned out not to be gay and developed a crush on Zhu Sha. Zhu Sha was always finding herself in that sort of situation where she was totally unaware that some man was falling for her; frequently the men were younger. She held a kind of Queen Bee charm for them.

At dinner with Eric, Zhu Sha wore a pair of newly-bought four-hundred-dollar pale gold sandals which frequently caused Eric's gaze to slip under the table, but although they spent a lot of time together before Zhu Sha left New York, she and Eric never went beyond lingering kisses and rumpled clothes. Her experience with a youthful, unfaithful and freeloading husband had turned Zhu Sha off younger men, even though someone like Eric was the best New York had to offer.

While eating lunch with her boss the next day, Zhu Sha wore the more expensive pair of shoes she'd purchased at Barney's, the five-hundred-dollar pair. At thirty-three and somewhat wounded by men, she could, of course, distinguish quite well between the importance of an appointment with one's boss and a date with a man one met on a trip.

One rainy day, carrying a box of FAO Schwarz toys she'd bought for her son as well as two pairs of shoes I'd bought for my parents, Zhu Sha left New York, a little the worse for wear.

During this time we never saw Nick, Eric's enchanting uncle. After that evening at the Bowery Bar, like a rare butterfly, we caught no further glimpses of him. According to Eric, he'd gone to Europe on business.

18

Diary of Living Together

To love is to suffer. To avoid suffering one must not love.
But then one suffers from not loving. Therefore to love is to suffer,
not to love is to suffer. To suffer is to suffer. To be happy is to love. To be
happy is then to suffer. But suffering makes one unhappy. Therefore, to
be unhappy one must love, or love to suffer, or suffer from too much
happiness. I hope you're getting this down.
Woody Allen, *Love and Death*

The more you know, the less you understand.
Lao-Tzu

May in New York. The grass was tall and there were nightingales in the air.

The cherry blossom along the street had started to wither and scatter at last, and occasionally tiny pale pink petals blew in on the warm wind through the open window and fell into my mint tea.

I sat in a small French café on the Upper West Side, writing in a red leather-covered diary. After a few months living in New York, the diary had got increasingly thick. I rejoiced that I'd been able to keep up this habit for so long regardless of which country or which city I was in, and regardless of whether my life was as sparkling as fireworks or as shitty as a pile of dog turds.

Living with Muju included quarrels as well as joy. When two people get so close that there is no distance between them, the blemishes that you couldn't see before inevitably show up.

I took a look at what I'd recorded in my diary:

X Month, X Day. Got up this morning, sunlight was nice. Smelled the scent of fried eggs and thought I was dreaming, but no, it was Muju making breakfast. Highly unusual. He put a small sausage on my plate, but it seemed to be more of a friendly reminder than an act of love: 'You should be doing this sort of thing.'

In Japan the values still venerated by men and women of his age are:

1. Women mustn't get out of bed later than men.
2. Women mustn't let men enter the kitchen.
3. Women mustn't speak bad-temperedly or coarsely like men.
4. Women mustn't walk around naked for more than five minutes even after sex.

Muju's own personal erotic standards that are:

1. Sex that was too easy is not sexy.
2. Woman with exhibitionist tendencies is not sexy.
3. Woman who takes off her clothes in front of a man by herself is relatively unsexy.
4. But a woman who goes to the kitchen early in the morning with her hair hanging dishevelled in her face and a pair of dark circles under her debauched eyes and makes breakfast – now that's very, very sexy.

X Month, X Day. Busy again, but still feel as if I didn't do anything today. Didn't drink, didn't smoke, and didn't take any drugs that might muddle my thinking or even give me a feeling of success. Did a half-hour each of yoga and Taoist meditation, and spent an hour on the phone long-distance with Xi'er. She can't find a man in Shanghai. She really ought to come to New York, where no-one knows she was once a man. Though I suspect she is too beautiful and too precious for these self-important silly American men. At times when I can't suppress my rage against a certain man (for example Muju, when he's arguing with me, my lawyer or my accountant) and am itching to smash him to bits, I imagine introducing him to Xi'er, letting him fall in love with her, without letting him know the truth. But it's only a thought; I could never really betray my friend.

Muju came back from the office this evening and his complexion was poor, he looked really exhausted. The past few days he has been worried because they have gone over budget. After moving in together, I've gradually discovered that just because there's a smile on his face doesn't necessarily mean everything's fine. In fact he's human just like everyone else with many of the usual worries. It's just that his maturity can often conceal and even go a long way towards dispelling these worries.

. . . Regardless, it's obvious he doesn't like my habit of leaving things all over the place. In fact, today I made a special effort to spend an hour before he came home tidying up the apartment, but when he glanced at the living room he told me warmly but firmly: 'Coco, you forgot to pick up these things on the sofa and the coffee-table.'

I was dumbstruck. I almost wanted to flush myself down the toilet.

X Month X Day. God, at last I understand that I am inherently incapable of being a maid. I can't do laundry, and somehow didn't see the word 'bleach' on one of the bottles of laundry detergent! Thus I destroyed: a pair of embroidered pillowcases, a pair of multicoloured dishcloths, a pair of his black underpants and two pairs of my socks. The last time I lost one of his socks. This time the situation was even more tragic! The first words out of my mouth when I see him will certainly have to be 'I'm sorry!' and then I'll have to explain to him that I'll buy new dishcloths, pillowcases and underwear for him at Bloomingdale's.

X Month, X Day. Starting next week, his Jamaican maid will come three times a week instead of once a week to tidy the apartment and wash the clothes. I wanted to pay for two of these visits, but he insisted on paying for it. 'It's no problem, it'll be fine,' he said. But I don't trust myself, and I am incapable of enjoying housekeeping, so how can everything be fine?

X Month, X Day. 'You're such a princess!' he said. But it wasn't a compliment; I could hear in his voice a trace of frustration. I remember before moving in every night when I would leave his place, I would always request that he see me downstairs and walk me to Broadway until I got into a taxi. Once, late at night, because he was truly too tired he didn't see me downstairs to get a taxi, and as soon as I got back to my own apartment I called and picked a fight with him, until he said 'sorry' five times. This only made him more tired, and I'm sure he was thinking: 'Best see her downstairs, that'll always be better than having an argument.'

Now that we're living together, he is always calling me 'princess'.

In a cordial but candid discussion today, he pointed out that while I'm very feminine in appearance and style of dress (men are always intrigued by me at first), as soon as I open my mouth, I reveal that I'm too strong, so much so that I'm even more strident than American women (why compare me to American women?).

'It's just because of my English!' I explained at once in my own defence. 'My English isn't sophisticated enough, nor seasoned enough. I often choose the wrong words and use the wrong grammar.'

'You give the impression of strength, and at times it's pushing me away, giving me a signal that says: 'Mind your own business, I can take care of it all by myself,' he said, spreading his hands.

I really dislike it when he makes gestures like this. 'You know, actually I'm just a small girl.' I looked at my fingers desolately, becoming a troubled child in a split second.

19

The Ex-Wife in the Kitchen

What could it have been that gave Maria, whenever she removed her outer garments . . . a pleasantly and naïvely bewitching smell of vanilla? . . . Maria did not anoint herself. Maria just smelled that way. Oskar is to this day in love with this simplest and most commonplace of all puddings.
Günter Grass, *The Tin Drum*

All of a sudden I received invitations from affiliated Spanish and Argentinian publishing companies to go to Madrid, Barcelona and Buenos Aires in turn to promote the Spanish edition of *Shanghai Baby*.

My first thought was to refuse, but my agent pressured me, pointing out that Spanish is a very widely spoken language and so on. But the reason I finally accepted the invitations was that I was a bit fed up with Manhattan – a long and narrow island that seems to have been established upon an active volcano. 9/11 had changed things for a month or two, then all the garbage, residue and toxins staged a comeback, and people went back to their seasoned, worldly and despairing selves.

To show good faith, the publishers generously offered to pay for a friend or relative to accompany me. Of course I thought of Muju straight away. But when I told him about it, Muju looked as if he wasn't all that excited. He said he'd have to check his schedule first before confirming.

His mood hadn't been very good lately. The American economy continued to be weak after 9/11 and the economy of his native Japan was in a major recession. As a result Muju's company had consecutively lost four or five big commercial clients – the cornerstones that he used to sustain those highly praised but poorly attended documentaries and the public welfare classes which he taught at the health centre. But he still hadn't given up those financially unrewarding projects yet. He had uncommon stamina and a strange sense of vocation that combined, became a sort of intuitive wisdom that made him different from most people.

Muju was scheduled to complete that documentary about the Latin American singer Julio and to give yoga and meditation classes through several different organizations in New York. He could only squeeze three days into the tail end of my itinerary at most. He would meet me in Buenos Aires.

First I had to get the visas to go to these two countries. Muju was too busy to help. He asked an assistant, a chubby, very capable, sweet gay man named Peter, to help me gather the address of the consulates, office hours, application materials that needed to be prepared, how much time would be needed to get the visa, and visa fees. He even helped me communicate with the two publishers regarding invitation letters and reservations of air tickets and hotels.

Thanks to Peter, I had the patience to take care of all of these things one by one and got the visas on time. On the evening I got the last visa, I invited Muju, and his assistant Peter and the editor Carrie to dinner at the Shanghainese restaurant Old Zheng Xing in Chinatown.

That night, for some reason people were setting off firecrackers on the street outside. That sound like the crackling of gunfire and the pleasant but pungent aroma of sulphur drifted into the restaurant. The word 'China' spontaneously popped into my brain. That sound, that smell, and the shards of exploded, bright red wrapping-paper with gold foil that covered the ground – these had to do with distant memories. When you're young and trendy you can play video games, listen to hip-hop, drink Coke and wear Adidas, but as soon as those old-fashioned firecrackers explode, you can't help but respond because they've already seeped into your Chinese bloodstream.

I looked at the three people around the table and a strange, sentimental feeling welled up in me amid the sound of firecrackers. I felt that when this meal was over I would part with them forever.

I settled the bill and trailed behind Muju to the toilet. I quietly followed him in, startling him. I locked the door, walked towards him, held his face firmly and kissed him like a gale of wind or a cloudburst. Then I opened the door and stepped out. When I heard the sound of his laughter behind me, I couldn't help bursting out laughing too.

Just as I was about to leave for Spain, a series of unexpected events occurred. Muju's Jewish ex-wife came to New York from Atlanta, bringing her son and daughter to visit her seriously ill father. On a whim she dialled Muju's number.

I had a black Dead Sea mud-mask spread all over my face when I rushed out of the bathroom to get the phone. Both of us had the same reaction as I answered. We were taken aback.

'Hi, I'm Kitty.' A strangely childish voice, quavering slightly.

'Oh, hi, I'm Coco.' Coated with the thick, increasingly hard Dead Sea mask, I could hardly open my mouth to speak.

'Oh, let me introduce myself. I'm Muju Miyanaga's ex-wife . . . just arrived in New York – and just wanted to ask after him!'

'Oh, okay, I'll tell him.' Naturally, even without me introducing myself she could guess that I was his present girlfriend.

'Thanks.'

'No problem.'

With both hands holding my blackened, rock-hard face, I tried to figure out why exactly this ex-wife Kitty with her little girl's voice had called. I quickly decided not to give her another thought. When you don't care about a person or thing she (or he or it) no longer exists. By contrast, the more you care, the more she (or he or it) draws energy from your fear and anxiety.

I would allow myself to forget the incident, I decided. Muju didn't have to know about this 'greeting' from his ex-wife. But when he got home from work, I couldn't stop myself telling him just so that I could watch his reaction.

Very surprised, he raised his eyebrows, his eyes opened very wide. 'Kitty's in New York?' When he said her name, the tip of my tongue turned sour again.

'Did she leave a number?'

'You can check for yourself.' I walked towards the kitchen as I spoke, behind me the beep-beep sound of Muju dialling numbers on the telephone.

'Found it. I think it's this one.' You could hear excitement in his voice. He could never hide anything. At times I really wished my boyfriend wasn't quite so transparent. I wished he would embellish things a little, be a bit more of a charmer from time to time.

Kitty's dying father unexpectedly took a turn for the better. Some warm afternoon, according to the arrangements Muju and Kitty made over the phone, the three of us would meet at a Starbucks. I knew that this might be a pretty strange situation, but taking me along was Muju's idea. Although he'd invited me, he'd become thoroughly anxious during the days before the meeting when he thought about how jealous I am.

On the way to the coffee bar he said to me again and again, 'You know it's truly in the past, don't you?'

She was half an hour late and didn't bring the children along as she'd said she would. Dressed entirely in a greenish-black suit ensemble, with a floral-print scarf wrapped about her head and wearing a pair of light-coloured sunglasses, she looked delectable, like a juicy green plant, though there was something nervous about her manner.

She and Muju embraced, and then she just shook hands with me. 'Oh, God, you look fabulous!' She sat down in front of Muju, untying the floral-print scarf, but forgetting to take off her sunglasses.

'So do you.' Smiling, Muju also had a thread of awkwardness, nearly overturning the coffee-cup in front of him.

It was clear my presence made the two of them uncomfortable. For my part I hadn't known Muju's ex-wife had the face of a movie star, and a chest that was clearly several cup-sizes bigger than mine. She definitely wore a D-cup.

They began by getting bogged down in memories. So that I wouldn't feel left out, Muju frequently said things like: 'Oh, Coco, you know what? Kitty was once the champion of the all-American Hula competition. At the time her waist was so tiny that it would fit within two hands.' Or, 'Oh, Coco, you won't believe this but Kitty's mother once wrote a letter to Kitty, and at the end of the letter she said, 'Don't forget to tell Muju that the next time he has a meal in an American home he'd better not use the table napkins to blow his nose; he must use tissues.'

I gradually started to believe that Muju had had a pretty good marriage.

And to have this pretty good marriage to a Jewish woman, he'd infuriated his conservative parents and was nearly thrown out of the family. He still wasn't allowed to get involved in the family business.

I became distracted. The more they talked, the more I felt like an outsider. Muju inadvertently drifted over to join Kitty in marital memories. Marriage and love are vastly different, so that even a divorced ex-wife looks like she has a special kind of mysterious confidence and power when compared with a current girlfriend. Sitting there, Kitty was like a great monument to this.

I don't know how it happened, but as we were about to part company, in a surprisingly emotional atmosphere Kitty promised that she would bring the two children over to our apartment before she returned to Atlanta and cook us a meal.

My head was humming in the days that ran up to this. Muju's ex-wife was going to appear in our big kitchen and undoubtedly would put me in an awkward position again.

I couldn't stand this old-school romantic stuff about the

kitchen. The days when a man's heart was controlled through his stomach were long past. Perhaps they were coming back. I thought about changing my occupation from erotic novelist too cookery writer.

I called Jimmy Wong and urged Muju to invite Richard and his wife W. to come along too. That evening, our apartment was filled with people, like a family of nations. W. brought homemade sushi and Japanese dessert. Jimmy brought a bottle of good wine.

Kitty was busy in the kitchen, like a housewife, and wearing embroidered slippers I sat lazily on the sofa, like a mistress. The whole situation was a little off but amusing.

Kitty's two children were very mischievous. They were very enthusiastic about the toy peaches and naked women that filled Muju's apartment. Finally they broke the toy wooden elephant that Muju had brought back from India thirty years ago.

Kitty seemed to understand clearly how important this toy was to Muju. She walked out of the kitchen, agitated, and told off the children. 'Did you forget what Mommy warned you? Quick, tell uncle Muju you're sorry.'

'Really, it's nothing.' Muju held one reddened tear-streaked child's face in each hand. 'This elephant is really old. It was time for it to be broken.'

You could tell that he had a karmic affinity for children.

Apparently Kitty once studied for a year at a French cooking academy, then met and married Muju and became a housewife. After the divorce she quickly remarried into a wealthy family in Atlanta, and had a beautiful son and daughter. With that lovably mild nature of her's, her position in her husband's family was completely secure. Nearly every member of the family liked her.

But she missed the bright simplicity of the life she'd had before she'd married into a wealthy family – 'like the naked sky, with nothing on' was the richly poetic expression she used. She also missed Muju's kitchen. Even now she had the help of a maid, in her eyes Muju's kitchen had more personality than any other kitchen in the world. This nostalgia was the reason that she wanted to make us dinner that evening

I took a few pictures for her in the kitchen. I discovered I'd grown to like this woman. Her beauty showed all the more clearly in the kitchen amid the aroma of food. This is a kind of wonderful chemical reaction that can only happen to some women. My mother made this kind of reaction happen too. The kitchen made her even more feminine.

She hummed a song softly, moving with graceful footsteps and working with a light touch. She showed me how, magician-like, she used those herbs that seemed such a mystery to me: thyme, bay leaf, nutmeg, sweet basil and lemon grass.

I found that the English words for ingredients were always hard for me to remember and English menus in restaurants gave me a headache.

'Food, women and children are the most beautiful things in the world. I'm increasingly aware of how lucky I am,' she said as she placed vegetables on a dish. 'Oh, could I trouble you to bring out this plate?'

I took the big plate she passed me and left the kitchen. Muju's gaze fell on me and I just shrugged at him. I wasn't clear why he and Kitty had divorced as her philosophy of life and his seemed surprisingly consistent.

As the two of them stood in front of the house plant she'd given him as a divorce present, chatting and holding dishes, I tried to work out the scene but just felt even more sharply than usual the acute complexity of life.

Richard and Jimmy were pontificating loudly. They had similar interests and they kept up a steady flow of talk about art and life. At the moment they were well matched in ability – bosom friends.

So I led W. into the bedroom to see my wardrobe. The embroidered Chinese silk clothes caught W.'s interest and we exchanged the numbers of each other's tailors.

Clearly her kimono-maker in Tokyo charged more than my

qipao-maker in Shanghai. She said that while the economy was in recession fewer and fewer people made inquiries about expensive kimonos.

Late that night, her younger sister drove over to pick up Kitty and her children.

As she was about to leave, Kitty took my hand and said many complimentary things, 'You're the best . . . really, you're the best.' I gave her an enthusiastic hug and smelled alcohol. She was slightly drunk and a bit sentimental. I was happy to find such a beautiful woman had such a sincere fondness for the kitchen and happy to see her leave a little sentimentally. 'Goodbye, Kitty.' I waved to her.

On the day I was to fly to Madrid, Muju didn't have time to see me off. He never enjoyed going to the airport to pick up people or see them off. The one time his mother, who played such a decisive role in the family, came to New York he didn't bother to go and pick her up. He felt it was a waste of time. Considering this behaviour, I think I described him accurately during an argument when I ran at him shouting that he was 'the worst combination of Japanese men, American men and Latino men.'

I was wearing that Marc Jacobs Girl-Scout-style denim top and sitting in the taxi that Muju had called for me. I was a bit carsick the whole way. My face had turned a frightening shade of white.

When I got to the airport rows of stern security guards made me even more nervous. The bags of a Middle Eastern man in a ragged scarf had been tossed all over the ground like street garbage. A short American man at the check-in desk covered his head with his arms despairingly and wept, mumbling some sort of explanation to the stewardess behind the counter.

As for me, I wasn't so unlucky. They only turned my suitcase inside and out and put my eyebrow scissors into a clear plastic bag. Accompanied by a stalwart black woman wearing a uniform, I walked up to the check-in desk and then, when the paperwork was taken care of, they put the small scissors into the big case, pasted baggage-claim stickers on the outside, put it on the conveyor belt and watched it disappear.

The flight was an hour and a half late taking off. The passengers sitting on the plane were confused and worried. The radio suddenly squawked, 'Who lost a little baby? In the rear of the cabin by the bathroom there is a little baby. Please come and claim it.' Whereupon a young mother hurriedly got up and with everyone watching ran to the rear of the cabin. Everyone laughed.

Muju and I called each other every few minutes on our cellphones. 'I'm still here,' I said.

'Drink more water, that'll make it easier. Or you can read a magazine,' he said.

'What if something were to happen to the plane? You really should have seen me to the airport. You're indifferent to me . . .' I said, wounded.

'Don't let your imagination run away with you. Nothing will happen. I'll see you in Argentina. You're my baby.'

20

Two Monks

Those who know don't talk, and those who talk don't know.
Lao-tzu

Putuo Island – Autumn

The autumn colours gradually intensified. Little by little the leaves of birch, poplar and maple blanketing the mountain began to change. The dark red leaves looked even more vivid in the early morning when they were soaked in dew. The red glow of the sun lit up the surface of the sea, dark green like a large piece of jade. The whole island was at peace yet it brimmed with vitality.

In the mornings I did nothing more than watch the ocean, lost in thought, or lie on the bed reading a book. All the books I read were several hundred years old: *The Pillow Book*, *Dream of the Red Chamber* or Tang and Sung poetry. Every afternoon, after a simple meal at the inn's restaurant, I would wander the beach for a while before strolling towards the Temple of Righteous Rain, where I would pay a visit to the Master of Empty Nature – the old monk whom I'd run into that day who'd remembered my Buddhist name of 'Wisdom'.

The Master of Empty Nature usually spent half an hour listening to me tell the stories of my life, which were like wisps of smoke floating away on the air.

He was a hundred and one years old. As Chinese people often say: the bridges alone that he'd crossed in his life were longer than the roads I'd walked. He'd never been to America or to Europe or

Japan, but Buddhist disciples from all those countries came to Putuo Island to visit him.

The Master of Empty Nature had lived in seclusion on this island for the better part of a century. Time had passed but he stayed in one place. He knew the sort of transformations this boundless universe was capable of. His whole life, the Master of Empty Nature had been happy doing good and giving away whatever he had, and being deeply loved, respected and honoured by the people of the island. The most widely circulated tale about Master tells of the great Chinese famine of 1961 when the temple monks with great difficulty gathered half a kilo of dry white rice to give to Master to make a big bowl of cooked rice. The next day a monk asked Master if the rice was good. The Master said: 'I didn't eat it, I gave it to the elderly woman next door.'

According to the old folk on the island, Master was born to a venerable Shanghai family and as a young man he was known throughout Shanghai as very bright. He was good at music, Go, calligraphy and painting – all the joys of the literati – and loved to travel. He had travelled along most of the rivers and through the mountains of China, but after taking the ferry to Putuo Island, he recognized its hallowed atmosphere and immediately decided to become a Buddhist monk, choosing to settle at the Temple of Righteous Rain. He never left the little island again.

There was a time when I thought it took extraordinary courage to float from one place to another. Now, upon reflection, I realize it takes even more courage to choose a place and never leave.

The Master of Empty Nature's face always wore an expression that seemed like a smile without actually smiling. He seemed like he was asleep when he wasn't actually sleeping. His gaze when he looked at people was calm and warmly bright. When he spoke his tone was neither rushed nor slow. Confronted with this cordial old man, I felt reverence. Sometimes as I was telling him about things in the past that had troubled me, I would meet his profoundly tranquil gaze and, for a moment lose consciousness of the boundary between myself and the world outside . . . and in that moment have nothing to say.

I began to appreciate the absurd nature of all this talking. As soon as I told the Master about experiences which tortured me they became light and buoyant and left my body behind, becoming things that bore no relation to me. Amid that pile of ashes, I saw nothingness. It was karma. It was mercy.

I thought of the story Muju had told me, how he had followed an old Master day in and day out, sitting in silence beneath a tree, meditating by the river's edge. It was as if I was feeling those things that he had previously felt. The third time I went to pay my respects to Master I said practically nothing in that half hour. I bathed in his amiable smile and silent gaze. The stillness created a peculiar sense of safety.

The fourth time I went to pay my respects to the old Master, he said something of profound significance to me. Every form of suffering in the world derives from ignorance. In order to free oneself from ignorance one must develop the true view, meditation, action and compassion – and compassion is the very foundation of the true view, meditation and action. Be compassionate towards others, and be compassionate towards oneself because a person who doesn't know how to love him or herself cannot know how to love other people.

This kind of 'love' is not contained in the common meaning of the word. It is the love that is generated by the wisdom that comes from an open mind. To gain such wisdom, one must love those things about oneself which are seen as flaws, such as one's anger, fear, jealousy, obsessions and other negative emotions. According to traditional Buddhist doctrine, these negative emotions and those other emotions which people believe to be positive – such as courage, understanding, gentleness, and so forth – are innate parts of people; both are indispensable.

If you think of positive emotions, like love, as flowers in a garden, then negative emotions are rubbish in that garden. What you need to master is how to transform the rubbish into fertilizer which will nourish those beautlful flowers

Some people believe their good qualities have to struggle against their bad qualities, vanquishing negative emotions and expelling them from their heads and hearts. This is wrong. Suffering and affliction are not evil. They are an organic part of llfe. You only need to transform them and make good use of them.

One afternoon, the Master of Empty Nature's disciple – the young monk named Hui Guang who had played Go with him under the tree – stopped me at the door to the temple. He told me that the Master of Empty Nature was ill.

I came to a halt at the temple's grey-green stone threshold, my whole face showing my distress. 'What has Master come down with? Is it serious?'

'Last night he caught a slight chill. He's already prescribed himself a dose of medicinal herbs to sleep. It's not at all serious,' Hui Guang reasssured me.

I was only slightly relieved to hear this.

Hui Guang happened to be going to another temple – the Puji Temple at the southern end of the island – to get Buddhist scriptures. I didn't have anything to do, so I strolled aimlessly along with him, following the rolling, paved mountain paths and talking as we went.

I asked Hui Guang why he had become a monk. He said his mother was a devout Buddhist and because of many years' infertility she'd pledged to Buddha that if she had a son she would send him off to be a monk in the service of Buddha, and that if she had a daughter, then she would send her off to be a nun.

'During these years of training, do you miss your mother?' I asked.

Hui Guang lowered his head and said nothing. His fair-skinned face for a split second revealed that sharp expression you often see on the faces of monks and nuns that comes from the strict practice of asceticism. His light yellow robes danced softly in the humid ocean breeze. The skin of his head, shaved to a glossy sheen and slightly dark green, gave off that hormonal smell of the first blush of youth.

His expression already told me that he missed his mother with a longing that was very bitter, that at times perhaps even approached hatred.

At Puji gate, Hui Guang spoke to the guards and we were allowed in without tickets. There were many more pilgrims in Puji Temple than there were in the Temple of Righteous Rain so that walking along you occasionally bumped into someone next to you. The buildings were decorated splendidly in green and gold and magnificently bejewelled. Hui Guang quickly found Shen Tian, another young monk who had been his classmate at the Buddhist seminary, and received the scriptures from him. Shen Tian also gave him a small cake as a gift. The two of them were like brothers.

The cake was packed in a small paper box and on the way back Hui Guang carried it carefully in his hand. He would not eat it himself. He intended to save it for his teacher the Master of Empty Nature

Hui Guang said such small cakes were the only food Master would eat that was not part of the prescribed vegetarian diet for monks. The Master of Empty Nature grew up as the spoiled high-born son of a prominent family and the Russian exiles who cooked for them prepared the most delicious cream cakes in Shanghai, so from the time he was small Master loved cake. After becoming a monk he relinquished everything except for the occasional treat of a cake – which he called 'the perfection of my imperfection'.

Chuckling, I asked Hui Guang, 'Can monks eat cake?'

'As long as it's man-made cream it's okay,' he said.

'Then can they eat eggs?'

'Ah, that. Recently the monks here on the island have been discussing it. Half the people maintain that we can, but the other half believe we can't.'

When we reached the Temple of Righteous Rain we didn't dare disturb the Master of Empty Nature. Hui Guang boiled up a pot of green tea and sat down with me under a Bodhi tree. He taught me a few Go stratagems.

This black and white board game is the direct embodiment of Eastern wisdom. The purpose of the game isn't to annihilate your opponent nor to capture your opponent's King. The player who occupies the most territory wins, but technically it is impossible for one player to seize all of the enemy territory for himself. So the victory is relative and lenient. Winning is based on the co-existence of the two combatants.

Time passed quickly The clear, sharp sound of wooden clappers rang out. It was time for the monks to go to the meditation rooms to recite sutras and sit in meditation. The young monk Hui Guang gathered up the game pieces and the game board. I drank what was left of the tea in my cup, and we said goodbye to each other. I walked slowly down the narrow road and returned to the Happy Arrival Inn.

21

In Madrid

Let's face it, when an attractive but aloof ('cool') man comes along, there
are some of us who offer to shine his shoes with our underpants.
Lynda Barry

Madrid – Summer

As I got off the plane and walked into the bustling hall of
Madrid airport, I saw lots of people contentedly puffing
away in a huge cloud of cigarette smoke. This reminded
me immediately that I was no longer in America with its
puritanical prohibitions against smoking, but rather in smoke-
filled, sloppy, fuzzy Europe.

In that one instant, I relaxed. The car that the publisher had
sent was parked outside. The driver put down the paper sign
with my name that he'd been holding and heaved my luggage
into the boot of the car. Then he drove at lightning speed,
forcing his way through the traffic.

Having already heard wild tales about Spain, I opened my eyes
– which were slightly red with jet-lag – wide, searching for that
picturesque landscape, exquisite architecture and those slim-
waisted Latin girls. Of course I was also thinking about the
handsome faces of a couple Spanish matadors . . .

The noise of the engine died away as the car pulled up in front
of an elegant hotel. Muju hadn't come to Madrid, so the
publisher's entertainment budget was more than adequate. They
had reserved a room at the best hotel in the city as it was only for
a couple of nights.

The first interviews began two hours later. The publisher's editor, publicist and a vivacious female Taiwanese translator sat with me in the second-floor restaurant of the hotel. The table was brimming with food. My stomach's reaction to jet-lag was always overwhelming. It took the form of a kind of enormous hunger pang.

The interviewers tormented me at will, but I weathered one after the other. In the breaks between interviews, the publicist Susan and I played a simple sort of Chinese checkers. The waiter brought us over glass after glass of tea and coffee as well as individually wrapped chocolates. Thanks to the amenities all the interviews on the first day concluded successfully. Nearly everyone was satisfied.

Susan and I discussed where to go for dinner. 'Don't eat at the hotel,' she said, 'Perhaps you'd like to go take a look around Madrid?"

'That's just what I was thinking,' I said.

We strolled the streets of Madrid in not-too-high heels, browsing shoeshops, boutiques and jewellers. At her urging I bought a pair of hand-made ankle boots and two Lourdes Bergada skirts (a popular local label). Of course we also browsed in bookshops, and when Susan insisted that I stand in front of a long row of bookshelves with the Spanish edition of my book for a photo I got a bit nervous. Posing like this wasn't very cool. I looked like I was worried I'd get injured by falling books.

At times I preferred to look like someone who couldn't write at all, someone who would walk down the street with an expression of blisslul ignorance and the relaxed smile of a girl who doesn't care. Someone who would believe herself capable of taking the bus and getting married at the next station – just like in a best-selling novel.

We sat down in an old restaurant that was famous for its roast lamb. In the dim lamplight the floor looked slightly damp and the walls were hung with oil paintings. It was like being in a pirate ship thay had mysteriously sunk to the ocean floor years before.

Susan helped me look at the menu, but even with her translating Spanish to English, I still got quite a headache. 'Okay, I've decided. Please recommend something. I'm willing to try anything,' I announced, closing the menu.

She winked. 'Don't worry, you'll like it. Everything here is out of this world!'

I enjoyed listening to her speak English with a thick Spanish accent. When she spoke, it was always with a 'the sky's not going to fall in' kind of enthusiasm that inexplicably buoyed you up. Even when frowning into her cellphone and shouting at the top of her lungs to some journalist, Susan still gave you a bright and powerful feeling. And when she laughed with pleasure it was a ray of light that emitted a kilowatt of energy.

In short, I liked her.

After the soup and salad, the delectable roast lamb was served. 'Wow, great, the most delicious flavour on earth!' Susan cried, clapping her hands. I agreed that it was tastier than any food we might find at a Chinese restaurant in Madrid.

'That was a hard day, but believe me, you were really super.' Susan held up a glass of red wine.

I held up my glass of Evian water in reply. 'Thanks.'

'You really don't want some wine?'

'I really don't.'

'Pity. The lamb here is absolutely perfect with a glass of red wine. Has anyone ever told you that in reality you and the novel are two very different things? Oh, let's not talk about the novel. You've certainly talked so much already that you're squeezed out.'

'Anyway, I like hearing you talk.'

'The trick to it is the red wine. Red wine always makes you radiant.' I smiled and nodded.

At that moment, she did look radiant.

Then she put down her glass and suddenly leaned towards me. 'Whatever you do, don't turn your head – but I just noticed that there's a guy sitting at the table to your left who keeps looking at you.'

I swallowed a piece of lamb, opened my eyes wide and kept them on her for a few seconds. 'I can't help it, I have to turn my head and take a look.'

'No, no . . . hold on for a bit. We have to act natural. Oh my God! He's the most gorgeous man I've ever seen, believe me.'

My heart skipped a beat. God, her last sentence got me keyed up. Gorgeous men were like poisonous flowers. They left you attracted yet full of nerves. And when you can't turn and look and have to pretend nothing's happening, the idea of 'him' becomes especially enticing.

'Oh, God, he figured it out. He's smiling at me. Oh, he's standing up! And now he's coming over here!'

'Fine.' I took a breath, turned my head abruptly . . .

'Hi, is that really you? Coco?' He stood in front of me like a great sun throwing off the scents of alcohol, pot and testosterone. I felt both dazzled and infatuated.

'Nick?' Lightly touching the thump-thump in the middle of my chest and smiling, I did my best to make myself look more natural, but I was annoyed with myself for blurting out his name so impetuously.

'Amazing. What a coincidence! To see you again here . . . wow.' His eyes were fixed on me; their expression as transparent as the subdued but amorous smile on his face.

He extended his hand to Susan: 'Oh, sorry, I'm Nick.' Susan still didn't seem to know what had happened. 'Why don't we eat together? Would you mind if I, uh . . . and my friend joined you?'

'Of course . . . not!' Susan said without thinking. We looked towards Nick's table and saw that his dinner companion was a beautiful American girl with blonde hair and a furious expression on her face.

The four of us finished the lamb in uncomfortable silence. The others all drank a lot. Nick's eyes were glued to me. His female companion's eyes shuttled back and forth between the two of us and Susan watched us all with avid interest. I didn't look at anything, just kept smiling.

This kind of game was both stimulating and silly at the same time. I even felt a bit sorry for the blue-eyed blonde with the D-cup bra. Her male companion was rich, smart, attractive and astonishingly handsome – and therein lay the problem. It seemed as if he could never belong to just one woman. He belonged to many women.

'I think I have to go back to the hotel,' I said, finally opening my mouth.

The other three people looked at me. 'The nightlife in Madrid shouldn't be missed. You won't find such exciting nightlife when you reach Barcelona,' said Susan, but she didn't sound convinced.

'Don't go,' said Nick. 'I know a great place that will inspire you. You definitely need to check it out.'

'Oh, I'm tired too. Perhaps we should go back to the hotel as well,' said his blonde companion frostily as she waved to the waiter for the bill.

'Then you can go back first.' Nick clearly didn't like the girl gesturing to the waiter. He was the one who would settle the bill so he had the right to decide when to summon the waiter.

When the bill came, Nick paid for our meals, even though Susan explained to him repeatedly that the publisher would cover it for us.

When we discovered that all four of us were staying at the same hotel, I realized that things were getting complicated. Nick had the number of my room and he wrote the number of his room on an empty cigarette box and handed it to me.

I took a long, hot bath, followed by a sleeping pill for the jet-lag, then settled into bed. Just as I'd counted more than a hundred even-numbered sheep and was drifting towards sleep, the telephone rang shrilly.

I abruptly opened my eyes, took a deep breath, and picked up the receiver. Of course it was Nick.

'I want to see you,' he said.

'Now?'

'Sorry, this is definitely a little nuts, but I really want to see you.'

I didn't say anything, and actually I didn't know what to say.

'The girl left. We were arguing all the way back from the restaurant and I'm glad she's gone. I found her another hotel. A car is coming to pick her up so she should be fine. I want to see you.'

'Poor me!' I cried to myself. I sighed and held my heavy head, which had become muddled and swollen from the sleeping pills, in my hands. I didn't know how to deal with the self-centred and annoying but outrageously sexy guy on the phone. I'd already encountered too many poisonous flowers. Every time I was like a moth to the flame and in the end there was only ever a pile of miserable ashes left.

'This is no fun,' I said in a low voice. 'Tomorrow twenty Spanish reporters will be waiting to pulverize me. I have to rest a bit. Goodbye!' I was about to hang up the phone.

'Hold on. Then can we have dinner together tomorrow night?'

'I'm afraid not.' My voice was hoarse.

'Then how about after dinner. I'll meet you in the lobby at half past ten.'

'Half past ten?'

'Goodnight! Sweet dreams,' he said softly.

22

He's Attractive, But Poisonous

Women always spend too much time saying, 'No, no, no.'
Mae West

Elegance is refusal.
Coco Chanel

I don't know where I am.

The throb of the music is so loud it rips you to shreds. Different odours mingle together in the heat. Nick covers his ears and shouts something into his cellphone, smiling in spite of it all. I don't think he can actually hear anything clearly! He is permanently hyper.

All the people here seem to brim with unflagging energy except me. I don't know why, with the black circles under my eyes, I'm sitting in this place when I should've been in bed an hour ago getting my beauty sleep.

Nick is smoking, looking at me, smiling. I drink Evian and squint my eyes, saying to him abruptly: 'You're a very *self*-oriented person. You have high self-esteem and are self-conscious, but you also need to be very self-controlled.'

He laughs loudly.

'Why are you laughing?'

'Better to laugh than cry,' he says, stopping for a moment. 'You know that I like you, don't you?'

At that moment a wild girl starts to strip off her clothes until nothing is left but a G-string. As she dances, she lashes an equally wild young man with a whip. We look at the crazed duo, then turn to each other. 'I have to go,' I say.

'Oh, okay. You're like Cinderella with her glass slippers, running away before the clock strikes midnight and the magic wears off. Which part do you like best? The endless running away?'

I look at him, grab my bag and get up.

'Sorry, I'm not criticizing you. It's my fault, I never put people at ease.' He stops smiling, takes my arm and squeezes his way through the minced beef of the crowd and out the door.

As we walk down the street, a cool breeze smelling of plants sweeps over my head and leaves me feeling more awake, but a voice inside my body reminds me unceasingly, 'You need to sleep, you need to sleep! Just go back to the hotel, say goodnight to him, close the door, and then get right into bed.'

We can't find a cab.

Nick looks overjoyed. 'Such a great evening!' he says to himself, his hands stuck in his pockets like Shakespeare in love. Then, just as I fear, a second later he says, 'Let me serenade you.' He really starts to sing, in a loud voice, out-of-tune, gesticulating with his hands and feet.

'Baby, baby, I love it when you're silent, it's as if you're not by my side. Oh, you hear me howling, but my voice doesn't move you, baby. I really love it when you're silent,' he sings.

I want to take to my heels. He is making me flustered. It feels like a million invisible insects are drilling into my bones, tickling and tingling, making me feel rash but frightened. He spins back and forth in front of me, assessing my expression, and I stifle a laugh as I avoid his eyes.

One de luxe Jeep after another passes by carrying sloppily-dressed kids who shout at us in Spanish, applauding. An empty beer bottle is tossed overboard. There's a crash and Nick bends down with a groan. I am really frightened and immediately run to his side: 'Are you all right?'

He grabs me all at once. 'I'm all right, just hungry and thirsty. I need your attention, your kiss.' My eyes can't escape him. I am spellbound.

Then this poor girl falls into his arms, her whole body melting. A gift from heaven or a punishment?

In the lift of the most expensive hotel in Madrid, the big mirror reflected the figures of a man and a girl standing side by side.

We didn't talk. The heat of our passionate kiss lingered on the tip of my tongue. We avoided meeting each other's eyes, nervously watching the numbers for each floor flicker past as the lift rose. His room was on the tenth floor, mine was on the sixth. When the light stopped at the sixth floor, the door opened.

Hesitating for a split second, Nick followed me out of the lift. Neither of us said a word as our feet trod soundlessly on the lush carpet. We stopped when we reached my door. 'I . . .' I stammered.

'Oh, all right,' he said quickly. 'You're very tired, I can tell.' He pronounced the word 'tired' with deliberate emphasis, slightly teasingly, but his face looked very sincere. 'So I'll say goodnight to you – and see you tomorrow in Barcelona.'

'Wait a minute – did you say Barcelona?'

'I'm going to fly there, and then back to New York the same day you fly to Buenos Aires.'

I must've looked extremely surprised, because a self-confident smile floated onto his face. 'Susan told me that in two days there will be a master Flamenco performance in Barcelona. Maybe I can arrange front-row seats.'

I didn't say a word, just took out my keys and opened the door. And then slammed it shut with a bang.

'Are you okay?' he shouted, knocking on the door. I opened it abruptly. He was still smiling.

Suddenly I found my courage and, returning his smile, I said: 'I don't know if this is your idea of fun, but I do know that self-centred guys like you are a dime a dozen. This is crazy. Good night!' I closed the door behind me, once again slamming it with a bang.

23

In Barcelona

I think, therefore I'm single.
Liz Winston

Barcelona – Summer

The plane circled in the sky. Susan and I sat next to each other, flipping through newspapers from Madrid. Susan said the reviews were positive. 'Nobody knows which hotel I'm staying in in Barcelona, right?' I asked suddenly.

She looked a bit puzzled as if she didn't understand, and then made an 'Ah!' sound. 'You mean . . . ?' I avoided her look. 'Relax. No-one knows which hotel and what's more, you're registered under a false name.'

There was a moment's silence. 'Oh, the truth is, I don't know . . .' She looked a bit uncomfortable.

I said hurriedly, 'No worries.' I smiled, lowered my head and continued to look at my photo in the newspapers – the only part of the Spanish newspapers that I could understand.

I'd already resolved not to care whether or not I saw Mr Handsome. He was just some guy who'd been spoiled by money and women, a big player who knew how to please and manipulate the people around him. Right now all I wanted was to fly on to Buenos Aires and be with Muju.

Susan tapped me on the shoulder and pointed to the open sea and the spotlessly white city beneath the plane. 'Look, we're here.'

The people in Barcelona were welcoming and their Spanish sounded like song.

During a half-hour break, I sneaked off into the hotel's Business Centre and sat in the internet room checking my e-mail.

There were a lot of letters in my mailbox. I clicked on Muju's letter first. It was short and began with the weather as usual:

The temperature in New York has already hit 90 degrees and people are wearing their summer clothes. Everything has changed. Right now the office is a bit chaotic. I'll have to be patient. Things can only be dealt with one at a time. How are you? Don't worry too much about how long you sleep, it's the quality of the sleep that counts. It's best if you sleep really deeply. Miss you. See you soon in Buenos Aires! M.

I took a sip of chrysanthemum tea, gazing silently at the trees like green parasols outside the window. Spaniards rode their little motor-scooters back and forth on the street; in the bright sunlight I felt the relaxed, cheerful flavour of a foreign land.

I took another look at Muju's letter. This seemed to have become a habit. I would always read his e-mails several times. It was like double-checking the names and addresses on envelopes before dropping them in the postbox. It had almost become an obsession. I always worried that I would miss something. I had to confirm that everything was really the way I understood it to be, in all areas from romantic relationships to envelopes containing the monthly bill from the electricity company.

Reading Muju's letter confirmed a perception I'd had a lot lately. We were like an old married couple, having passed through the layer of passion and lust and fallen into the bed of familial affection. The weather, sleep and food appeared with increasing frequency in our conversations.

This wasn't necessarily a bad thing. The problem was that we weren't man and wife yet, let alone an old married couple.

When two lovers are caught feeling like an old married couple in this way, there are two likely outcomes. One is that they slowly separate, which is like recovering from a chronic illness. The other is that they marry quickly, leaping to their uncertain fate amidst the cracking explosions of Chinese fireworks.

Having thought through things to this point, I could only shake my head. I always think too much. If I never marry, it'll no doubt be because I think too much. If my body is a secret garden which attracts men to unearth desire, then the web-like maze of my mind is enough to frighten them off again. That's not good. According to Chinese medical theory, thinking too much can even affect the quality of your hair.

I took another sip of chrysanthemum tea and pulled my eyes away from the sunlit beauty of the street outside the window realizing there wasn't much left of my half-hour break. So I hurriedly skimmed the letters sent to me by my father and Xi'er.

My father told me he was going to be a visiting professor for six months in the history department of Singapore National University and would be leaving in a month and a half. My mother would go with him. He said that the New York shoes I'd sent back with my cousin Zhu Sha from New York fitted mother perfectly and that his pair were also the right size, though he complained that the heels were a bit too low. He wasn't very tall to begin with, and wearing shoes with slight heels made him look much better.

When I read this I had to grin. The older my father got, the more attention he paid to his image. Ever since he sprouted his first white hairs, he'd had my mother dye his hair black every month. He had more than forty ties, and more than twenty pairs of shoes, but he only smoked one brand of cigar – the Chinese-made 'Imperial Crown' brand.

'You have to be extra careful when you're walking around alone in a strange place. You can buy fewer shoes but never economize when dining out. If you can bear to then spend money on food, it's the shrewd thing to do.

In the end he couldn't resist imparting the philosophy of gourmet living to me.

Xi'er's letter was the longest, giving endlessly detailed accounts of recent developments: her restaurant had become one of the hottest in Shanghai, and people were lining up to go there; it was making more and more money, but there were fewer and fewer lovers to share her bed; she was wealthy, but unhappy without a boyfriend, and felt her life had become a cliché.

> *When are you coming back? If you don't come back, I'll die. Shanghai's so boring now. All the foreigners who come here are not only broke but insincere, and let's not even talk about how boring they are. Way worse than a few years ago, when it was the turn of the century and people were all DKD* [which means Death, Depression and Decadence] *crazy but naïve. People now are too practical. All they think about is earning money and then sleeping with a girl for free, and then earning more money. They come to Shanghai to earn money. They've heard that Shanghai is the last place left in the world where there are still opportunities to get rich overnight. 'The last virgin territory' as one foreigner told me yesterday.*
>
> *Oh, right . . . lots of minor news: After Lee lost her job at the Buddha Bar, she went to Parliament which was re-opened by a Taiwanese, and in the end got fired again. Recently she was arrested by the police, I hear it was for selling drugs to clients. And that British interior decorator Andy Smith just left Shanghai; I heard he got AIDS.*
>
> *Also Qiqi's going to get married. I got the invitation and your name was written on it, looks as if he doesn't know you're away from Shanghai. I'm going to go to the wedding and look around and then I'll tell you how his wife looks. Stay wet! Xi'er.*

As I left the internet room, I thought about the letters I'd just received. My mind was in a whirl. It was as if a door had been opened in my brain, and half of my awareness had flown back to Shanghai, while half of the other half was with Muju and the remaining fourth was still in Barcelona, answering questions with a smile, striking poses for the cameras, diligently and tirelessly continuing to work.

The Qiqi to whom Xi'er had referred at the end of her letter was Qi Feihong, who was young and successful and had made a lot of money trading in international futures. He was often at work when other people were asleep and sleeping or spending huge sums of money when other people were at work. He'd once been voted one of Shanghai's 'Top-Ten Outstanding Youths', but because he flaunted his profligate lifestyle, he never again received any official recognition. By contrast he frequently appeared in the headlines of the celebrity gossip rags and his name was never missing from lists like the '50 Diamond Bachelors of Mainland China'.

We'd gone to the same middle school. He was four years older than me. When he was voted into the 'Top-Ten Outstanding Youths of Shanghai', he also became my fiancé and we lived together until one morning several months later when I discovered in mailbox an unwrapped CD with his name written on it. When Qiqi saw it his expression changed dramatically, and he admitted to having gang connections. Soon afterwards, he mysteriously disappeared for a month and I moved back into my own flat.

At the time, nothing was going smoothly. I'd reached an impasse with my writing, and one evening, disaster having followed upon disaster, I tried to slit my wrists. It wasn't just painful but also terrifying – not in the least bit fun. Dripping blood, I managed to call a boy who'd secretly been in love with me for years and he'd rushed over and saved me. It was only five years ago, but felt like fifty. The bloodstains on the bath had long since yellowed, my face in photographs had blurred and my former fiancé was finally going to marry. I was neither hurt nor happy for him. I didn't care in the least. I just couldn't help thinking of those fading memories, thinking of that girl collapsed like a dying bird in the bathroom on that terrible night. A chill ran down my spine.

That evening I tactfully declined Susan's well-intentioned invitation and didn't go out for dinner. Instead I stayed in at the hotel and ordered room service. Then I watched the BBC for a while, getting a taste of British English. Speaking this kind of English aloud is like holding an invisible egg in your mouth – you have to be very careful not to break it. It has the effect of making you seem sophisticated.

Half an hour in the bath, then half an hour with my legs crossed practicing the meditation that Muju had taught me.

I don't know why, but halfway through this type of meditation I'm always sexually aroused – it only lasts a few seconds. Perhaps after the whole body has relaxed and your energy has been activated, it spontaneously migrates within your body and when it gets to the sexual zone, you feel that thing that people call 'sexy'.

After taking some sleeping pills, I lay down on the bed and called Muju. All I got was his voice-mail recording. It looked as though those problems at the office were keeping him really busy.

I turned out the light at the head of the bed and lay flat on the soft, smooth mattress with my left hand at my navel and my right hand holding my left breast. It was the position that made me feel most comfortable. I began to count sheep slowly.

Suddenly, the telephone rang. Almost instinctively I broke into a light sweat. 'God!' I cried softly, reaching over to pull out the telephone line, and then turned over and continued to count sheep. I don't know when, but at some point the sheep turned into a man called Nick.

One Nick, two Nicks, three Nicks . . . it wasn't a problem. I'd take another sleeping-pill.

24

Like a Hollywood Movie

Every little girl knows about love. It is only her capacity to
suffer because of it that increases.
Françoise Sagan

On the day I left Barcelona, I was told my book had the top
spot on Argentina's bestseller list, ahead of *Lord of the
Rings*.

Muju called. He'd already confirmed his ticket to Buenos
Aires. He would arrive two days after me.

Susan took me to the airport. She'd bought me a small box of
chocolate-covered dried orange slices from a little shop called
Gugu near her house. 'I guarantee you'll get addicted to these.
Chocolate with dried orange is the best combination. There is
only one shop in the entire world that has them and that's at that
little store Gugu next to my place.' Her laughter bubbled up like
the fizz in a series of soda bottles, up and up . . . I really couldn't
bear to say goodbye.

'Can I eat one now?'

'Oh, of course. They're for you.'

'Thanks.'

I opened the wrapping of the box and took out a piece for her
and then put another piece into my mouth. Wow. It really was
the best chocolate I'd ever had. Chocolate coated only half of
each slice of orange, so the feeling of the chocolate melting in
your mouth mingled beautifully with the resilient texture of the
orange slices. 'Very sexy,' I said.

Susan giggled. If I met girls like her all the time, I reflected, I could travel round the world and never feel lonely or tired.

The cab to the airport took a shortcut via City Hall, but the road was blocked by Palestinian demonstrators. Already quite a few cars were stopped there. Numerous police were coming and going, which only made matters worse.

'What are they doing?' I asked nervously.

'Protesting.' Susan looked worried too.

'Why are they protesting?'

'Hard to say. Probably the problems in the Middle East.'

'Yeah, must be,' I said. In my heart I knew that Susan and I would never understand those politics, those wars with their wild bursts of testosterone. Why was the situation in the Middle East always so violent?

'Human beings have the harmful habit of manufacturing tragedy,' I said as I bit into another chocolate-covered orange slice.

Susan nodded her head. 'But we can't miss the flight,' she said firmly, as she opened the car door and walked into the street.

I watched her walk back and forth a few times, looking for a way out. Time passed and I got worried. I hated missing flights and that really awful feeling when you're utterly helpless as your travel plans are messed up. Perhaps it had to do with my astrological sign. I liked making plans but never liked my plans to be thrown into chaos.

I asked the driver if he could find another route and he uttered a stream of words I didn't understand, but the gist seemed to be there was no hope. A long row of cars was lined up in front and behind our car, and backing out of the alley would be no small feat.

Susan came over. 'This isn't working. We're going to have to change cabs!' she shouted.

'Okay, but how do we find another cab?' I said, starting to pull my luggage with all my might from the boot of the car.

'Don't worry,' said Susan as she flipped open her cellphone, her face anxious. We forced our way out of the small alley. Susan screamed curses into the phone – several lines were busy or nobody was answering, suggesting that the Spanish were all calling their lovers or on the beach getting a tan. This was supposed to be a romantic and passionate country after all.

We stood by the side of the road beckoning to what seemed like every car. And then, with a whoosh, just like a scene from a movie, a black Mercedes-Benz came to an abrupt halt in front of us.

The glass car-windows slid down to reveal a charming, smiling face. 'Get in, kid!' He opened the door for the two dumbstruck women on the side of the road. 'Hurry up.'

A man who always wore black Armani suits in a black Mercedez-Benz limo, who was more handsome than George Clooney . . . a man who always appeared when and where you least expected him to. Who could compete with that?

I kept my mouth shut. Sitting beside me, Nick frequently smoothed his thick hair with his hand and made small talk with Susan.

'What a coincidence,' said Susan.

'Yeah, what a coincidence,' said Nick.

I didn't know you were going to the airport too. How on earth do such coincidences happen?' said Susan.

'Uh-huh, it's divine intervention,' said Nick.

Then it grew quiet in the car for a while. There was only the faintly discernible sound of jazz coming from the stereo drifting in the air around us.

'Oh, what's this?' said Nick, as if discovering a new continent, when he saw the box of chocolate-covered orange slices I held in my hands.

I didn't speak, I just opened the box. He shrugged at the chocolate, looked at me and smiled, and without saying a word took a piece and put it in his mouth.

'Oh!' He shook his head. 'Very sexy!'

Susan laughed heartily, and I laughed too, even though I felt that I shouldn't laugh then. That time with the static electricity when we had kissed in New York, Nick had said the same thing Muju had said: 'New York's too dry!' and now, once again, he'd said the same thing I'd said: 'Very sexy!' Imagine how infinitesimal the probability of this kind of coincidence.

I couldn't help but wonder if there was some kind of connection linking all of these coincidences. There's a spiritual bestseller called *The Celestine Prophecy* which claims that all coincidences have an underlying spiritual or mystical logic.

Before we got to the airport, we'd eaten the whole box of chocolates and also by the time we had reached it all three of us had relaxed a bit.

Susan and I hugged tightly, reluctant to part. Everything on this brief Spanish tour had gone smoothly, with a few moments of drama along the way which had made for a lasting impression.

Nick then hugged Susan goodbye, and from Susan's expression you could tell that he really was a ladies' man.

Susan left, and the two of us went to check in at different counters. After that, Nick hurried with me to the gate. The plane had already started boarding. He quickly handed me his business card, on which he'd written all his personal phone numbers and a private e-mail address that his secretary wouldn't check. After confirming that he had placed all possible means of getting in touch with him in my hand, he gave a sigh of relief.

I don't want to let you go, but we'll see each other again, I promise,' he said. I didn't doubt his words – if he said he would see me again, then he would.

As we were about to leave he leaned down and kissed my cheek, hesitated for half a second and then kissed my lips.

His lips were both hot and soft and his breath smelled sweet. It was the kind of smell that could make you wet instantly.

I changed planes in Paris and on the night plane from Paris to Buenos Aires I wore earplugs and eyeshades and slept surprisingly well. Perhaps I slept because I was so tired and no longer had to worry about the telephone ringing loudly or someone knocking on my door after midnight.

The next morning, my chastity intact, I arrived in the Southern hemisphere in Buenos Aires.

25

A Portion of Love Disappears in Buenos Aires

No matter how big or soft or warm your bed is,
you still have to get out of it.
Grace Slick

Just remember, we're all in this alone.
Lily Tomlin

If we want everything to remain as it is, it will be necessary
for everything to change.
Giuseppe di Lampedusa, *The Leopard*

Buenos Aires – Summer

People were as enthusiastic and friendly as in Spain. Although they were in the midst of a terrible economic crisis, the Argentinians showed their inherent decency and warmth of character. And they were passionate about reading. On a bleak, chilly night, reading a book by the light of a small lamp revived an old-fashioned mood amidst the economic disaster; fortune in the midst of misfortune.

In this wonderful city, with its wide blue sky and gigantic trees, where the great writer Borges was born, I spent two busy days – in the Marriott Hotel.

All the interviews were carried out in the ground floor café of the hotel and occasionally we would go out into the garden beside it to take some photos. The atmosphere was enthusiastic, emotional and sincere. I discovered that I was using my heart and not my head to get on with people around me.

I was entranced by the sombre but sparkling expressions on people's faces; entranced by the towering trees that can only be found in South America; entranced by the dreamy scents in the air, entranced by the church with its great expanse of lawn close to my suite.

In the twilight, I imagined shadows on the lawn outside, walking, dancing, speaking in whispers. Perhaps they were spirits from the church. They were mad with loneliness. They wanted someone to talk to them. They paced back and forth curiously on the lawn outside the young Chinese woman's door. They rarely saw Chinese people here. The media claimed that I was the first Chinese writer to visit.

On the morning of the third day, I was floating in a strange dream when I heard the door to my room open. The trace of sedatives that remained in my brain made it hard for me to open my eyes, but I knew he'd arrived.

He stayed in the living room for a while, gave the attendant a tip, and then I heard him go into the bathroom. After a series of splashing sounds, I heard the door to the bedroom being pushed open. Lightly he walked over to the bed, leaned over and kissed me. The scent of the morning air outside lingered on his lips, slightly cool, like mint.

I kept my eyes closed and reached out my arms to hold him tightly.

Muju had brought several cans of Japanese green tea as a gift to give the publisher's editor and PR, keeping a can for ourselves to clear our heads in the morning when we got up. Japanese green tea and Chinese green tea are practically the same thing, although the Japanese prefer the tea leaves to be crushed into powder.

While I was busy with my affairs in the café, Muju made his own way through the streets and alleys of Buenos Aires with a backpack, a map and a mini-camcorder.

At nightfall he returned, and sat in a distant corner of the café drinking tea and watching me. This was the first time he'd seen me at work and I could see the adoration and pride in his eyes.

After I finished work, a group of us went by car and small boat to a riverside restaurant for dinner. On the way we passed the wealthy part of town and Lucy, who went with us, pointed out a luxurious mansion that took up the entire street and said: 'Look, that's where our President lives.'

Another person added, 'In fact, our President is always busy in the office making a total mess of our country.'

We got to the riverside and boarded a boat. I can't remember the name of the river but it was famous for the people of Buenos Aires. Lucy said the dense forest at the river's edge had once sheltered wanted men – quite a few exiles during the revolutionary period, many of whom were radical artists, writers and poets. The water was rough right there as the river's course split and shifted back and forth almost as if it was a separate world; an ideal place of refuge and seclusion.

We sat in the little boat as it chugged along, staring attentively through the gathering darkness at the dense cluster of trees and scattered houses on either shore as we passed them in perfect silence. A full moon hung in the sky. It was reflected on the surface of the river, rippling with the waves. It seemed you could reach out and touch it. The sky of the Southern hemisphere was bright and clear.

The boat got to the restaurant, slowly dropping anchor at a simple wooden wharf where the engine was turned off.

In this restaurant, called the Calico, there was a fat calico cat, and two waiters. One of the waiters was extremely short and plump with a bald head and theatrical features. His squat, high nose caught one's eye especially. He looked like some kind of caricature. The other was very tall and also bald. In the centre of his forehead he seemed to have an injury as it was covered by a thick bandage. He had an unhappy expression. You couldn't help but wonder about the relationship between these two peculiarly contrasting people.

We were the only customers in the restaurant and sat out on the platform by the little wharf in the open air.

Apparently their deep-fried cheese was the best in Buenos Aires. To me, with less-than-perfect teeth, it tasted like rubber. I fed my share to the calico cat, who gulped it down in a matter of seconds. No wonder she was so fat. The waiters brought out one dish after another, shooing away the cat every so often as she gorged herself beside our table.

It was late autumn in Buenos. Sitting outside in the evening you could feel a slight chill in the air. The damp air from the river seeped quietly into one's clothing, sticking to one's skin like a distant memory.

The people with us were all smoking. Muju chatted with them about current affairs in the country and Lucy and I talked about Susan in Spain. Lucy had lived for ten years in Madrid and she and Susan had known each other for a long time.

A night wind blew intermittently into the silence. We sat by the river as if it were time itself. Its vast, powerful currents passed by, flowing quietly forward until they merged with the ocean, but something of it wouldn't vanish. It was life, it was love, it was dreams.

Everyone liked Muju. His warm smile and great big heart made it possible for him to make friends anywhere he went. He was the kind of person for whom the whole world was family and everyone was a potential friend. He always reminded me of that kind of knight-errant of old in the East who would go forth with his sword to the ends of the earth; the kind of man whose solemn vow was worth a thousand pieces of gold, who would ride the fastest horse and carry the sharpest sword and even cut off his own head to save a friend; and for whom friends were usually more important than women. There's an ancient Chinese tale about a man who, in order to save a group of starving friends who'd been surrounded by the enemy in an isolated city, killed his beloved concubine for them to eat.

Muju always wore the trendiest, coolest clothes, but inside was hidden an old-fashioned soul, perceiving women, his friends and everything in the world through the traditional attitudes of centuries or even millennia. His existence was a mixture of time and clay. He was like an unwilling but curious panther making his way tentatively through the modern-day urban jungle, discovering that the joyful childhood of humankind had long since come to an end.

The next morning, we sat on the lawn outside the hotel drinking Japanese tea and reading the English-language newspaper that had been delivered early. The third section had a report on the Argentinian economic crisis which mentioned that yesterday was the first day in a month that Argentinians could get money from the newly re-opened banks. Frighteningly long lines had formed outside several of them. When they closed at the prescribed hour, the corpses of three elderly people were discovered. They had dropped dead from hunger and weakness while waiting in line.

The peso had once been worth one US dollar but it was now only worth thirty-five cents. Lucy said to us: 'Now's the time to shop in Argentina.' The Marriott was full of Mexican and American tourists taking advantage of the opportunity; and perhaps the Argentinians needed the income, but to be a foreigner there was always to smell the traces of desolation and tragedy in the air. You couldn't help but feel thoroughly apologetic.

After a waiter from the hotel had pushed the breakfast trolley out onto the lawn, accepted a tip and left, Muju and I had a small argument about a matter of principle.

As a preface Muju suddenly said to me: 'Why did you look at the waiter like that?'

I put down the piece of toast I was holding, completely taken aback. 'What do you mean?'

Muju took a sip of tea. 'Perhaps you weren't aware of it, but for a second there you demonstrated unnecessary arrogance.'

I nearly spat the bread out of my mouth. 'I've no idea what you're talking about.' My voice trembled and my hands clenched themselves into fists to stop them from grabbing anything within reach and throwing it.

Muju avoided my stare, cut a slice of bacon and put it on my plate. 'I'm just being honest with you. It's just my feeling, something I've felt for a while now, and it's better to speak up. Perhaps I'm being too direct, sorry.'

I placed my napkin on the table, got up and went up to our room.

I rinsed my face with cold water and, as I looked in the mirror, I suddenly felt something collapse inside me, not totally, unlike the economic collapse of a country. It was the first time Muju had criticised me in such a direct way, and in an unimaginably tactless time and place. The real hurt came from him saying it was something he'd felt for a while now. It made me feel ashamed. Why hadn't I known about it for so long? I replayed my smile to the waiter again and again, saying thank you, and giving a tip, but I still couldn't understand what I'd done to cause Muju to judge me so harshly.

I hated the way he said he was sorry. Every time he said he was sorry it only made me feel a kind of impossible distance between us. He wasn't really apologizing. He only felt apologetic for what didn't seem right to him about had happened. More than once I'd felt that he was practically the perfect man, but this time I felt desperate and indignant. He *was* practically the perfect man, but in fact it was him who was exercising the privilege of arrogance in front of me. You can say to a woman 'You don't love me enough,' but you can't just say 'You're needlessly arrogant towards other people' so lightly. Only the gods can take that tone of voice.

Or was it my own fault? Because I always admired his honesty I'd seen him as a god all along, seen him as a force that could help me grow up.

I changed clothes and went down to the café. Muju had stayed on the lawn to meet the Spanish teacher recommended by Argentinian friends.

My head hurt throughout my morning interviews with journalists. Often I forgot the question halfway through my answer.

I would have three free hours in the afternoon, but that night I was scheduled to lecture to an audience of three thousand at the International Book Fair in Buenos Aires.

As an apology for causing unhappiness in the morning, Muju arranged for a car to take us for lunch to a highly recommended restaurant by the harbour during our free afternoon.

Unfortunately the driver got lost, turning this way and that among the streets and alleys, until somehow a whole hour had been wasted. The driver only knew the odd word of English and looked upset. Muju, masking his anxiety, tried to communicate directions to the driver using a map and almost non-existent Spanish.

I just stared expressionlessly out of the window. When the car passed through a slum, I saw boys wearing ragged soccer kit shouting and playing football in an empty lot; being Maradona seemed their only hope of escaping such a poverty-stricken neighbourhood.

We drove for another half hour, but still couldn't find the restaurant Muju had chosen. Suddenly I said to the driver: 'I'm sorry, please stop here.' He didn't understand English, so I had to gesture again.

The car came to a halt outside a restaurant that looked scrubbed but tacky. Tourists passed along the street. Not far away a splendidly dressed couple danced the tango in the sun. The girl was lovely, with long legs, a high bottom and voluptuous breasts, perfect in every way. If she'd been in Shanghai, she could have danced at the best social clubs or married a rich man. When the dance ended and the man held out his hat for money, the crowd evaporated.

I sat in gloomy silence.

Muju suddenly spoke up: 'Didn't you notice? Just now you were arrogant with the driver!' As he said this an earnest but puzzled expression appeared in his eyes.

I dissolved into tears. I hid my face behind my Chanel hat and my big Armani sunglasses, cheeks worn away by tears and self-esteem in tatters.

The hot summer sun of the southern hemisphere shone down on the crowded street. I sat quietly in that sunlight savouring the feeling of being hurt and wronged. Muju tried to speak gently. 'Don't cry, baby. Let's get something to eat now or we'll soon be late for your lecture. Some things we'll have to talk about later.

I said nothing. I was like a snowman melting slowly and inexorably gradually disappearing in the sun.

Muju held me, kissed me, encouraged me, and consoled me, apologizing profusely, but to no avail. I felt nothing but fear and sorrow. I felt that love was leaving me behind and I didn't have the strength to hold on to it.

That afternoon was the emptiest, bleakest time I could remember. That afternoon, the gods were warning me that even someone who genuinely loves and cherishes you – even if it's a close to perfect, wise and warm person – that someone at some point will become your hell, your fatal enemy. No one is perfect in this life, and because we are only human and not divine, it's inevitable that there will be hurt, misunderstanding and prejudice.

I didn't eat anything and rushed to the book fair about five minutes before the lecture. Lucy and the others were crazed with worry. I don't remember what I said to that crowd of three thousand. I only barely noticed that at the edge of the front row a familiar figure was aiming his mini-camcorder at me. One of the fingers of his left hand was missing the tip. He truly loved me, but sometimes he hurt me carelessly. I loved him, but at times I didn't understand him at all.

On the last day in Buenos Aires, we went to a soccer field to watch a match. An ocean of people flooded the pitch waving and cheering. It was perhaps the only really vital thing left in the country.

Then we went to the best department store in Buenos Aires. I took a break in the café on the ground floor, while Muju browsed the boutiques on his own. When he returned with seven or eight shopping bags in his hands, he had changed into new shoes and a new jacket.

He handed one of the smaller bags to me. 'For you,' he said. Inside the bag was a smaller bag, and inside the smaller bag was an even smaller box. When I looked inside, I saw that it held a pair of ruby earrings and a white gold necklace set with a heart-shaped ruby.

They gleamed with a deep and delicate light. The red was beautiful like a drop of virgin blood. I looked at him. 'Thank you.'

'You worked hard,' he said. 'You deserve it.'

Lucy drove us to the airport. The flight was on time, and before it left, we scoured our pockets and bags, using up all our pesos and spare change in the airport stores. We bought two packs of bitter Argentinian tea and a packet of chewing gum.

When only American dollars were left in our wallets, we went back to the US.

26

Sunlit Fragrance

You would notice the scent of the flower,
but not know that it came from me.
Rabindranath Tagore

Putuo Island – Autumn

The Master of Empty Nature gradually recovered.

But he still ate startlingly little and furthermore didn't eat anything after noon in accordance with Buddhist doctrine. Every day he ate only breakfast and lunch. In the morning he ate only a bowl of rice gruel with no vegetables. In the afternoon he had a meal of rice and vegetables, consisting of tofu with a few greens, peas and mushrooms, but without meat or fish. Only these two meals a day.

One sunny afternoon, I accompanied the convalescent Master on a stroll all around the grounds of the Temple of Righteous Rain.

When we walked past the Pu-ti tree in front of the Guanyin Hall, several birds chirped sweetly in the branches like notes plucked on a Chinese zither.

'Master, do you hear the birds chirping?' I asked.

'Yes.' Master nodded, raising his head to glance at the tree branches. Several small birds flew out of the dense crown of the tree with a flapping sound and disappeared from our sight.

'Now can you hear the birds chirping?' Master asked me casually.

For a moment I didn't know what to answer. I knew

instinctively I couldn't say 'no,' even though that was how it was in actuality. This question of Master's was on another level entirely.

Master turned and continued to walk forwards. I followed behind him, watching the shadows of Master and myself slowly moving in the sunlight, one in front and one behind.

'I'm sorry. I didn't grasp your meaning,' I said at last.

A smile drifted to Master's face. 'But your Buddhist name is Wisdom!' he said.

I burst out laughing. 'That's because wisdom is what I lack,' I said.

Master, with his snow-white whiskers, said evenly, 'Sounds are created like dust and are extinguished like dust. The ability to hear is not created when sound is created and is not extinguished when sound is extinguished. True insight ignores the coming or going of sound.'

I came to a halt, gave a little clap. 'I get it!'

But Master seemed not to have heard. His footsteps continued forwards. I rushed after him, supporting him with my hand as he went up the steps.

The young Buddhist novice Hui Guang was just then bustling off down a corridor to one side. When I went over to look, a layer of paper had been placed on the stone benches, and a big, freshly-plucked bouquet of wild chrysanthemums was spread on top of it. Hui Guang lowered his head and with single-minded attention used a stalk of bamboo to spread the chrysanthemums out more evenly to catch more of the sun's rays.

'Oh, Master you've come!' Hui Guang looked up, just then seeing us. He stood up quickly.

The Master of Empty Nature patted him on the shoulder. 'You went to a lot of trouble to remember, and got these flowers so promptly.'

'As your pupil should, 'Hui Guang said with his hands pressed respectfully together.

The Master of Empty pointed to another stone bench and said

to me, 'Why not rest here a while.' And smiling, he said to Hui Guang, 'Let's play Go.'

'Your pupil will leave right away to get the game pieces and the tea.' So saying, Hui Guang took off.

Soon Master and Hui Guang were setting up the Go board, drinking tea and starting to play. I watched the battle from the sidelines, periodically turning the chrysanthemums on the stone bench, the better to let the sunlight seep as quickly as possible into the delicate and beautiful petals. When the wild chrysanthemums had dried in the sun, they would be placed in a cotton bag as a fragrant chrysanthemum pillow for Master. Apparently sleeping on such a pillow could make your ears and eyes clearer and sharper, and dispel harmful heat and dampness. Last night the Master of Empty Nature had casually mentioned the effects of this kind of pillow, not anticipating that the young monk Hui Guang would remember it and get up bright and early to spend the morning in the mountains picking chrysanthemums.

I turned to look as Hui Guang played against Master, a serious and absorbed expression on his young face. The young novice monks in the temple were like apples unblemished by wormholes, with a pure and unparalleled decency of spirit.

I remember once asking him: 'Have you ever thought about what sort of person you want to be?'

He said: 'Someone like the Master of Empty Nature.'

I sat with the two monks, one old and one young, for a long time, aware of the fragrances wafting softly over and seeping directly into my heart. It was not only the fragrance of wild chrysanthemums drying in the sun; it was also emanating from the man who had lived for a hundred years and the youth who still possessed the innocence of childhood with the soul of a flower.

In the Buddhist scriptures it is written that fragrance emanates from the bodies of those who practice Buddhism.

27

Leaving New York, Leaving Him

> You have to be very fond of men. Very, very fond.
> You have to be very fond of them to love them.
> Otherwise they're simply unbearable.
> Marguerite Duras

> Go, it's time to go.
> Lao-tzu

New York – Summer

The green poplars cast quiet shadows and the streets and buildings gleamed in the sun. New York was already full of the scenes of early summer.

I sat wearing my trendy Chanel sunglasses at a café on a street on the Upper West Side, writing in my diary, watching passers-by, drinking tea. A Chinese person who drinks nothing but tea in a Manhattan café – this image already marked me as alien. It's almost a curse. In Shanghai wearing leather pants and sleeping with Western culture marked me as an outsider. In New York I was also an outsider drinking tea and wearing Chinese silk *qipao* dresses. I had travelled much of the world, yet no matter where I went I was always an alien, rushing past lugging my suitcases and clutching a boarding-pass.

Sometimes I felt a sharp ache in my throat, as if the lack of a sense of belonging was a thorn sticking there.

More and more often I dreamt of the little island where I was born, Putuo Island, and of the temples there. Usually the dream began with me floating utterly exhausted on the surface of the sea looking everywhere for the little island, then as I was on the verge of giving up, a voice from the depths of the heavens would say something to me. I would listen with all my might, but couldn't quite make it out. I kept having the same dream with the voice from the heavens, night after night. And whenever I woke up I'd feel puzzled and lost and frustrated that I couldn't hear clearly what that mysterious voice was saying to me.

In another dream I became a child of two or three years old trying hard to step across a threshold. The threshold was too high for me, so I had to concentrate hard and put all my energy into it. It was a great strain for me but still I seemed to feel no fear. Nobody was around and all was quiet but very bright.

Muju was still busy at the office. If there ever was a day when he stayed there less than twelve hours, he felt guilty.

Neither of us mentioned the argument in Argentina, but it didn't mean that he and I understood or forgave each other. Instead we'd reached a sort of tacit agreement to ignore the things it had raised for the time being. We'd concentrate on each other's best side. We would nest in this peaceful space like birds worn out from flying.

At the same time, we both had a premonition that I wouldn't stay in New York much longer.

In the mailbox downstairs were books sent by my publisher, some contracts, a postcard from Muju's ex-wife Kitty (wishing Muju and me every happiness), a number of bills and several pirated editions of *Shanghai Baby* that Xi'er had sent from Shanghai (she'd already collected more than thirty pirated books for me, all with bizarre covers), as well as a *Spiderman* DVD that you could get for a dollar on any Shanghai street corner.

In the enclosed letter, she warned me: 'Don't spend ten dollars in New York to see the latest trashy Hollywood movie; when you return to China, ten dollars will get you ten of those movies!'

Muju arranged a farewell dinner, not for me, but for the sweet and able Peter in his office.

Peter had found his dream job, teaching at a university in San Francisco. Meanwhile Muju's company was struggling to stay afloat as clients dwindled, leaving him no choice but to consider reducing the size of his staff, so it was a good move for both of them.

Nonetheless the mood at dinner became sentimental. Muju made an exception and got a little drunk, holding Peter's hand and talking non-stop, his eyes glistening with tears. They'd worked together for a decade.

As Muju's said, 'I love him like family.'

Muju developed family feelings towards people who worked for him easily, his friends, towards his former girlfriends and ex-wife, and even towards the subjects of his documentaries. As for me, perhaps I was hanging somewhere between family and lover? Muju had an unhappy childhood and then was cut off by his family when he married a Jewish girl. At times I couldn't help but wonder which Muju needed more, a family or a lover? Which kind of love had he had with his ex-girlfriends – familial love or romantic love?

The dinner ended around midnight. While Muju was still feeling tipsy and sentimental, I made a quick pot of tea in the kitchen and then the two of us sat on the living room sofa and talked.

'A little boy lives inside my body . . . sometimes I'm very childish,' he said.

'I know,' I said. That much was obvious. I glanced around at the small nudes and peaches arranged round the room, glanced at the crazy but cute style of clothing he wore and glanced at his round face and curving eyes as he laughed loudly.

'Sometimes I can make an ass of myself.' He took a sip of tea, put down his cup and reached out to rub my back. Through my clothes I could feel the heat on his fingers left by the teacup. 'You can make an ass of yourself too, Coco, though I've always believed you're smarter than me.'

I chuckled. 'Thanks, you're wiser than me.'

He didn't laugh. His hand continued to stroke my back lightly. Even when it was unintentional, his touch was out of the ordinary and I had to suppress the desire to purr like a lazy cat.

'We're not competing. We're always learning and looking for something that's possible together, no?'

'What sort of possible?'

'You don't know? Marriage, kids, those things that most men and women think about when they're together.'

When I heard him mention these sensitive subjects so frankly and openly, I panicked. Thoughts about them floated through my mind almost every day. I tossed them this way and that like vegetables frying in a wok. But when Muju came out with it like that, I suddenly didn't know what to say. I got up and went to the kitchen. I stood there staring at nothing for a few minutes, then acting like I'd just washed my hands, walked back.

'What do *you* think is possible between us?' I asked, trying as hard as I could to keep my tone even as if I were prepared for anything he might say.

Lying on the sofa, Muju reached out his hand and pulled me to him. Then he tugged my whole body down on top of him.

We lay there on the sofa for a while, but didn't speak. Silence between us always meant something. Held by him gently and firmly, I smelled the scent of alcohol and testosterone; sweet and disturbing.

'We won't get married, right?' At last I opened my mouth, unhappy with the trace of meekness and cowardice in my tone.

'I . . . don't know,' he said.

I fell silent. Although he said 'I don't know,' I guessed what he really meant. 'Why don't you know,' I mumbled, trying to climb off his body, but he held me firmly to him not letting me leave.

After struggling unsuccessfully, I relaxed on top of him. When my face touched his, I realized my cheeks were damp. I was crying. 'Useless!' I cursed myself silently. Damn the tears on my face, damn the man who said 'I don't know' but still held me tightly and wouldn't let me go.

'Baby,' he purred, 'in the time we've been together, I'm sure there have been times when you've felt confused. I'm sure there are things about me that you dislike. You're very special, and many men could fall for you. You're a princess. But sometimes I feel kind of confused. It is so difficult to please you. No matter what I do, you're angry.' His tone was tactful, but a more direct translation was that ever since we'd met, Muju had felt bewildered; he found me so spoiled and hard to please that he couldn't imagine a happy ending for us.

I got up from the couch, went into the bathroom and closed the door. I turned on the tap, splashing my face with the running water. My skin hurt slightly. It's lucky we can feel pain; it proves we're still alive.

I walked out of the bathroom and said to Muju, 'Perhaps it's time for me to go back to Shanghai to write my new book.'

The next morning I called the travel agent. She said it was the peak of the summer season and that most flights to Shanghai were fully booked. 'I only want one seat,' I said, 'Surely you can help me find just one seat. I don't mind if it's a bit more expensive.'

I put down the phone and life suddenly became clear. I was like an asteroid that had been lost in space and had now come back on its orbit again. Even if this wasn't the direction I most wanted to go in, still it is always better to have some direction than none at all.

I slowly began to put my luggage in order, walking from one room to the next, a list in my hand.

On the list was everything that I would need to take with me, big and small items alike. Barney's Kiehl's brand moisturizing lipstick; power cord for my laptop computer; a roll of film I hadn't had time to develop; all the porn magazines that I'd bought for Xi'er (featuring well-hung naked guys); American dramamine for my rock 'n' roll friend Piao Yong. Piao Yong was the guitarist for a Beijing rock band, a fanatic about tattoos and women. He had a sexy pair of hands that gave off the scent of marijuana; hands which could play the guitar amazingly fast. A lot of women wanted to be that guitar in his hands. His only weakness was that he was often travel sick and Chinese medicine didn't help him; only Japanese or American dramamine helped.

As I was walking backwards and forwards packing, I suddenly noticed the cabinets in the living room. I'd never seen them opened. I guessed the contents weren't important, because Muju had never put a lock on the doors. It felt easy to pry once I'd managed to convince myself that the items inside didn't have much value.

I opened the door of the cabinet. Inside were drawers. One of them contained old shoeboxes and, curious, I opened one box. Inside was a big pile of photographs of women I'd never seen. Some were alone, some with Muju. All his ex-girlfriends were here!

An inner voice said to me: 'This is pointless, you're grown-up now.' But another voice said: 'Go on, look at those ex-girlfriends, perhaps you'll be one yourself soon!'

I looked. But after a while I didn't feel as excited as I'd expected. Some of them were prettier than me, but the majority were only average-looking. Yet all of them were quite cute in some way and without exception all wore happy expressions. I got about halfway through the pile and then stopped. Muju had a right to his privacy. Trying to understand our relationship by spying on his past only showed my clumsiness.

I closed the box and was about to shut the drawer when an album labelled 'Muju' caught my eye. I opened it: inside were pictures of Muju. I was drawn to an old picture of him in college. He looked like a handsome bad boy, wearing leather, leaning against a wall smoking, his eyes deep and vague with an intense longing. The aging black-and-white photo had a surreal beauty. In it Muju projected a wildness and fragility that he'd long since lost. Wildness with fragility is the hallmark of youth.

I pulled out the photo, closed the drawer and the cabinet and went over to my big trunk. I took out a box full of mementos: notes that Muju had written to me, ticket stubs from concerts we'd been to, plane tickets from trips we'd taken together and other souvenirs. Carefully I placed Muju's old photograph with them.

During my last few days in New York, I had meals in turn with Jimmy Wong, the editor at my publishing house, Columbia professors, my aesthetician Natasha, Richard and his wife W., and Eric the book critic. Having a meal together is a good way to say goodbye.

'I have to return to Shanghai. I need a Chinese background for my new book. Right now I'm still writing Chinese.' This is what I always said over dinner. It seemed writing had become a good excuse for leaving New York.

My friend Jimmy Wong had his own troubles then. He'd just discovered his cute and clever daughter Nancy and her controlling mother had reached an all-time low, like fire and water. Nancy had scrubbed the toilet bowl with her mother's toothbrush and afterwards taken to running away from home. Once she couldn't pay for a pizza at a pizzeria in New Jersey and had to work in the shop for three hours before she called her daddy Jimmy to come rescue her.

Another time she ran away for a week and Jimmy and his ex-wife nearly went mad with worry. In the end they discovered their precious daughter throwing wild parties at the summer house of an equally wealthy classmate: fourteen- and fifteen-year-old rich kids skipping class, smoking dope, popping pills and having orgies.

Not only that, but Jimmy was also worried that he was being investigated by the Government. He'd never dared to do anything illegal, but it was inevitable that among his clients some would have counterfeit documents or credentials. He'd never looked at a white girl, either, because he was afraid of undercover agents – sometimes he was so naïve.

The result of all this was he'd got so anxious he'd started seeing a therapist.

Jimmy's story only strengthened my resolve to leave New York. There's a time for everything and now it was time to leave for a while.

To my great surprise, Eric had resigned from his job at the *New York Times*. He planned to go to Shanghai in a month and then go to that place he held so sacred – Tibet. It'd be his first trip to China.

He said he'd already sent an e-mail to my cousin Zhu Sha in Shanghai; he wanted to see her. In fact, since he had first fallen for Zhu Sha, he couldn't get her out of his mind. He was desperate to see her, whether or not she liked him; even if she was married.

I looked at Eric's youthful and enthusiastic face and didn't know what to say. Was this a comedy or a tragedy?

The tragi-comedy of male-female relations inevitably follows this pattern: you love me, I don't love you; I love you, you don't love me; and on and on. But my and Muju's relationship was, I still love you and you seem to still love me, but we'd better separate for a while and wait and see what happens.

That day, Muju made an exception to his rule and took me to the airport. It was ten years since he'd taken anyone to the airport. I was anxious the whole ride, because I was sure that I would cry when we said goodbye. I didn't want to cry; I believed in the superstition that crying when you say goodbye brings bad luck and can turn it into a permanent farewell.

The moment arrived. Big, tall Muju leaned down, tugged me and kissed my lips. I hadn't anticipated the little sparks that cracked and left a mildly painful tingle on my lips.

'God, static electricity again,' I mumbled.

'New York's too dry,' he said. We looked at each other and smiled. We had to be a pretty special couple to generate static electricity on both our first and last kisses in New York.

'Drink lots of water on the plane,' he said. 'Get up periodically and do some tai chi in the aisles.'

I laughed again.

When I'd settled into my seat on the plane, I realized I hadn't cried. Perhaps it was a pretty good sign.

28

The Master Says: Smile! Smile!

Question: 'How is one released from worldly cares?'
The Zen Master replies: 'Who has put you in bondage?'

Putuo Island – Autumn

After a burst of autumn rain, the weather on Putuo Island suddenly grew much colder. The flowers and plants withered and drooped. Deep browns and reds appeared amidst the green of the mountain forest. The view was suddenly bright and vivid.

Without realizing it, I'd spent two weeks on the island. The day of my return approached and the Master of Empty Nature sent word via Hui Guang that I should visit him once more before I left.

The Master of Empty Nature lived in an abbot's room in the north-western part of the temple. The whole room was simply and neatly decorated with an old bench, an old table and a low wooden bed covered with a thin blanket. Beside the table a small shrine had been set up complete with a statue of Guan Yin. It was a lifestyle from an earlier century.

This almost spotless room had an indescribable fragrance and warmth. What caught my eye was the big white scroll hanging next to Master's bed. On it was written in coarse, dense strokes of black Chinese ink the single character 'Death'. Every time I looked at this character, my heart beat fiercely. The first time I entered this room I'd been quite startled by it.

I asked Master why he'd hung this particular character on the wall. Master stroked his whiskers, and replied: 'Many people are so concerned with bustling through life that they neglect to prepare mentally for the inevitability of death. They forget to live a meaningful life before death arrives.' Another time he'd said: 'Everyone is afraid of dying, but without knowing death, how can you know life?'

The reverence I felt for Master increased with each passing day. In my eyes, this kind old man stood for wisdom. He was like a grandfather who unselfishly blessed and protected the younger generation. With him there, it seemed like all my troubles could be easily solved. Panic, confusion, sadness, restlessness – all the negatives would naturally disappear. He was a giant refuge. In a world in love with youth, sex and power, he was precious, an older person with an uncommon power that ordinary people couldn't see.

On the afternoon I bought my return ticket to Shanghai, I went again to the rooms of the Master of Empty Nature at the temple of Righteous Rain. From a distance I saw Hui Guang with his sleeves rolled up wiping the windows in the walls outside Master's room, a wooden bucket of water by his feet.

I called out a greeting to him. He turned his head, his round face flushed from working, and smiled at me. 'Master is expecting you.' He turned back and went on wiping the glass of the wood-framed windows.

Master was sitting with his legs crossed on the wooden bed, wrapped in a grey robe. The word 'Death' still hung there on the wall as shocking as ever. From the angle I was looking, it sat right over Master's head like something that could drop from above at any time. Master looked slightly drowsy and his body beneath the robe was so thin and small that it was practically invisible.

I brought my hands together under my chin in greeting.

'You're leaving?' he said, motioning me to sit on the old bench.

'Yes, I'm taking the ferry tomorrow morning,' I said, somewhat hoarsely. 'I'm not sure, I don't really feel like leaving, but . . .'

'You can come back at any time.' Master smiled. 'When I was your age, I wished earnestly that I could run around day in and day out, remaining nowhere.'

Master's smile had healing powers and in that instant I no longer felt so sick at heart. I couldn't help but smile. 'Where there are gatherings, there are dispersals; once dispersed, there will be time for gathering again,' said Master.

'I'll come to see you again, Master. Next time I'll certainly bring cream cakes. There's a great vegetarian restaurant in Shanghai called Gongdelin – they also make cream cakes for monks.'

Master nodded, looking me over with a smile. 'You look a bit healthier than when you came.'

'I slept very well here. Didn't dream so much and when I did it wasn't nightmares,' I said.

'Tell me what kind of dreams you had.'

'Oh, some recurring dreams, for example, of me floating in the sea trying to find an island; I guess it was Putuo Island, but I couldn't ever find it. Sometimes a mirage would appear, and then a voice from the sky would tell me something that I could never quite hear. Also I dreamt I was a small child trying with all my might to cross over a threshold. Twice I dreamed of situations in New York, about my friends.' I paused for a moment. 'But none of them had any feelings of terror.'

Master didn't make a sound. His expression was again one of laughing without laughing, sleeping without sleeping. At this point Hui Guang came over carrying two cups of green tea and then softly withdrew from the room.

After gesturing for me to take tea, Master picked up the cup of tea by his bed with both hands, lightly blew on the leaves floating in the water and took a sip. I followed his example and took a sip too. Excellent tea; it was picked and cured by the monks themselves.

'How long have you been studying English?' Master suddenly changed the subject.

'Five or six years, give or take. I'm still studying it.'

'It requires patience,' said Master. 'Behaving properly to improve one's character requires even more patience. You might spend your entire life on it. Spiritual growth takes a lifetime.' I gazed fixedly at Master's kind face. It's hard to describe, but a profound feeling of familiarity and connection surged up in me.

'I have something for you.' Master pointed under the bed. I hurried over and pulled out a wooden box. When I opened it, it was filled with sutras. Master took out a thin volume called *Incantations of the Great Mercy* and handed it to me. 'Read it when you have time. It is helpful for gaining wisdom and calm.'

I quickly brought my palms together. I felt very moved, but couldn't think of any words of thanks, suddenly inarticulate.

'This little booklet was given to me by a monk I met once when I was young and travelling around. Now I give it to you. May it be of help.' At this point I was not only moved, but astonished. The gift was without a doubt extremely precious.

When I got up to leave, Master struck his staff forcefully on the ground and said in a voice as if reading the sutras: 'Smile! Smile!'

I held back my tears at leaving and up floated a smile. 'Child, all of life's secrets are in a smile. You're so young; don't always keep a straight face. You must smile, and even better sometimes be playful!' Saying this, Master waved at me. I bowed deeply.

Hui Guang escorted me out of Master's chamber and out of the temple.

Standing on the lichen-covered path outside the temple, I looked at him and said, 'I'll miss you.' He lowered his head, kicked a small piece of stone off into the distance. Again I could smell the pure and slightly acrid odour of his body, like the smell of burning mugwort. It was the special smell of a young and ascetic monk.

After a long pause he broke the silence by saying, 'You take care.'

I smiled happily. 'Take good care of the Master of Empty

Nature. And don't fall asleep when you're meditating.'

He smiled back. 'In this morning's class I almost fell asleep.'

'Why?' I asked him, laughing.

'Yesterday at three in the morning I couldn't sleep and sneaked out of the dorm to the public telephone at the temple door and called my mother.' He was chewing his lip lightly, his face lit up. 'She thought she was dreaming.' He grinned, absorbed in the happy feeling his mother brought him.

The wind suddenly blew one red leaf after another from a nearby maple. The flitting leaves were so red, so eye-catching, exceptionally beautiful.

I waved at Hui Guang, then turned and walked past the highly-decorated archway of the Temple of Righteous Rain. I sat awhile on the beach, then went back to the inn for dinner.

Early next morning, I got up and washed, ate breakfast and stored my luggage behind the hotel counter. Then I went to the Temple of Righteous Rain and burned incense and worshipped before the various Buddhas.

I passed an exceptional number of tourists that day. They came and went across the Temple threshold like migrating fish.

29

Everything Comes Quickly
in Shanghai

People of the world are as if struck with malaria:
cold for a short while, hot for a short while,
and before they know it their life has passed.
Master Fa Yan

Shanghai – Autumn

I returned home to Shanghai. First I checked my voicemail and
e-mail messages. Not a trace of Muju. But I didn't feel as
lonely or insecure as I had when I'd got back from New York. I
would even remember to smile even when I was alone. The
world wouldn't stop turning just because I was on my own.

Over the next few days, I tidied up the apartment myself,
which I hadn't done before I left for Putuo Island. Cigarette ends,
pill bottles, tissues, dirty plates, old magazines, socks and shoes
were scattered all over the place, and gave the place a rancid
smell. I never knew I had so many things to be thrown about.

Some tasks are pretty much the same: tidying an apartment,
lying in a beauty parlour getting rid of dead skin, resigning from
a job, breaking up with a boyfriend. They're all uncomfortable at
first, but leave you feeling better in the end.

In the two short weeks that I'd been away, Shanghai had
changed yet again. The fourth great bridge across the Pujiang,
the world's largest steel arch bridge, had been finished and would
soon open for traffic. Shanghai's bid to host the EXPO of 2010

had been successful and the booming of the excavation machines at a site in my neighbourhood echoed around the clock. The age driving licences expired was lifted from fifty to seventy and a rapidly increasing number of people had cars for personal use. A new variety of tangerine appeared in the markets. They were called Shatang Ju, the size of pigeon eggs and very sweet.

And Xi'er now had a generous Australian boyfriend with a generously-proportioned dick. His name was Adam. He was the Asian regional director for a world-renowned IT company. He worked hard and played hard, always wore brand names, flitted from one hot club to another and never left till he was drunk. Most of his time he wasn't in Shanghai and he didn't have many friends there, so Xi'er hoped that he didn't know her secret.

But I didn't think much of the relationship. On the phone, Xi'er kept going on and on about how great he was. I listened to her love story as I tidied up my wardrobe. They'd met in her restaurant, it was love at first sight, he was so great, he wanted to see her all the time, oh, he was so great . . .

In the end I couldn't stop myself shutting her up: 'You've been talking all day but I still haven't heard what exactly's so great about him.'

'Forget it. You never like my boyfriends.' She gave up.

'Don't talk nonsense. Of course I want you to have a man who really treasures you, and that you love him and he loves you and you love each other till your hair turns white. In which case I'll feel there's still hope in life.'

'I really like him,' said Xi'er.

'If you're happy, I'm happy,' I said.

'He's the best man I've ever had, not just physically and intellectually but financially.'

I just listened and didn't make a sound.

'Hey, I deserve to have a successful, wealthy, well-hung man!' Xi'er said. 'I spend three times as long taking care of my skin as most women. The money I spend on clothes alone could buy a small island in the Pacific. Shouldn't I have that kind of a man?!'

Because her Australian boyfriend wasn't in Shanghai, Xi'er dragged me with her to a wedding where I didn't know anyone. The bride was a regular customer at Xi'er's restaurant and was always very generous. She wasn't the first to invite Shanghai's famous female proprietor 'The Cut-throat Concubine' to be a guest at a wedding. In fact, Xi'er had already been to a lot – I'm not sure exactly how many – of her customers' weddings. Overnight she'd become a total wedding nut.

Like Xi'er, I enjoyed having the chance to show off elegant evening clothes and believed that going to other people's weddings brought you good luck. Also like Xi'er, I despaired of ever getting married myself. But Xi'er had attended far too many weddings. On any given day she knew which weddings were scheduled and where.

First I went to Xi'er's place, where she was bustling around enthusiastically to a Maria Callas aria. 'Hey, Beautiful!' Her face covered in a homemade mask, she greeted me and then looked me over carefully. 'God, Putuo Island really affected you . . . All of a sudden you look like a nun!'

I laughed and looked at myself in the mirror. I was only wearing light make-up, black-framed glasses that I didn't normally wear and a simple white cashmere outfit.

I looked at Xi'er again. She was like a dramatic and pampered movie star. On her face was a nourishing mask of natural pearl powder, yoghurt, tea-tree pollen and lemon juice. A red silk cord held her hair high and she wore creamy silk pyjamas custom-made by her clever tailor, with high-heeled red satin Gucci sandals. In her left hand she held a pale gold frock modelled on a Vera Wang original, and in her right a copy of a Dolce & Gabbana ankle-length dress, both made for her by her tailor.

She couldn't make up her mind which outfit to wear. I'd helped her choose the material for the pale gold Vera Wang copy. It was strapless and had butterfly-ties around the waist. The original Vera Wang outfit had once been worn by Sarah Jessica Parker in a photo published in a magazine; Xi'er admired both of them a lot. She held the dress up against her body, grinning broadly so that the thick mask on her face the wrinkled slightly.

Xi'er was proud of these two secret weapons, which gave her a sense of security: the little Subei tailor who could duplicate any fasionable outfit; and the facial that she'd invented herself.

In Shanghai, Xi'er and I went to the same hairdresser, the same yoga instructor, the same tennis coach, the same travel agent – but our tailors were different. Hers was extremely clever and could make an almost exact copy of the latest style shown in any fashion magazine. Mine excelled at making Chinese-style *qipao* with complicated patterns of buttons that drew admiring glances.

Xi'er had a special knowledge of beauty secrets. She knew that small facial pimples could be cured by dabbing them with boiled green tea leaves, blackheads could be banished by rubbing them with balls of cooked rice, static cling in skirts could be eliminated by spreading moisturizing cream on silk stockings in cold, dry weather, and so on . . . Xi'er even knew of a Tibetan musk balm that could prevent pregnancy when applied to the navel before sex (obviously, this was of only academic interest to her).

Xi'er enjoyed these things.

I glanced at my watch and reminded Xi'er we'd better hurry. She walked towards the bathroom saying: 'We can be fashionably late by fifteen minutes.'

'Whatever!' I went into her kitchen and found half a container of yoghurt in the fridge left over from her face mask. I carried it into the living-rroom and ate it slowly as I sat on the sofa.

The wedding wasn't special. It took place in a supposedly six-star hotel, but even the food was below par. I disliked its greasiness (perhaps the result of the recent drop in oil prices?) But Xi'er said the problem was that my stomach had become enlightened too and it couldn't digest human food any longer.

Xi'er knew nearly everyone at the wedding and people revolved around her talking non-stop. At my request she introduced me only as her friend Sophie. I was happy to sit in a corner keeping out of trouble.

Xi'er secretly pointed out some of the guests to me. The pair of twin sisters dressed head to toe in brand-names were born into a poor family. The younger married a Malaysian trillionaire and the elder sister lived with them; sometimes when her brother-in-law was drunk or pretended to be drunk he'd go into the elder sister's bedroom. That woman in flats with the hairstyle of a university teaching assistant was actually a high-class call girl. Apparently she only accepted foreign currency. And the middle-aged man with a charming manner was an arms dealer from Taiwan.

It reminded me of New York.

I didn't want to be reminded. I'd come back from Putuo Island, but what had really come back was a body. There were still some other parts of me that hadn't returned. I needed time.

My head hurt, so I said goodbye to Xi'er and went home.

A few days later my cousin Zhu Sha brought her fourteen-month-old son Little Worm to have dinner with me at a newly-opened Japanese restaurant.

This was the first time I'd ever met the little guy in the flesh. I was a little nervous about taking the baby from Zhu Sha. Holding him carefully in my lap produced a miraculous, heavy, soft sensation. I liked him immediately and almost didn't want to give him back until he began kicking my stomach with his chubby legs and crying loudly.

'Actually he loves being held by pretty aunts. Men never dream of touching him, even his father's reluctant,' said Zhu Sha looking at her son with admiration.

We tried to talk about other things but the pretty little two-legged animal constantly moving in her lap caught our attention. Most of the time was spent talking about him, and what time was left over was spent talking about his father.

Zhu Sha mentioned how she and the father of her son were already sleeping in separate rooms. She and her son had one bed, and his father slept in the guest room. In the morning when she went to work, the nanny would look after the child and the father would paint vast, hazy paintings in his studio, and then when he felt bored he'd leave the studio and play for a while with his son.

'Once Ah Dick stood the child up on the palm of one hand holding his clothes, and paraded the boy around the room spinning in circles like a madman.' Zhu Sha reached out an arm and made a gesture in imitation. 'He's really crazy.'

Even though Ah Dick expressed overwhelming love for his son, Zhu Sha suspected that he didn't, in fact, really like him, but rather was jealous that he'd stolen so much of the attention that once was his.

'Perhaps you should treat Ah Dick a little better,' I said, remembering the twenty-one-year-old, ponytail-wearing, cartoon-painting Ah Dick of four years ago. Then he was a luscious bad boy all the older Shanghai women wanted to take to bed.

Zhu Sha fell silent.

When she fell silent she was at her most beautiful. In the words of Eric, who'd fallen in love with her at first sight in New York, she was 'beautiful like a Chinese Buddha'. Her facial features and temperament were gentle and refined, classically Chinese. If she'd been born a hundred years earlier she wouldn't have become so hardened by her successful career or shrewd as she was now. Used to giving orders in the office, she was a cold fish at home. If she'd lived a hundred years ago, she'd be wearing silk, sitting delicately by a carved window embroidering, burning incense and waiting for her husband to return at dusk. Of course, a hundred years ago her feet would have been bound into three-inch golden lotuses; which one wouldn't have enjoyed.

Little Worm was saying something to himself very noisily and Zhu Sha put a little steamed egg into his mouth. His bottle was still on the table. Zhu Sha didn't feed him mother's milk. Her chest was very flat; there was no milk for him.

'Life changes completely once you have a small child. If you haven't fully prepared for it psychologically, it's best not to,' Zhu Sha said to me in the tone of voice of someone who knew what she was talking about.

I thought to myself: here's an example of a small child wrecking a marriage. She kissed her son a hundred times a day, but the child's father wasn't so lucky.

'Eric's coming to Shanghai, did you know that?' I changed the subject.

Zhu Sha sighed, but her expression was unconcerned. 'Can you believe it? Why's it always these young guys? I'm not the headmaster of a boys' academy.'

'It's *because* they're young that they fall in love at first sight, doing crazy things like travelling across the seas to Shanghai to see you. When's that kind of thing going to happen to me?' I sighed too, thinking of Muju.

Little Worm suddenly started to giggle, kicking his legs on his mother's lap, reaching out a hand to me. I picked him up and gave him a kiss.

That evening when I got home I turned on all the lights in the house, put on a CD by the Latin jazz great Gilberto Bebel called *Tanto Tiempo* that I hadn't heard for a time, threw some rubbish out and sat down on the greenish-black cloth sofa. I didn't know what to do next.

I didn't feel like sleeping. My mind was alert and I wasn't at all drowsy. I felt lonely, that loneliness like lamplight that pierces glitteringly through your consciousness to the deepest part. Bebel's singing voice was so soft it made you want to find someone to share the evening with.

I hummed lightly along with the music, amazed to discover that in the soft light I suddenly couldn't see any shadows anywhere. I was sitting alone on the sofa, without even my shadow.

There was nobody softly calling my name, no-one touching my knee.

Humming along, I went slowly into the bathroom, filled the

bath with water, added a lot of strongly-scented crystals and climbed in after them.

Lying in the hot water, I scrubbed myself with a round pink sponge. The CD player was playing track eight, 'Lonely', and Bebel was singing again and again: 'Lonely, lonely, lonely.' Every pore of my skin sang 'lonely, lonely, lonely' along with her. A fish struggles in a net, a rose struggles against being plucked, a woman wet in ecstasy approaches oblivion. But there are always one or two things which stay absolutely still. In the silence drops of vapour condensed into little pearls of water and dripped down from the ceiling making faint *dha* sounds.

I got out of the tub, wrapped a big towel around myself, and stumbled, exhausted, towards the bedroom.

The phone rang. I picked up the receiver and heard a pleasant voice say in English: 'Have we met?'

I panicked. The voice sounded familiar, the tone was familiar too.

'Excellent. So you're in Shanghai . . .' He laughed. 'I told you I'd see you again.'

Suddenly my head began to spin. Every time he appeared I went blank. Maybe his body had a special electro-magnetic field and the wave he gave off had a destructive, seductive quality. And he appeared like a UFO, whenever you expected him least.

'Nick!' I exclaimed without meaning to. 'You're in Shanghai?'

30

Ferragamo Christmas Tree

Can officially confirm that the way to a man's heart these days is not
through beauty, food, sex, or alluringness of character, but merely the
ability to seem not very interested in him.
Helen Fielding, *Bridget Jones's Diary*

He was dressed all in black, Armani. He stood in the cavernous lobby of the Ritz-Carlton hotel, watching as I passed through the revolving door and crossed over the waterway on a little arched stone bridge.

Nick was smiling and running his hand through his thick hair. Then he came over to greet me, gently catching my waist and lightly planting a kiss on my lips. Proper, elegant – people were looking at us.

'We're the perfect couple,' he whispered in my ear, his smiling eyes occasionally moving from my face to my clothes. I was all in black too, my whole body sleek in black silk.

'You look gorgeous in silk.'

'Thank you,' I said.

'It's like a dream seeing you again. You've no idea how happy I am.' He took my hand, leading me towards the second-floor banquet hall where a huge charity benefit was being held. It was the reason he'd invited me here.

'I'm happy too,' I said. 'But it doesn't seem real, You make life seem like a Hollywood movie, too comical.'

'Ever since I was a kid I've liked being different. Everyday life doesn't suit me,' he said. We reached the door to the banquet hall and the waiters nodded and bowed, addressing him by name. They obviously recognized him.

'Tonight we have more time to get to know each other, but the important thing is for you to get to know me. I regret that I didn't write a book for you to read so you could get to find out about me.'

Nick meant that he'd already read my book.

'You think you already understand me?' I asked in a low voice. A young woman escorted us to a table near the rostrum. He waved and smiled at people, greeting them. We sat down.

'Shanghai's development is really amazing. My parents weren't even sure at first where Shanghai was until I sent them a copy of your book. I told them I might marry you.' He finished speaking, watching my reaction.

I took a look at him. 'I just saw a Japanese cartoon with an Italian story. There was an American whose catchphrase was "I want to marry you".'

'So you're refusing me?' he asked.

'Were you proposing?' I retorted.

He laughed. 'I like your glib tongue.'

Just then a man walked in front of us. I looked closer. I wasn't completely sure, but I thought I knew him. Oh my God! The man with the stiffly sprayed hair, wearing a smart suit and looking slightly too neat was none other than my former fiancé, Qi Feihong. We hadn't seen each other in five years.

He seemed to have recognized me already. 'Ai ya ya, look who it is!' As he stretched out his hand, a flood of memories came back. When he said 'Ai ya ya' his tone hadn't changed a bit; it was still sarcastic, effeminate. I felt like punching him on the nose, but then he might say: 'Ai ya ya, what are you doing?'

I took a deep breath, put on a neutral expression – this was a camouflage that I sometimes used – and said, 'Oh, how are you?' I extended my arm and shook hands with him.

After a disorderly exchange of greetings, his glance fell on Nick. Clearly Nick's near-perfect exterior left a deep impression. 'Is this your husband?' he asked in English.

I quickly shook my head and Nick guffawed, clapping him on the shoulder. 'That's a very good association of ideas!'

Qi Feihong called over a woman wearing furs appropriate for winter. She was his new bride. Her features were flawless, but her face was the kind that was hard to remember. I was reminded of Xi'er's account after the wedding: vain, docile, good-looking, totally lacking in sex-appeal.

We all exchanged greetings, after which they sat at a neighbouring table.

'Small world.' I forced a smile.

'He doesn't like me,' Nick said. 'Could you tell?'

'Not too many men would like you,' I said, giving him a sideways glance. In this banquet hall, handsome and suave, Nick stood out from the crowd. Sometimes God wasn't fair.

The banquet began. The host made a speech; the waiters began serving food for each table, but the guests' minds weren't on it.

One after another illustrious figures made speeches at the rostrum, from the Mayor's wife to the president of the charity; to diplomats from all the countries stationed with their wives in Shanghai. Children from welfare institutions performed a number to unanimous applause. Then the auction began. Judging from the programme in my hand, there would be a scarf signed by Placido Domingo during a recent recital in Shanghai; some expensive vintage of French red wine; a signed poster from the 2002 Tennis Masters cup in Shanghai; a Ferragamo Christmas tree; a home-cooked meal for ten by the chef at the Ritz-Carlton; a piano lesson with a world-famous pianist and much more of the same.

The auctioneer rhythmically called out the items. When he got to the Ferragamo Christmas tree, Nick joined the bidding. 'I want to give it to you,' he said. 'That way even if we don't spend Christmas together you'll think of me.'

Bidding for the tree started at 8000RMB and began to rise slowly until finally only Nick and Qi Feihong were competing.

'Give up!' I whispered to him.

'This isn't about a tree anymore.' Nick's hands were clenched,

'This is about male pride now. It's ridiculous.' Amidst the auctioneer's shouts, Nick raised his hand again to signal, increasing the figure.

'You're crazy,' I said in a low voice, 'You could buy seven pairs of Manolo Blahniks with that money.'

'I don't like the way your ex-fiancé keeps staring at your legs,' he said. I shifted them self-consciously.

'Remember, we came here to donate money to those cute children.' He winked and flashed me a smile. I glanced over at the children from the welfare institutions sitting happily to one side and shut my mouth.

When the banquet was over, the waiters asked where the super-expensive Christmas tree should be delivered. Nick said: 'We'd best go to your place now. I could make a few suggestions about the best place to put it.'

I interrupted, 'Perhaps we should put it in your room first, then when you leave you can send it to my place.' Nick looked at me as if he was seeing right through me and smiled slightly. 'Don't worry, kid, we'll do whatever you want.'

He turned and said to the waiter: 'Please take it to my room.' I thought this was a good opportunity to say goodbye to him.

'I have to go,' I said. 'Thanks for inviting me, I had fun tonight.'

He grabbed hold of me. 'Just ten minutes!' Practically staring into my eyes he said, 'Let's go to my room. I forgot to give you your present, it's right there, you can leave when you've got it, okay? I promise.'

I couldn't say no.

Following like a procession behind the huge and extravagant Christmas tree, we took the lift and walked along the corridor. Wherever we went people saluted us. When we reached Nick's four-room suite, the two young waiters, huffing and puffing, laid the huge, brightly-coloured tree down by the living room sofa. 'Excellent!' Nick gave the waiters a tip and closed the door. He stared at me amorously.

I stood terror-stricken by the tree, with my arms folded tightly. Now what should I do? Even a stupid woman could predict what was going to happen next. 'But not tonight . . .' I said to myself. 'I have to preserve my chastity at least tonight.'

'Want something to drink?' he asked. There was audible tension in his voice; the desire was already rising from the soles of his feet.

'No thanks,' I said, parched, looking helplessly at the clock on the wall.

He was clearly sensitive to this and said quickly: 'Oh, ten minutes I said! Right now I've probably got four minutes left.' He rushed into one of the rooms where his luggage was, searched around in a flurry and then brought out something wrapped in purple paper.

'I don't know if you'll like it. It's a book I've read many times.'

I opened it and looked at it. It was *Steppenwolf* by Hermann Hesse. He watched my expression. 'Don't you like it?' he asked.

I didn't know how to answer. It was another stunt! He never played according to the rules; he always surprised me. But this was more dangerous. The weightiness of the book had turned the matter of the two of us into something serious. To give a woman a book isn't the action of a Casanova. I didn't want to associate him with ordinary and accessible happiness.

He would always be a UFO disguised as Casanova, appearing when and where you least expected him, but then disappearing again.

'No,' I said cautiously, 'I like it. Thank you.'

I didn't tell him that Hesse had recently become one of my favourite authors.

'I still have one minute,' he said in a low voice, 'Let me see you to the lift.'

We walked out of the room. 'You really don't need me to take you home?' he asked again

I smiled. 'Shanghai is safer than New York.'

He sighed. 'It makes me sad.' But he quickly decided to cheer up, and smiled again. 'For the next few days, would you be willing to show me around Shanghai?'

There were dark circles under his eyes. Perhaps it was jet-lag.

That evening when I got home and had gone to bed, insomnia appeared like a wisp of smoke from Aladdin's Lamp and surrounded my head.

I suddenly decided to get up and call Muju in New York. After dialling the numbers, I heard the sound of his voice on the answering machine. I didn't leave a message, but hung up the phone and dialled again. Still no answer. After listening to his message again I hung up. Just listening to his voice was helpful. Muju's raspy voice on the answering machine was now my only physical connection with life in New York.

Then I called Xi'er. Right then she was busy at Shanghai 1933. I didn't want to take too much of her time, just to tell her simply that I'd run into my former fiancé at a charity auction at the Ritz-Carlton.

'You ran into Qi Feihong? Did you see his wife? What did you think?' Xi'er spoke rapidly.

'Nothing in particular,' I said indifferently.

'That's exactly it,' she said approvingly. Men like to choose that type of woman for a wife.' After half a second, she suddenly remembered something. 'Aiya, what were you doing at a charity auction at the Ritz-Carlton?'

'Um,' I stammered, not knowing how to tell her about Nick. The whole thing was too much like a soap opera, I was afraid it would arouse her curiosity. 'Actually it was nothing,' I prevaricated, 'a friend invited me.'

'Wow, wait until I have time, you have to tell me all about this mysterious friend.' She laughed loudly. We said goodnight quickly and hung up.

Then I looked for the thin volume of *Incantations of the Great Mercy* that the Master of Empty Nature had given me when I left Putuo Island. I read it slowly and just as slowly calmed down, gradually drifted off to sleep.

The next morning, I was still dreaming when I was woken by the phone. I knew even in my toes who it was.

'I have a meeting all day, but have turned down everything for the evening. Can you suggest a place we could have dinner?' said Nick.

'Shanghai 1933.'

The proprietor Xi'er was decked out like last night's Christmas tree. Her whole body shimmered. The hordes of female customers dressed to kill made it feel like we'd wandered into a fox's den by mistake. As luck had it, that evening there was a party called 'Night of the Temptresses'. Xi'er told me on the phone: 'Actually it's a game where you buy men.' Nick was excited when he heard this.

'You really want to go?' I asked. 'It'll be full of women who despise men, gays and some rotten old paedophiles.'

'Let's go,' he said.

Adam, Xi'er's new boyfriend, sat at the table with us. The green-eyed Australian had ruddy skin and a conspicuous nose that made you think of that other part of his body. He was dressed tastefully enough, but his speech and manner seemed wired wrong; something wasn't quite right. His sense of humour was sometimes really tasteless. The last time I'd called Xi'er, he answered the phone. 'Xi'er? Oh, she's busy with something in my lap right now. Ha ha, just kidding, she's coming,' Adam had said.

Xi'er was busy with the crowd. After half an hour, she came over, surreptitiously threw a coquettish glance at Nick and then sat down and gave Adam a kiss. 'It's about to begin!' she said.

We started to eat and drink. The music suddenly stopped. A man in make-up cracked a few jokes and then a row of young guys suddenly appeared under the lights. There were men of every skin colour, but most were white, all were handsome, and one was a dead ringer for a young Tom Cruise.

'God, where did you find them?' I asked.

'Half of them are waiters in my restaurant, half are overseas students. I put an ad in the English-language classifieds, and immediately got fifty responses. Lots of poor foreigners in Shanghai right now,' said Xi'er, taking a drag on her cigarette.

Nick shook his head, saying to me: 'Don't stare at those boys so obviously.'

The women customers began to go wild. They'd order a boy they had their eyes on and the boy would go over to their table and be the waiter for that table, pouring them wine, lighting their cigarettes and keeping them company. Of course for the privilege they had to pay a big tip. 'Tom Cruise' was spotted by several tables at once and a bidding war broke out. In the end the one with the most money won.

'Hopeless,' said Xi'er, emptying the wine in her glass in one gulp.

'But this was your idea,' I said.

'The clients like it,' said Xi'er.

'It's about energy. It's the energy of our age. The desire for women's rights is really unusual. Ultimately it'll destroy the world,' said Adam.

Xi'er and I went to the cloakroom together. As soon as we were inside, Xi'er squealed, 'Where did you find a guy like that?' She placed both hands on her chest, closed her eyes and groaned. 'Oh, he's too fucking charming.' She used uncharacteristically coarse language. 'I love him too!' She hugged me.

'Then the guy's yours,' I said, raising my eyebrows as I started to do my hair in the mirror.

'Seriously, he's better than all your old boyfriends put together.' Xi'er started to do her hair in the mirror.

I looked at her oddly. This was the very first time that Xi'er had not only not attacked a man I was with, but generously despatched truckload after truckload of praise.

'You don't need to think about Muju, and you don't need to think about everlasting love. A guy like Nick is worth it even if it's only a one-night stand.' She carefully applied lipstick in the mirror. 'If you don't feel like it, how about lending him to me for a night?' Xi'er giggled.

I was reluctant to admit it, but I agreed with what Xi'er said. Most women would think so. In life it isn't likely you'll ever run into a man as able to satisfy your dreams as Nick. He had it all, like flowers that bloom at night: so splendid, overwhelming, inconceivable, and then disappearing without the slightest trace.

'What do you think of Adam?' she asked.

'Better than I thought,' I said. 'Since you like crazy men.'

We walked out of the cloakroom and sat back down for a while.

'We have to go,' said Nick. Then he turned to Xi'er. 'Do you want to meet up at some other bar or shall we say goodbye now?'

'Oh, this is going to finish up pretty late.' Xi'er winked at me. 'Have fun, you two.'

31

Do You Need a Reason to Love?

Don't threaten me with love, baby.
Let's just go walking in the rain.
Billie Holiday

In his sumptuous suite, the multi-coloured lights twinkled on
the Christmas tree.

We sat on the sofa watching a DVD we'd just bought: *The Bourne Identity*, with Matt Damon and Franka Potente. There was a big pile of disks on top of the TV. When foreigners first come to Shanghai they're dumbfounded with delight to discover that a dollar can buy you a DVD on the street. I didn't like the movie but liked Franka. When I was in Munich I'd spent the afternoon chatting with her and then we'd had dinner together. She had a certain bookishness you didn't often find in Hollywood. And I thought she was really cool in *Run Lola Run*. Nick was also a fan of hers.

I suddenly got a headache about halfway through the movie.

'I have to go,' I said.

He held his face and groaned. 'Since we've met that's the phrase you've used most often.'

I looked down.

'You don't like me a bit?' he asked, his eyes fixed on the screen, a desolate expression on his face. 'Can I make you like me before I make you say "I have to go" again?' He still didn't look at me.

His despairing expression made me agitated. The truth was,

I'd been poisoned the first time I saw him as though I wanted to be destroyed.

'Do you like me?' I asked. Clearly it was a foolish question.

'What do you think?' He turned his head, smiling, clearly enjoying that I was being foolish.

'Why?' I asked.

'Do you need a reason for liking someone?' he retorted.

'I'm still getting over someone else,' I said. My tears fell.

'Oh!' he sighed, holding me, touching my hair. 'When you're like this it makes me want to fall in love with you. I really want to carry you over to the bed, but I don't want to take advantage of someone's distress, unless someday you want to sleep with me yourself.' He placed my hand on his lower abdomen. He was rock hard. There was even the faint trace of moisture on his trousers. Instantly I snapped out of it and pulled back my hand.

'Can I take you home?' he asked softly.

We said goodbye at the door to my place. 'Are you free tomorrow? I want to see you every day before I leave,' he said. 'Think about it. When we're together, every second is fun, even when we're watching a DVD together! That must mean something. I seriously like you, otherwise I wouldn't have given you Hermann Hesse. Look at me, listen to me. Baby, you're different from the rest, full of contradictions, and I'm enchanted by it.'

After that, we went out every night to different restaurants and bars around Shanghai. Sometimes he'd bring his assistant, an American guy with glasses, so I invited Zhu Sha and Xi'er to join us.

Nick knew that Eric was coming to Shanghai. He said to Zhu Sha: 'I'm worried about Eric. He may seem rational on the outside but in fact he's addicted to fantasy.'

Zhu Sha said: 'I'm worried about myself. I feel numb towards men now.'

Xi'er said: 'I just read an article that said people with thin lips are cold-hearted and people with thick lips are trustworthy.'

Then in unison we all turned to look at Nick's lips. He smiled at us, revealing a set of snow-white teeth.

Nick described Shanghai's nightlife as 'typical big city nightlife'. It's true, Shanghai's nightlife had become even more sensually dissolute and complicated, but it had changed greatly in the three years since I'd written *Shanghai Baby*. Now there were fewer convention-defying artists and more CEOs in suits as tight as rolled umbrellas.

Wherever I went I checked out the cloakrooms. I believe that you can tell the quality of a restaurant by the style of its toilets – it's known as judging the whole leopard by one spot.

In the cloakroom at TMSK there was a large crystal lotus. When you touched it, fine jets of water would spray out automatically from the pistils. Apparently it had some religious significance for the proprietor.

The cloakroom at the Number 7 Club had photos on its door, including a shocking shot of a fat man leaning over counting a thick wad of cash. The club was the former residence of the 1930s and 40s crime-boss, Du Yuesheng. The cloakroom at The Doors had baroque mirrors where you could see countless reflections of yourself, but that was relatively common. The Va Va Room had an entire wall full of butterfly specimens that was quite magnificent, but after a while looking at it gave me the creeps. The outside wall of the cloakroom in Grand Hyatt 88 was clear glass, making you feel like you were peeing in front of the entire city. Park 97's cloakrooms were the trendsetters of Shanghai: pink lamps, a large red sofa, white flowers. It was like a bordello from old Shanghai. In that warm pink light a woman's skin looked sleek and free of blemishes; even the bags under her eyes disappeared. When it first opened, a middle-aged Shanghainese female attendant in a white shirt stood at the door. For a small fee she would seat the guest in a chair for a massage.

I remember that white-shirted masseuse with fondness. She worked with a neutral expression, but the folds of her baggy white shirt always gave off the scent of dried lavender, as if it had just been pulled from an old, lavender-scented wooden trunk.

That day, it rained heavily and the weather suddenly turned cold. I sat in my study writing in my diary.

The heater was on. It was quite warm in the room, but beyond the glass window was another world altogether. I don't like the cold weather, but I've always enjoyed rainy days. Muju once told me that this had to do with my body's excessive Yin energy, though I thought it had to do with low blood pressure. Muji had also said he'd never seen a woman with so many contradictions that my body was filled with conflicting energies – in Taoist terms there was 'an abundance of Yang, as well as an abundance of Yin'.

I closed the diary, stood in front of the window and watched the rain. Torrents pounded down and the whole world seemed on the verge of disintegrating. This only served to accentuate the feeling of tranquility and safety inside. I couldn't help smiling.

It was Nick's last day in Shanghai. In an hour, he would pick me up and take me to dinner at an Italian restaurant. The whole time he'd been in Shanghai we seemed to dine together constantly – but nothing else.

This time would be a bit different. We had a tacit understanding. I wasn't afraid to sleep with a guy – quite the opposite, I took pleasure in it. But confronted with Nick, strangely, I would think of the word 'chastity', a chastity that could have symbolized me.

Surprisingly, Nick was even more restrained than he'd been in New York or in Spain – or we wouldn't have been able to spend so many easy days together.

I wandered from one room to another. I'd already changed clothes, as usual into black silk with a touch of green and very close-fitting. Then it occurred to me something was missing. In the bathroom I found the ruby earrings that Muju had bought me in Argentina and hooked them into my ears. I couldn't wear the white gold necklace as it didn't go with the outfit. I smiled at the girl in the mirror – she certainly liked complicated situations and she was full of contradictions.

The telephone rang. Nick was waiting downstairs with the car.

I changed into high-heeled Via Spiga shoes and went down. He pushed open the car door holding an umbrella and ran over to me. 'Hurry up, kid, or we'll have to swim to dinner.'

The driver drove slowly in the pouring rain. It was rush hour. Nick twisted and turned, looking impatient.

I touched his hand and smiled at him. 'How do you feel?'

He kissed my hand. 'Much better.' He no longer stared at the rain-drenched cars crawling along in the heavy traffic. Eventually he said, 'You know what? You're different from when I first met you.'

I looked at him with a smile, wondering what he would say next.

Then he said: 'Look at you, you smile more than you did in New York or in Spain.'

I smiled until my eyes squinted. 'Oh? Actually you're different too.'

'How?' he asked curiously.

'You notice things more than you did before. It's still "me me me", but you're slowly starting to observe things beyond yourself.'

He laughed loudly. 'Oh, you're so sweet.'

The restaurant was called Shanghai's #1. It was an Italian restaurant, and celebrities like Pavarotti would go there when they were in town.

We sat down. Our waiter walked over, all smiles. 'Do you have white truffles and a good vintage red wine?' Nick asked. 'I'm going to help you learn to enjoy something besides Chinese food,' he assured me.

'Never mind,' I said picking up the menu. There were Chinese translations of the dishes' names.

We didn't say any more, as we ordered food and began to eat.

'Say something.' I put down my fork and looked at him. I wasn't accustomed to a silent Nick.

'Be with me tonight,' he said, his unblinking blue gaze boring into me and the corner of his mouth curling upwardss. He looked as though he would crush anyone who stood in his path.

When we'd eaten and settled the bill, Nick carried me piggy-back down the stairs from the third floor to the first floor. At first I struggled and tried to make him put me down. Then I became afraid of tearing my tight dress, so I gave up. I let him carry me on his back, my legs sticking inelegantly out from the side slits of my *qipao*; once again a public spectacle. Don't forget, Nick enjoyed standing out in a crowd.

I sat on the sofa next to the Ferragamo Christmas tree, my feet on the coffee table in front of me, switching channels with the remote control. A news item on CNN said the White House hadn't excluded the possibility of military action in Iraq. The BBC was talking about the problem of nuclear weapons in North Korea. Finally I turned to MTV and watched some girls dressed like lollipops singing and dancing.

Nick was carrying items from room to room. 'I hate putting my luggage in order,' he said. 'If we get married, will you pack for me?'

'If I pack for you, will you marry me?' I replied, eyes glued to the television.

He placed carrot juice and a chocolate bar under my nose. 'Thanks,' I said, 'You're really thoughtful.'

'Tonight, I am your slave,' he said. 'If at any time I don't satisfy you, you can spank me.'

We used different bathrooms. He gave me the cosier-looking one. I sat in the bath chewing my fingernails and staring into space until he knocked on the door.

'Five more minutes,' I said. I could sense him waiting outside and after five minutes he knocked again.

'Coco, are you all right?'

'I'm fine.' Saying it, I rose slowly from the bath, dried myself and smoothed on some skin lotion. Then I slipped back into my black-with-a-hint-of-green dress and put the ruby earrings back on.

I opened the door and Nick looked at my clothes in surprise. 'What are you going to do?'

I lay on the bed. He touched the slippery silk encasing my body. 'So beautiful. A pity to tear it.' He watched me, gasping with excitement.

I give him a lingering kiss, and then released him. 'Go ahead, please. The sound of silk being torn – it's the best aphrodisiac in the world,' I murmured.

'What will you wear home tomorrow?' he asked suddenly.

'I have spare clothes in my bag,' I said. We looked at each other for a few seconds, then burst out laughing.

'God, I've never seen a woman like you before,' he said. 'I'll be right back.' Bare-chested, he went to the drinks cabinet.

After downing several drinks Nick became Bacchus, suddenly ruthless, tearing the silk that clung to me with skilled movements. The torn silk floated down like petals, classically decadent. The tearing sound was incomparable, delicate, dainty, arousing ecstasy deep within the flesh.

Excited by desire, we surrendered everything, everything . . . the world had already been torn, we were the tattered fragments floating soundless in the air, floating unconsciously, floating . . .

Gasping. Consciousness came back; horrified, I felt wetness between my legs – he hadn't used a condom. I jumped out of bed and charged into the bathroom.

He followed holding me from behind. 'God, are you all right?'

I shook my head. 'I don't know.' He turned on the tap and helped me wash. He was very gentle and I felt much better. 'Now help me,' he said as he turned off the tap.

'What?' I said.

He stood in front of the toilet.

I stood next to him, holding his cock with one hand to help him pee. 'Pervert!' I said. 'I've never had a man ask me to do this before.'

'You spoil me,' he said, and then with a groan, 'It's not working, it won't come out, it's just making me hard again.' I glanced down and sure enough it was.

He roared like a tiger, picked me up, spread my legs and put them around his waist. I closed my eyes and felt him enter me again.

The next morning, we kissed a quick goodbye. He went to the airport and I went home. Soon after, the hotel staff moved the Ferragamo Christmas tree to my flat.

32

One Leaves and One Arrives

Question: The wind blows and the flag moves.
Is the wind moving, or is the flag moving?
Zen Master Hui Neng: Neither the wind nor the flag
is moving; rather it is your heart that is moving.

The morning I said goodbye to Nick, it was cold and
overcast and the smell of burning coal filled the air. The
birds had vanished, the last leaf had fallen from the trees.

I went home exhausted and went directly to the phone.

When I heard Muju's voice on the answering machine a wave
of helplessness rushed over me. I didn't understand what was
happening around me, I could only accept it.

Muju said he'd be in Tokyo at an independent film-makers'
festival, he'd entered his documentary about the Dominican
singer Julio. Recently he'd been insanely busy polishing the final
edit. He had some new commercial clients too. Purely for the
money.

Muju said he'd be in Shanghai in two days' time, a last-minute
decision, because he suddenly wanted to see me. He left his
number in Tokyo and made a kissing noise. 'See you in
Shanghai!' he said.

I replayed his message again and again not just to hear his
voice but to try to conjure up the scent of him. How did he feel
about us now, what was he thinking? Was he coming to Shanghai
to be reunited with me or to pronounce us totally separated, and
just become ordinary friends?

I phoned Xi'er. She was still asleep and answered groggily, 'I beg you, Beautiful, wait till I wake up, I'll definitely call you back.' She hung up the phone.

I called Zhu Sha. She was in the middle of an important meeting. I left a message with her secretary and hung up.

At that moment there was no one to share my puzzled excitement.

I decided to have breakfast and then bathe, and then to meditate in the lotus position, praying to the gods above.

Xi'er flew down the expressway in her little green Beetle. I sat beside her. We were on the way to Pudong Airport. The music was blasting, distracting me a little.

Xi'er chattered constantly: 'I want to get a good look at exactly what kind of person it is that merits the honour of our royal entourage meeting him at the airport. To tell the truth, it troubles me a bit that you care so much about a man. Think about – when you were in New York he wouldn't meet you at the airport at all. Damn it, why are there are so many cars? If this traffic continues it will take over an hour to get there.'

I chewed gum and said nothing.

'Why? Why?' Xi'er said in a sing-song voice. 'Why are women so stupid?'

Xi'er pulled into the airport's short-term parking. I powdered my face, turned and asked, 'How do I look?'

'As if you weren't wearing make-up,' she said, looking me over.

'That's the effect I want,' I said.

The waiting area was crowded. A meticulously made-up woman stood holding a bouquet of fresh flowers.

'I'd die before I bring flowers to meet anyone,' I said quietly to Xi'er.

Then the loudspeakers announced that Muju's flight had already arrived.

Immediately I began to worry, pacing back and forth, my palms sweaty. Xi'er pushed her sunglasses onto her head. With piercing, spirited eyes she examined the stream of travellers pouring through the gate. 'I have to get a good look at him,' she whispered.

We waited a long time without any sign of Muju. But when I turned my head, suddenly I saw him. In the Asian crowd he stood out by his height. He seemed to have lost a lot of weight. He'd come out of another exit. He saw me at the same time and came striding towards us, pushing his luggage.

We were strangely shy with each other. We hugged a bit hastily. It wasn't as overwhelming as I'd imagined it would be on the way to the airport. Then I introduced him to Xi'er and Xi'er extended a hand, but Muju leaned over and kissed both of her cheeks. She didn't expect this, and her face grew red. Xi'er looked especially cute when she blushed.

Xi'er noted Muju's missing fingertip with sympathy. Later she mentioned that she thought he had a mysterious, old-fashioned air about him.

It took us another hour to drive back to the centre of the city. The green Beetle manoeuvred slowly through the stop-go traffic, with two thin girls in the front seats and a great bear-like man folded into the small rear seat. This car was designed for women and by its size excluded large men. But Muju endured the discomfort happily, pleased that two pretty girls had driven to the airport to meet his plane. Any man would feel overwhelmed by such an unexpected favour. Muju thought Xi'er and her car were really adorable.

When we reached my place, Xi'er reminded us of our dinner date, then drove off. I helped Muju carry his luggage inside. Muju seemed amazed by what he saw once we were inside. 'I never thought it would be this neat,' he said. Surely he was remembering New York, where I instantly made the space unrecognizable. 'You've changed since New York.' He added, 'Your apartment is really attractive.' He was referring to the style of the 1930s French villa with its wooden staircase and huge balcony. Once many similar villas existed in Shanghai's former foreign concessions, but now there were fewer and fewer.

Then Muju saw the Ferragamo Christmas tree, looking like a prop from *Star Wars*. He walked over and examined it for a moment, saying nothing. As I emerged from the kitchen with a cup of tea and saw his expression as he considered the tree, I feared that some sixth sense of his picked up on the existence of another man.

We took our tea with us as we toured the house. 'I like your house,' he said.

'This is your room.' I pointed to a room with a desk, a chair, a beautiful reading lamp, a fax, and some toy peaches. He glanced at the peaches, then looked at me. I smiled slightly, walking away as if I hadn't noticed.

Muju put his arms round my waist from behind. 'I can't not love you,' he said. He blew warm air into my ear and I melted. I trembled all over, my heart beating extra fast and my eyes closed. It was a chemical reaction and, even more, a psychological response.

We spent the entire afternoon in bed, making love, making pillow talk and making love again.

It was Muju's first time in Shanghai. My Shanghai self, my old French flat, a giant, soft bed giving off the scent of light rain and flowers – all this formed an irresistible and magical ambience: a sentimental spell of Oriental love and lust no one could break.

We lay naked under the pale gold silk cover, silk pillows the same colour under our heads. He twisted several loose strands of my long hair around his fingers, playing with them peacefully.

It seemed ages since we'd seen each other. I knew he still loved me and that his love was more deeply rooted than before.

'You smell wonderful,' Muju commented. He always said this after we made love. He was very tuned in to the scents I emitted after orgasm. Women are basically like a kind of incense and making love is like burning this incense and letting its scent float out.

I snuggled quietly into his arms.

Much later, I said softly, 'Leave your mark on my body.'

He looked at me.

I turned over and moved close against him and kissed his neck forcefully for a while. An impressive red welt appeared. 'Like this.' Gently I said, 'Do that to me. You can do anything you want to my body, it belongs to you, but you have to love it, you can't stop loving it.'

He closed his eyes, holding me absolutely still. 'I can't stop loving you.' Much later he opened his mouth and said, 'Sometimes when two people have separated, it may look to others like their love has faded or they themselves may think their love is gone, but that's not true. Love is still there. Even if you're not aware of it, love doesn't disappear, it persists.'

I closed my eyes and felt an intangible, tempestuous wave surge through the room. We were floating on that wave and the extraordinary fragrance of water-lilies permeated the room. There was no other existence, just this unhurried world, the two of us, him and me, tenderly attached to each other, snuggling close.

'I love you.' I heard my voice as if in a dream. Love is somehow intertwined with dreams.

We walked to Shanghai 1933. Muju had only two days in Shanghai, so walking would show him some of the city that couldn't be seen by car. The centre of Shanghai was the same as Manhattan – good walking gave one flavour and a sense of is energy.

As we strolled past a small alley, we saw a group of people. Muju walked over with his camera and took a shot of four old men playing mah-jong. Their cumulative age must have been three hundred years. This event pleased Muju enormously. The old men and the mah-jong satisfied part of his image of Chinese culture.

The little alley was squeezed between several tall buildings, so tall that you couldn't see the tops even if you craned your neck. Beside them was a half-built building, the exterior wall enclosed in a giant green safety net.

We wandered down Huaihai Road. Muju said: 'Shanghai women are more sophisticated than Shanghai men.'

'Perhaps you think that because you're naturally more sensitive to women, more observant,' I teased him. But in fact what he said was true – it was a woman's city.

We arrived at Shanghai 1993. Xi'er had reserved us a cosy corner with soft red chairs with softer green cushions – a very Chinese feel; from it you could see the bright streetlights.

Xi'er, all in black, emerged from several screens of green bamboo holding an empty birdcage. She looked a little sad. 'A little bird died,' she said, embracing us. We could smell her Opium perfume.

'I'll be right back.' She disappeared again behind the bamboo. Xi'er had a unique sway to her gait and Muju kept taking pictures. 'Everything is like a movie here,' he said, training the lense on me.

'Welcome to Shanghai 1933!' I blew a kiss to the camera.

The waiter brought our menus. Muju could only read a little Chinese, but the dishes were also listed in English. The most expensive among them was called 'The Cut-throat Concubine'. He asked what that was, and I explained that this was another name for the proprietress, Xi'er, insinuating that she'd fixed an especially high price for it; a hidden knife to rob the customers. The dish was originally called 'Buddha Jumps the Wall'. It was the main course of the legendary Manchu and Han Banquet. According to custom, the Manchu and Han Banquet is eaten for three days straight and altogether there are 108 types of dish. Its ingredients include sea cucumber slices, shark's fin, abalone, pigeon egg, tendons of pork, chicken, duck and more than twenty other delicacies, plus a marrow broth, rice wine, turnips and other vegetables blended with spices according to a centuries-old recipe. The duration and degree of heating when you cook it requires meticulous attention. Then it is sealed in a large liquor-jar with a lotus leaf and baked at a low heat until it's done. The juice is mellow and rich, aromatic and intoxicating, hence the expression 'When the scent of food wafts over to one's neighbours, even the Buddha ceases his meditation and comes climbing over the wall.'

Muju listened, his whole face full of yearning. 'I can't stop salivating,' he said. 'Let's try it.'

'They don't always have this dish. For one thing it's so expensive that people don't often order it, and some of the rarer ingredients aren't always available – you have to ask the chef first,' I said.

At that point Xi'er and her Opium scent came over.

'Do you have "Buddha Jumps the Wall"?' asked Muju.

'You mean "The Cut-throat Concubine"?' Xi'er quickly corrected him. 'That dish is a lot of trouble.' She beckoned a blue-eyed waiter. 'Go ask the chef if we have "The Cut-throat Concubine".'

'If you order that, then you're not going to want anything else,' I said, reaching an arm around Xi'er's slender waist and switching to a cat-like voice: 'Xi'er, the Cut-throat Concubine . . . Shanghai Princess.'

She was tickled speechless, pushing aside my hand. 'Okay, okay – if you pay for the dish, I'll give you any other dish as well as a bottle of the best rice wine, and provide you with unlimited superior-grade tea – if your stomachs can fit that much in.'

Happily, the kitchen had the dish. It was being prepared for a regular customer but something had come up and that person couldn't make it. So we got it.

Before tasting anything, Muju took pictures of the large tray overflowing with old-fashioned delicacies in ceramic pots. 'Later when I'm feeling greedy I can watch the tape,' he said. 'Too bad you can't shoot the smells as well.'

Xi'er did send over a number of extra dishes, until Muju said 'Stop.' In Muju's eyes, conserving food was the first principle of a true gourmet. All food was a gift from the earth.

'People are greedy by nature,' said Xi'er. 'Sometimes you have to use people's greedy hearts to earn money.'

Then with rapt expressions Xi'er and Muju discussed the mysterious and unparalleled complete Manchu and Han banquet.

'I heard that in order to keep eating for three days and three nights, some people take laxatives and some people swallow tapeworms,' said Muju.

'Ha,' said Xi'er. 'That's nothing. A hundred years ago when a restaurant in Guangzhou made the complete Manchu and Han banquet, someone had living centipedes and baby rats rolled up in a pastry to eat. You know that people from Guangzhou will eat anything.'

'I'm going to vomit,' I said, getting up and heading for the lavatory.

When I returned, Xi'er had already had someone make me a pot of Wulong tea. She looked at me. 'Are you all right? Was it the food? You always eat a lot.'

Muju said too: 'You look pale.'

'Cut the nonsense, it's just confusing me. All I want is a cup of tea,' I said.

That evening we hit a few hot-spots together. The camcorder in Muju's hand ran constantly. He wanted to derive wisdom and energy from every second of the experience, otherwise he felt his life was being wasted. He joined a crowd of dancers. He waved to me, exaggeratedly swaying his shoulders and bum, grinning broadly like an adolescent.

Xi'er stood next to me drinking tequila and smoking a cigarette. 'He's very cute,' she yelled over the music.

'I know,' I shouted back.

'Which one will you pick? Nick? Or him?' Xi'er continued to shout.

I glanced at her in surprise and shrugged, and then leaned my mouth close to her ear. 'You think I have the right to choose? Destiny will choose, darling. All we can do is keep smiling and pray!'

'You know what? If it was me, I would choose both of them!'

Xi'er laughed heartily, chin high and head thrown back. Unlike Zhu Sha, Xi'er never covered her mouth with her hand when she laughed.

'But then you woudn't get either of them,' I said softly, which of course she couldn't hear.

The next day – Muju's last day in Shanghai – we spent looking for good restaurants, going to the most expensive department stores and visiting the Museum. At nightfall, exhausted from walking, we went to a foot-massage parlour – the one on Fuxing Street where Xi'er had taken me when I'd just returned to Shanghai. Xi'er said that the fifteen-year-old had quit. No one knew where he'd gone.

'This is the best foot-massage parlour in Shanghai,' I told Muju.

'Great!' said Muju, plopping himself down on the plush sofa. Immediately two girls came out and served us cups of tea. Then they brought out a brown-coloured Chinese herbal bath and we stuck our feet in it.

'Feels great,' Muju sighed, 'perhaps I should move to Shanghai.'

I closed my eyes and imagined living with Muju in Shanghai, having a dog, a couple of goldfish and four or five plants. His study would be downstairs, mine upstairs; the humming washing machine would be wafting out the subtle fragrance of clean clothes; we'd hire a domestic who was good at cooking, and a good-natured chauffeur with a stubbly beard who would drive Muju to work in the mornings and take me to the beauty salon or a café or bookshop in the afternoons; in the evenings we'd watch DVDs or play mah-jong with Xi'er and Zhu Sha; then one day we would wake up and suddenly discover that we'd aged and become the legends that people were always talking about.

I heard a soft snore and opened my eyes to find Muju fast asleep on the sofa, the young masseuse still rubbing his feet with her hands

That evening, he packed the luggage that he'd only just

unpacked two days earlier. I helped him take his dry underwear and socks out of the washing machine. We looked busy as we went from room to room, keeping occupied with small tasks to fill the void of impending separation.

Casablanca was playing on the TV in the living room. When I walked past I glanced at it. It was the final scene at the airport where the lovers are saying farewell. Humphrey Bogart says to Ingrid Bergman, 'We both know you belong with Victor. You're part of his work, the thing that keeps him going. If that plane leaves the ground and you're not with him, you'll regret it. Maybe not today, maybe not tomorrow, but soon and for the rest of your life.' Bergman asks: 'But what about us?' 'We'll always have Paris,' replies Bogart.

We didn't say anything as we lay on the bed. Two brief days had passed in the blink of an eye. Like a dream.

I tossed and turned next to him and the bedsprings creaked. 'Are you okay?' Muju finally asked.

'How do you feel?' I asked.

'What do you mean, how?'

'How do you feel about the past few days in Shanghai?' I said, slightly annoyed that he was asking a question when he already knew the answer.

'It's been delightful. There's a good woman here, and good food. It's the best few days I've had since I saw you that last time at the airport,' he said.

'A good woman and good food,' I muttered, unsure inside whether I was willing or able to become that kind of good woman.

He held me and began to slowly kiss my ear and my neck.

'What should we do now?' I asked, struggling to stay alert beneath his kisses.

He said nothing, but went on kissing me. There was a lot of feeling in his kisses, and a lot of caring – it wasn't just desire. After I felt these things, my whole body instantly became relaxed and warm. I began kissing him back.

Then my skin started to burn with desire. Passionate sex with Muju always helped melt away my anxieties and left me perfectly content, able to rediscover all the love that was still there, a natural part of all the things between Heaven and Earth that give off energy and light.

Suddenly, without warning, I felt Muju come inside me – the first time he'd ejaculated since I'd known him. I was so shocked I almost fainted.

33

The Fruit of Love

I cannot choose the best. The best chooses me.
Rabindranath Tagore

As the weather grew colder and the expressions on people's faces became bleak, they shrank into their thick clothing, rushing past on the street with their heads down. The trees by the roadside were bare and the curling branches looked astonishingly beautiful in the streetlights. Their mass of strange lines conjured up strange images like details in a surrealist painting.

I like observing the differences presented by each season, the varied kinds of beauty. It increases my ability to understand and value life.

After Muju left, I didn't feel particularly lonely or hurt. Some subtle change had taken place within me.

I remembered something that the Master of Empty Nature had told me on Putuo Island. Within everyone is their own perfect little world. It's a pity that many people, not grasping the perfection that exists within them, are ruled by confused emotions. They torture themselves and others with their insecurities.

I wasn't sure how far I had to go before I would see the perfect world hidden within me, but I'd already mastered smiling when you are alone, living each day to its fullest.

The second day after Muju left I developed symptoms of a cold: sneezing, cold extremities, slight dizziness. I drank hot water constantly, turned up the heat, and put on four woolly sweaters. But I found it wasn't having any effect on my good mood. As usual I read, meditated, and went for a walk.

Three or four days later, Xi'er called to complain tearfully that her Australian boyfriend Adam had gone cold on her. She suspected that he'd finally found out about her transexuality: rumour and slander circulated in Shanghai even quicker than flu.

I listened patiently as she alternated between crying over Adam and crying over the people she suspected of spreading the news; then she said she couldn't remain in Shanghai, too many people knew her secret. She was going to emigrate to America and never come back.

'Okay. We can live in New York together. You can open another restaurant in Manhattan and dozens of rich American men will chase you. Even though they're no better than the men here, and maybe even worse. But still, they won't know your secret,' I consoled her.

She said: 'I'm serious.'

I said: 'But why don't you talk with Adam? Perhaps he's gone off you for some other reason.'

'I should be a lesbian. Starting now, I'm only dating women,' she said. I laughed out loud, then cleared my throat.

'Are you sick?' she asked.

'Feels like a cold,' I replied.

'Ha,' she cried, and then said something that took my breath away: 'You could be pregnant.'

'Why?' My whole body broke out in goosebumps.

'Listen,' she said, cheering up. 'A female customer told me that for the first few days after she becomes pregnant she gets all the symptoms of a cold. She's been pregnant three times and each time was the same; now whenever she gets a cold she worries.

I clutched the receiver silently, unsure how to react. Xi'er got a lot of strange information from her customers.

'Believe me, ever since I became a woman my intuition has got better and better, more sensitive than that of a natural-born woman,' she said emphatically.

'What should I do?' I finally asked.

'The pharmacy sells pregnancy tests. Shall I buy one now and bring it over?' Xi'er was suddenly cheerful, enthusiasm ringing in her voice. For years Xi'er had begged me to swear that she would be the only godmother of any child I had. She, not my cousin Zhu Sha, who had a child of her own. Since Xi'er lacked ovaries and a womb, she said that her only chance to mother a child would be to place her hopes in coming back in her next life as a 'real' woman who could get pregnant and give birth. Of course I couldn't refuse her. Xi'er looked forward to the arrival of a precious little baby even more than I did, to the point where she once even told me: 'It's no good, just find a sperm donor. I'll pay half of the child-support.'

'Wait a few days and see!' I said hesitantly. 'If my period doesn't come in a few days, you can definitely take me to the hospital for a test.'

'You have to let me know,' she said.

'I will,' I said.

When I put down the receiver my whole body was feverish and my face was hot. My cold symptoms suddenly disappeared. 'Perhaps it's not real,' I said to myself. But thinking carefully about those nights with Nick and Muju, I couldn't rule out the possibility of pregnancy at all. But pregnant by whom? Whose child would it be?

I sat on the sofa with my face in my hands and groaned. Then I leaned back on the cushions and stared at the ceiling. Nick's and Muju's faces appeared, those nights, those caresses, those orgasms and screams. Oh! I closed my eyes again and let out another groan.

God, God, I couldn't think of it. I had to go outside for a walk, get a breath of fresh air. But wait a second, would cool air be bad for the baby? I should put on more clothes. The world had changed completely, everything was different. Although I didn't have the final proof, it seemed pretty likely I was becoming a mother.

I put on a thick down coat and a Burberry hat and scarf I'd bought two years before but never worn, and walked down the street for a few minutes, then suddenly hailed a taxi, giving him an address. I was going to see my tailor.

I'd just given my tailor some silk to make tight-fitting Chinese *qipao* dresses; now I could discuss the measurements with her again. Chest, waist and bottom would all have to be bigger.

When she asked ine how much bigger, suddenly I couldn't find the words. 'Just . . . bigger,' I said. Inside I thought, even if it was a false alarm, I should still be able to wear *quipao* that were slightly bigger. She lowered her head and wrote the larger measurements on a slip of paper.

It pleased me that the tailor was quiet and reserved. She never asked her clients questions. Even when famous faces from the news or television appeared in her shop, she was unruffled, taking their measurements and making clothes to order with her usual professional attitude. I was sure she'd run across female stars whose bust-size had suddenly increased by two cup-sizes, but bet she calmly recorded the new bust-size, never making jokes, no matter how witty.

That was my tailor in Shanghai.

A few days passed and my period still didn't come. I went to the bathroom almost every hour to look for red on my underwear.

Finally I phoned Xi'er. 'Let's go to the hospital,' I said, my voice hissing like a snake.

'I'll be outside your place in twenty minutes,' she said decisively.

The hospital was full of unsmiling people, shoulder to shoulder, slowly and haphazardly coming and going amid the noxious smell of disinfectant, abruptly reminding you there are 1.3 billion people in this country. However the great advantage of hospitals here is that they are cheap; I spent approximately half an American dollar on registration fees and then another half a dollar for a little plastic cup.

I handed my bag and jacket to Xi'er, went into the slightly dirty bathroom and peed into the little plastic cup, getting my hands dirty, though in the hospital, self-respect and grace aren't essential.

I washed my hands and carried out the cup of urine. Some men were passing by at that moment and they unconsciously glanced at what I was holding. Xi'er handed me her newspaper, which I used to block the view of the cup.

'I'm losing my patience. I feel awful,' I groaned.

'You're the one who wanted to come here. I told you there are pregnancy tests at the drug store.' Xi'er frowned. She was wearing an unseasonably warm Eskimo-style hooded fur jacket and boot ensemble. It looked like we were going to a fashion-show in a refugee camp. Everyone was staring at her.

'It's best to be cautious about this kind of thing. I'm always afraid if I did it myself it'd be inaccurate.' I sighed. Holding the cup of urine carefully I went to the lab window.

You could see the results in three minutes.

I stood outside the lab window stamping my feet. I could hear my heart beat. I never knew three minutes could be so long. Xi'er smiled and put my clammy hand into the pocket of her furry overcoat. I seized the opportunity to put my head on her shoulder. 'I've never seen you so weak. It's very womanly,' Xi'er said into my ear.

Then we got the lab results: I was pregnant!

Xi'er squealed all at once. She was beside herself with excitement, but I just watched her quietly. My mind was a blank.

When we left the hospital, I declined Xi'er's offer to drive me in her car and insisted that I wanted to walk. 'Okay. I'll call you tonight.' She hugged me, smiling and drove off with a wave.

I walked down the street trying to breathe deeply from my abdomen. I couldn't see anything different about my belly. But whether I could sense them or not, certain changes were taking place. Such changes were very subtle, but astonishing. They would alter the course of my life.

I felt like wailing and then like laughing to express my feelings on this momentous occasion. It was a line of demarcation between two lives, like the equator dividing the Northern and Southern hemispheres. I felt I had to give it a voice.

But in fact I neither cried nor laughed. I just walked quietly from one end of the street to the other. The sounds of the stream of people and the cars beside me and the smell of the dust had no effect on me. I walked calmly on, gazing at everything in sight but not really registering anything.

I came to a street where people were running out of a smoke-filled old house. Someone screamed 'Fire! Fire!' and a sheet of flame suddenly leapt from the building and lit up the sky. The fire grew fiercer and the crowd of spectators grew increasingly restless.

I stopped walking and stood across the street staring, mesmerized, at the burning building. The building was swaying; encased in the blaze, it looked as if it might crumble at any moment.

Suddenly I was flooded with a nameless wave of intense emotions. I found I'd started to cry, and cry hard, slowly squatting down on the pavement.

Through my tears I saw that the fierce fire seemed to have spread everywhere, stirring up a heap of memories and the deepest and most basic emotions. To the one side was destruction, and to the other new life.

Life moves in cycles, like the seasons recurring in their unchanging order. A young woman like me, the fertility of spring inside her, travels on he own journey through summer and autumn until she reaches the mystery and awe of winter. Memories pass through the clean white forehead, and in the womb – baptized by fire and blood – a seed germinates, so still and quiet . . .

Epilogue

I think of other ages that floated upon the stream of life and love and
death and are forgotten, and I feel the freedom of passing away.
Rabindranath Tagore

Xi'er got up her courage and went back to her home, which
is in a conservative village in the south of Hunan. It was
the first time she'd been home to see her parents since her
operation. Her mother was unwilling to see her, but her father
took her to the best restaurant in town to have dinner. The next
day the little village was buzzing with the gossip that Xi'er's
father and a young woman had been on a secret date. When Xi'er
returned from the village, she was brave enough to tell her
boyfriend Adam about her secret.

At first, Adam decided to just be friends with Xi'er. But he
found that he was still attracted to her. 'I'm helpless,' he said.
'Maybe it isn't the world that has changed, it's me.' With Adam's
help, Xi'er finally got a visa, and now they were holidaying in
Adam's home town of Melbourne.

Eric came to Shanghai, and after finding Zhu Sha stayed on
for a while. At the end of his trip he took a few days to visit Tibet
in search of his spiritual home.

According to Zhu Sha, she and Eric still hadn't done anything,
but there were rumours that she was about to divorce Ah Dick.
At the same time, because of her achievements at work, she
hoped to rise quickly through the ranks and become the
company's regional manager for China. But success didn't seem

to be what Zhu Sha really wanted. When she was small and going through a very strict girl's education, what she'd had drummed into her were the phrases 'to be a woman you can't be too strong' and 'it's lonely at the top'.

My father finished his lectures in Singapore. He and my mother returned to Shanghai. I went nearly every day to join them for dinner. In their eyes, I was a little fatter, even prettier than before.

I thought I needed a little more courage before I told them about the pregnancy. An unmarried pregnant woman is a difficult topic of conversation in China.

But I mentioned it in a letter I wrote to the Master of Empty Nature on Putuo Island. Master replied by sending me an ink painting of a rainy landscape. Beside the painting was inscribed a *koan*: 'With rain comes widespread growth, and the scenery of a thousand mountains is so delightful – if you are satisfied and comfortable in yourself, you will achieve great joy.'

As for Muju – I still loved Muju, just as I said at the beginning of this book. My love for Muju was more than love, it was a kind of self-redemption.

And Nick . . . I think I also loved Nick in some sense, in spite of his unfortunate reputation as a philanderer.

But neither of them knew I was pregnant. And for the moment I couldn't be sure which of them was the child's father.

One evening, I dreamed again that I was adrift on a boundless sea, looking for the heavenly island of my heart's fondest desire. When that familiar feeling of powerlessness hit me, the voice from the sky once again rang out. This time, I finally heard it clearly.

What the voice said was: 'Marry Buddha.'